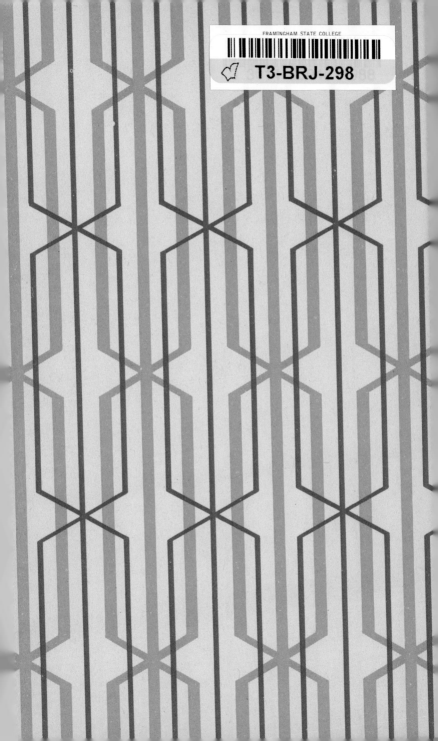

SEVEN SCOTS STORIES

SEVEN
SCOTS STORIES

BY

JANE HELEN FINDLATER

Short Story Index Reprint Series

BOOKS FOR LIBRARIES PRESS
FREEPORT, NEW YORK

First Published 1913
Reprinted 1970

STANDARD BOOK NUMBER:
8369-3498-9

LIBRARY OF CONGRESS CATALOG CARD NUMBER:
75-121542

PRINTED IN THE UNITED STATES OF AMERICA

CONTENTS

THE BAIRN-KEEPER

THE BAIRN-KEEPER

" Y'RE ower wee," said Kate McLeod, contempt in both words and looks.

" Aye, I'm wee, but I'm that bauld and firrm," said little Easie Dow, facing her would-be employer dauntlessly. She was indeed small for her thirteen years : she looked almost like a child of ten. Kate eyed her again, calculating whether any work worthy the name could be got out of such a tiny creature ; yet the child's air and her words were impressive. She stood there bolt upright ; thin arms like bits of stick held in to her sides, fingers clenched :

" I'm wee, but I'm that bauld and firrm," she repeated.

At the distance they stood from each other, Kate could not hear the frantic thumping of Easie's heart, which might have given the lie to these brave words. Kate herself was a mountainous woman, tall, bulky, big-boned, almost masculine in appearance. Her face looked as if it had been roughly hacked out of a bit of wood, her skin was like hide, and her hair like coarse black linen thread ; her voice was loud and gruff—altogether an alarming personality.

3

The Bairn-Keeper

They stood looking at each other, this woman and this child, for a full minute after these opening words had been spoken ; then Kate added :

" It's no a sairvant I'm seekin', ye ken—jist a bairn-keeper."

" I'm fine wi' bairns," said Easie. " Hoo many's o' them ? "

" Jist the ane," said Kate, a trifle hastily ; then she added, " But there's an auld body, an' what are they but jist bairns ? "

Easie nodded sagaciously. " Jist bairns," she agreed. Apparently neither the care of youth nor age had any terrors for Easie ; she seemed to consider herself quite adequate to either task.

The interview was taking place at the " Huts," as they were called, a temporary cluster of shanties set up for the navvies who had been making a new line of railway in the neighbourhood of Kate McLeod's home. Easie Dow had two or three times been sent to Leeks Farm with messages, and Kate, casting an eye upon the child, had thought to drive a bargain. She questioned her closely one day as to her belongings, and finding that Easie had now no relative in the world except the uncle who had grudgingly supported her for the last two years, Kate decided to see if she could be · " got cheap." Easie, it is true, was under age ; but the school was going to be shut immediately—in about a month's time—for the summer holidays, and in the meantime the Huts were being taken down, as the line was completed and the navvies were

4

to be moved on to another job. It would be generally supposed that Easie had moved on too.

Leeks was a lonely farm, four miles away from the school, at least : ten to one no one would hear anything about Easie being there—and a year soon passed. So Kate McLeod argued ; and so she had placed the matter to Easie's uncle when she first spoke to him. The moral standard of navvies is not proverbially exalted. John Dow saw no reason at all why his niece shouldn't take a good situation when it was offered to her ; she had been a burden on him long enough.

As for Easie, she was dying to begin to earn her own living. There burned in her little soul a bright flame of independence. Too long she had eaten the choking bread of charity ; she yearned to join the great army of wage-earners.

No wonder then that she blew her own trumpet so boldly to Kate McLeod ; no wonder that her heart thumped with the terror of rejection, that her small hands were clenched in determination to win this prize of her first situation !

" I maun get ye cheap, y're that wee," Kate persisted, trying, after the traditional manner of the buyer, to depreciate the article she was determined to obtain. But Easie was too good a woman of business to let this remark pass unchallenged.

" It's no the size ye pay for ; it's the work I'll can dae," she said eagerly.

This seemed unanswerable. Kate ruminated for a minute or two longer, then made Easie a princely

offer of " a shilling a week and her meat." It did
not take long to clinch the bargain. A shilling a
week and her meat ! Easie's soul sang for joy ;
here was independence at last, and more than that.
She did not know the words "social status," but she
well knew the feeling of not possessing the mysterious quantity. As " a navvy's bairn " from the
Huts she had been well kept in her place at
school, and made to feel by the other children, in
some subtle way, that she was an outsider from their
little world. Things would be altered now ; she
looked fully an inch taller when she felt herself a
duly engaged bairn-keeper at a shilling a week and
her meat : no one should look down upon her now.
She rushed in to tell her news to the next-door
neighbour, a kindly, untidy Irishwoman who had
always been the recipient of her joys and sorrows.

"Eh, Peggy, I'm to be bairn-keeper to a wife
frae Leeks Fairm, an' I'm to get a shilling a week
and my meat," she cried, bursting with pride.

"Faith thin, Aisy me dear, it'll be missin' ye
we'll all be," cried Peggy. "And what will ye be
knowin' about a wean ? "

"I'll can learn," said Easie sturdily.

"The Saints preserve ye ! there's a deal to learn !"
said Peggy.

Surely never did bride pack up her wedding
garments more gaily than Easie " sorted " her " bits
of things " for the journey to Leeks Farm.

Of course there was no question at all of a trunk.

6

The Bairn-Keeper

In the first place Easie did not possess one, and in the next place she would not have had anything to fill one with. But her poor little clothes must be carefully folded and tidily pinned together, for Easie had been brought up for the first eleven years of her short life by a careful mother, and her instincts were orderly.

Then the question arose: in what were her garments to be rolled up?—in a skirt or in her mother's Paisley shawl? The shawl was really almost too precious, Easie thought, yet it would make the tidier bundle. She stood by the side of the bed on which all her tiny possessions lay, and dubitated long, making an inventory of her goods.

Item: her Sunday frock, bought before her mother's death three years ago, made up ingeniously (by these clever motherly fingers) so as to admit of Easie's slight yearly growth. A tuck had been let down each year since, and next year Easie knew that she would need to add to the length of the skirt by that mystery of the dressmaker's art, a false hem.

Item: a hat. Of the changes which this hat had undergone it would be difficult to write, for it would require a history all to itself.

Item: a bundle of undergarments.

Item: Easie's black leather bag. This was really the child's dearest possession. She had picked it up on the road once when on her way to the village. It was a fairly sized reticule of the cheaper sort, lined with red calico; but to Easie's

7

eyes it was simply priceless. Honesty had made her hurry with it immediately to that representative of law and order, "the pollisman," who suggested that it must have been dropped off the coach which had long ago rumbled off on its way to Stirling. But the "pollis" was a human being. He saw the glint of longing in Easie's eyes when he took possession of the bag, and he remembered it. After a suitable time had elapsed, as the bag still remained unclaimed, the "pollis" appeared at the Huts one morning, and handed the bag into Easie's skinny, eager little hands. The joy of that day! She sat snapping and unsnapping the bright brass clip of the bag till it was a wonder that it did not break. What did it matter to Easie that she had nothing to put in it?—strong in faith, she carried her empty bag on her arm till Providence began to fill it for her.

"The gods give threads to the web begun." Easie went to the village shop one day, bag in hand. She was a favourite with Mrs. Adams, the old woman who purveyed for the neighbourhood.

"That's a grand bag ye have the day, Easie," she said. "It'll be to hold the messages?"

"Deed no," said Easie, almost indignantly. "It's ower fine for messages; it's jist a bag."

Pressed as to its history, Easie gave this in detail, and it is not surprising that Mrs. Adams at once drew out that fascinating drawer in which she held reels of silk and cotton, fancy buttons and various odds and ends, and began to consider its contents.

"There's two-three pirns and buttons here, Easie,

that's not much asked for ; maybe you'd like to be puttin' them in yer bag ? "

Easie flushed with joy, yet drew back shyly from the counter.

" I canna be takin' yer pirns, mistress," she faltered.

" They're just in my way here, ye see," said Mrs. Adams, picking out one or two of the more sun-faded reels. They were not exactly the most useful colours, but what did that matter ? Bright blue faded into green, yellow turned white, white turned black with time—three pretty little reels—in they went to the bag.

" And here's a few buttons for the other pocket," said the good woman, placing a card of quite use-less but ornamental metal buttons beside the reels.

It was wonderful after this how Easie's bag was stocked, " here a little and there a little," with the most heterogeneous medley of objects. It mattered not to her what the thing might be ; in it went, with the invariable formula, " I'll maybe find a use for it." She never, of course, found a use for one-half of these strange oddments ; that consti-tuted part of their charm.

But this is a long, too long, digression from Easie's packing. Well, the Sunday dress, the hat, the bundle of undergarments, and the bag lay on the bed waiting to be packed somehow and con-veyed to Leeks Farm. Easie decided that the Paisley shawl must enfold them. Then what rapture to produce from the bag a huge, rusty safety-pin (found some months ago, like the bag, on the road), and with it to secure the ends of the bundle after everything had been folded up inside the shawl !

It had been arranged that McCallum the baker should be asked to give Easie and her bundle "a lift" on the way to Leeks. McCallum was a jovial, kindly man, and knew Easie well ; he came round twice a week in his cart to dispense bread to the Huts, and what more natural than that he should drive her to Leeks ? John Dow had boldly asked this favour of him, adding that Easie was to be bairn-keeper at the farm.

"Bairn-keeper ? She's but a bairn hersel' ! " said the baker.

"She's fourteen year auld," said Dow stolidly. He was not going to stick at a lie or two.

"Fourteen, is she ? She's gey wee for that," said McCallum, a little incredulously, whistling to himself as he arranged the loaves on his tray.

"Weel, that's her age, an' time she was earnin'," Dow retorted.

"A' richt, ma man ; I'll gie her a cast ower tae Leeks," said McCallum ; but he drew his own conclusions about the matter.

So it came about that on this Friday afternoon, when her packing was all done, Easie sat down to wait for the arrival of McCallum and his cart. And suddenly, in this period of inaction, apprehensions began to crowd into her mind. Though she had called herself bold and firm, Easie was

The Bairn-Keeper

in reality very timid by nature, and now that the
excitements of packing were over, a terror of the
unknown seized upon her. The Huts had not been
much of a home, it is true, but at least she had not
been among strangers here. Now she was leaving
her uncle, the only relative she had in the world,
leaving the friendly Peggy Donovan next door,
leaving everything that was familiar, and going out
alone into the world. She had bid a very unemotional good-bye to her uncle before he went off
to work in the morning ; now the time had arrived
to say her farewells to Peggy. When the baker's
cart came in sight, Easie looked into Peggy's dis-
orderly kitchen and announced that the hour of
her departure had come. "I'm awa', Peggy,"
she cried, with a great show of briskness and
courage.

Peggy was washing, because it was the wrong
hour of the day (she always did things at wrong
hours), but she drew her soapy hands out of the
tub and flew to the door, calling down blessings
from half the saints in the calendar on Easie's
head. She was a kindly woman, and there was something in the sight of Easie's forlorn little flitting
that might have touched a heart of stone. Just
the child, standing alone there by the roadside with
her bundle, no one looking after her, no one launching
her on this her first voyage upon the sea of life.
Tears rose to Peggy's eyes, and she gave Easie a
smacking kiss and an almost painful thump on the
back to show her goodwill. " Good luck to you,

The Bairn-Keeper

Aisy me dear, an' long life and happiness," she said.

McCallum, too, was touched by the sight.

" Is that a' yer things, lassie ? " he asked, as he hoisted the bundle into the cart.

" Aye, that's a'," said Easie, in a choking voice. All her courage had disappeared, and she was sobbing openly now. There seemed to be nothing more to be said or done, so McCallun bade her climb up into the cart and off they went. The vehicle was a high spring cart of the usual sort, with a board across it on which the driver sat ; the stout black horse trotted briskly along, and from under the tarpaulin cover at the back of the cart there crept up a delicious smell of new bread. At any other time this drive would have been an ecstasy to Easie, and even now she had a feeling that she was wasting something very delightful ; yet cry she must—it was impossible not to. McCallum took no notice of her tears for some time, but spoke a great deal to the horse, and finally, as they began to ascend a long hill, he asked Easie if it would be possible for her to hold the reins while he looked over his account book.

" Aye," said Easie, with a sob.

" No' ower tight, then ; jist let him ken y're there," said McCallum, surrendering the reins into her small hands.

He got out his book and a pencil and seemed very busy for a little ; the horse went steadily onwards, and Easie held the reins proudly. By the time they

The Bairn-Keeper

reached the top of the hill she was equal to a remark and soon found herself munching a " cookie " which McCallum had produced from his basket.

" I'm tae be bairn-keeper at Leeks," she volunteered.

" Aye, there's a puir, misthriven bairn there," said McCallum.

" An' there's an auld body there too that I'm tae mind," Easie pursued.

" Aye is there ; auld and blind tae."

" Blind, is she ?—it maun be awfu' tae be blind ! " Easie exclaimed. Curiosity then made McCallum ask Easie what her age might be ? It seemed a simple question, and she answered without the slightest hesitation :

" Thirteen, come the second of July."

McCallum whistled and flicked at the horse with the whip. " Ye'll hae passed the sixth standard at the school then ? " he queried.

" Na," said Easie, " I'm gey far back. Ye see, I've been moved aboot sae muckle frae the ae school tae the ither these three years back."

" Aweel, schoolin's a fine thing," said McCallum. The subject seemed to be much in his mind ; but Easie was exercised quite otherwise.

" The mistress at Leeks was unco big and stoot," she said timidly. " I'm feared she'll be ill tae dae wi', Mr. McCallum."

" You jist be doin' yer ain work, Easie, and never heed her," he advised.

" I'm a wee thing feared," Easie said.

13

The Bairn-Keeper

" You'll get on fine, nae doubt," McCallum assured her. " Ye'll feel strange a wee at the first ; but I'll be roond come Monday, and Alex Ferguson the flesher is on the road on the Tuesdays : it's no as if ye wouldna see some kent faces."

He broke off his attempted consolations and glanced at the child ; her tears were falling again.

" Hoots, Easie, it'll no dae tae greet that gait ; wait till ye have the bairn and the auld body tae mind, that'll help ye."

At this point Leeks came in sight, a little, square, grim-looking stone-built farm by the roadside. The byres stood to the back, and at one side of the house was a great midden grown round with nettles and dockens. A few twisted plum-trees and some cabbages represented the garden. At the other side, a little burn ran down into a spout ; but the soil around it was pashed into ill-smelling mud by the ducks that were always dabbling about there, and feathers floated in the pool below the spout. Leeks was a dreary, God-forsaken-looking place altogether.

" Here ye are, Easie," said McCallum, and Easie, with a tremendous effort at self-control, gulped down her tears and prepared to descend from the cart.

A dog ran out barking at the sound of wheels, and then Kate McLeod herself appeared. She stood by the cart and spoke with McCallum about some loaves before she welcomed Easie—if that word could be applied to the curt sentence :

" Come in by."

The Bairn-Keeper

The Leeks kitchen was as forlorn as the outside of the house. A big, stone-floored room, lamentably dirty and smelling indescribably of boiled cabbage, braxy mutton, dogs, and byre. The only pleasant object in the room was the wide old chimney where a wood fire burned. At one side of the fire sat "Grannie," the "old body," while at the other side a wooden cradle was placed, containing the bairn —the future object of Easie's care. Such a Grannie —such a bairn!—it would have been difficult to say which looked the older of the two. Grannie was only eighty ; but the bairn seemed to wear the burden of centuries on its little wrinkled face : it was astonishing that a thing so young could look so old. It lay in the dirty cradle keeping up a constant low, whingeing cry.

"Wheesht, ye limmer that ye are!" said Kate McLeod, in her gruff voice, giving the cradle a push with her foot that set it rocking too violently. The child cried more loudly, and old Grannie by the fire piped out to know what ailed the bairn ?

"Hoots, she's jist a fair torment," said Kate.

"I whiles think if I had her here on my knee—" the old woman began ; but Kate interrupted her with a coarse laugh.

"Na, na, Grannie, it's ower lang sin' ye've had a wean—and wha wad be lookin' aifter the twa o' ye tae see ye didna let her fa'? But here's Easie Dow that's tae mind the bairn." She pushed Easie forward to the old woman's chair as she spoke.

"I'm tae mind the bairn, and maybe I can help

you tae, mem," said Easie, anxious to mind her manners. But Kate burst into her rough laugh again at this ceremonious style of address.

" Hoots, it's jist ' Grannie ' she gets frae us a'," she said.

The old blind woman put out her hand and felt for Easie.

" She's gey wee," she said. " Will she can lift the bairn, Kate ? "

'' Weel, if she canna lift her, she maun gang," said Kate, with much finality. Easie's heart stood still for a moment, then she drew all her forces of mind and body together for the struggle.

" I'm fine at liftin'," she said. " See here." And with that she bent over the cradle and grappled with the baby. Now, as everyone knows, lifting is much more a question of science than of actual muscle. Easie really had quite strength enough to lift the poor misthriven child comfortably if she had known exactly how to do it ; but then she did not, and to add to her difficulties she was nervous and dreaded failure. The baby seemed to be made of lead. For one moment she thought she could not manage to lift it at all ; the next minute, swaying, it is true, under her burden, she got the child out of the cradle and carried it across the room. A thousand terrors leaped into her mind in that short journey across the uneven floor of the Leeks kitchen. What if her arms were not strong enough, and she let the baby fall ? What if it jumped out of her unsteady, unskilful grip? What if she stumbled and fell? It was an awful moment as she stood there before the fire, swaying under the burden she carried, panting, flushed, trembling, but clutching the baby like a vice.

"Aye, she can lift her," said Kate. "Weel, I maun be off til the byres. See you tae the bairn, Easie, and tae Grannie or I come back."

Thus suddenly the bairn-keeper was plunged, so to speak, up to the neck in her new duties. A feeling of perfect despair came over her, for the baby was screaming now, and making strange jerking movements in her arms. She did not know what to do to quiet it, and there was no one to appeal to save the helpless old blind woman propped up there in the chimney corner.

"Would ye haud the bairn on yer knee a minit, Grannie, till I sort the cradle?" she asked timidly.

"Aye, my lassie; I like fine tae haud a bairn again; but Kate, my good-dochter——"

She paused, turning her head in a listening attitude for a moment.

"The mistress isna here," said Easie, drawing nearer; and the old woman went on:

"My good-dochter canna be fashed wi' an auld helpless body like me, and she aye says gin I tak' the bairn it's mair fash tae look aifter baith o' us."

Easie deposited the child on Grannie's knee, and drew up a stool beside her; she thought she discerned a helper.

"I'm willin' tae dae my best," she said, "but

The Bairn-Keeper

I've nae skill wi' bairns, an' they're gey ill tae lift, I see. Maybe you could teach me hoo it's done ? "

" Seeven sons I had," the old woman began, in a strange, chanting voice—" Seeven sons—an' they're a' in their graves but William—Kate's man, that is. Aye, I ken weel aboot bairns, lassie—an' I ken this ane's ower wee, an' it's aye greet-greetin' a' the day."

She stopped again, with the same frightened, anxious look behind her.

" Is't no' weel ? " Easie asked.

The old woman leant forward in her chair till her shrivelled lips nearly touched Easie's ear.

" It's no' cared for, lassie," she whispered.

Glancing at the tiny, grey, wrinkled face of the baby, Easie understood the situation all of a sudden : the baby was ill-treated. A wave of pity swept over her ; she felt as bold as a lion.

" I'll care for't," she cried. Then she addressed herself afresh to the practical question of how to learn to lift her charge. Bending down, she gave another clumsy grab at the child, which made it begin to scream afresh.

" Eh, she's awfu' tae lift ! " Easie cried. " And what'll the mistress say, tae hear the bairn cryin' this gait ? "

" She'll no hear, and she'll no heed," said Grannie. She was sitting forward in her chair, balancing the baby on her knee with all the skill of a practised hand. Her old heart warmed in this exercise of a long-neglected art.

The Bairn-Keeper

"See, lassie, tak' her up firm like under the oxters. Dinna be feared o' the bairn," she directed.

Easie made a desperate lunge at the baby, got it into her arms, and began, under Grannie's direction again, to pace up and down, rocking it gently. Half an hour of conflict followed. Easie felt that now or never she must learn to hold the bairn— yes, if she died in the attempt ; yet she could not manage to hold it comfortably.

"Get a bit shawl, lassie, an' pit it roond yer shouther, an' pit the bairn intil't," grannie suggested. "Hae ye a bit shawl onywhere ?"

"Aye," said Easie, "I've a fine shawl oot by."

"Gie me the bairn, an' gang for't then," Grannie commanded.

Depositing the bairn on the old woman's knee, Easie ran out to the door where her bundle still lay. There, kneeling on the floor, she unpinned the big safety-pin and got out her precious Paisley shawl Far too good she knew it was for such a purpose, but she was desperate.

"Here, Grannie—here's the shawl. I ken fine what ye mean. I've seen the tinkler wives carry their bairns that way," she cried.

"Aye, it taks the weicht aff the airms," said Grannie. "Pit it roond ye—aye, like yon—aye, that's the way o't. Noo' tak' the bairn."

Again more easily said than done, but at last it was accomplished. Grannie was by this time almost as much excited as her pupil, but together they got the shawl arranged and the baby laid into its right position. Then Easie began to strut up and down the kitchen as proudly as a peacock. Gradually the crying died down, the little creased face relaxed.

" Losh, Grannie ! she's asleep," Easie whispered, delight—almost ecstasy—in her voice.

" Lay her doon in the cradle then," said Granny.

This difficult feat Easie accomplished by kneeling down very cautiously till she got on to a level with the cradle—then ever so gently unfastening the shawl and somehow or other slipping the baby in between the blankets. Oh, the relief of that moment ! But it was the moment chosen by Mrs. McLeod to re-enter the kitchen.

Easie, who was brooding ecstatically over the sleeping child, sprang to her feet at the noise of the opening door.

" Mind, mistress, the bairn's sleepin' ! " she exclaimed, raising her hand with a warning gesture.

" And what o' that ? " Kate inquired, tramping across the floor noisily, to swing the great kettle off the chain it hung on, with one twist of her powerful red hand.

" It was gey hard tae get her ower," Easie explained.

" Aye, she's a bad sleeper : she's aye greetin'—that's the way I wantit a bairn-keeper—I canna dae wantin' my sleep."

A pleasant prospect this for poor Easie, but enthusiasm for her new calling sustained her—enthusiasm and something else she was unaware of herself, and could not have named—that rose up suddenly in her heart as she looked from the piteous old-young face of the baby to the hard unmotherly face of the woman who stood beside it. In certain natures the instinct of helpfulness is born instantaneously out of the emotion of pity ; with them to see distress is to try to relieve it. Easie was too young to understand the emotion that influenced her or to form any resolutions of helpfulness ; but in the depths of her nature something stirred, and she responded blindly and unquestioningly to it.

" Come up the stair," said Kate brusquely. " And whaur's yer claes ? "

" They're oot by," said Easie.

She stepped to the door and gathered up all her belongings as well as she could in her arms. Kate seemed to find no fault with this rather curious proceeding, as a more orderly housewife might have done. She preceded Easie up the little wooden staircase that shook under her heavy tread, flung open the door of a tiny room lit by a skylight, and informed Easie that these were her quarters.

" An' ye'll hae the bairn wi' ye ; whiles she screams awfu'. Grannie'll need a hand up the stair tae ; she's that stiff noo an' blind she's a body's work tae mind—and me wi' seeven kye tae milk an' the hens an' ducks an' a'."

She paused, breathless.

" Aweel," she pursued, as Easie made no reply, " the maister'll be in for his bite the noo, and ye'll can hae some parritch." She turned away, slammed

The Bairn-Keeper

the ill-fitting door behind her, and went downstairs again, leaving Easie alone.

There was no chest of drawers in the room, so Easie began to pile all her little garments in a corner. The Sunday dress and hat were hung upon a peg, the bag upon a nail at the back of the door.

Then, all things being done, the little bairn-keeper sat down on the edge of her bed and wept.

.   .   .   .

Easie got a full view of the Leeks family as they ate their supper that evening. William McLeod, Kate's husband, was a big, hulking, silent man, who shovelled in his food at a great pace, then rose from the table, lighted his pipe, and went out into the night without having exchanged a word with anyone. Grannie, as Kate expressed it, "got her meat" given to her on her knee by the fireside, for, said the tender daughter-in-law, "it's ower muckle fash trailing the auld body across til the table." So a very uncomfortable meal Grannie had : she could not see to feed herself, and many a spoonful found its misdirected way on to her shawl or her skirt. Easie noticed all this, and marvelled. Kate had a strange, restless manner ; she would eat a few mouthfuls standing, then cross over to the other side of the room for a plate or a spoon, then sit down and look round the table, eat a little more, get up again muttering to herself—and so on. Easie sat like a mouse at the corner of the table, eating whatever she was offered, her active little brain noting all she saw. She could not quite make out

The Bairn-Keeper

this household ; something was amiss, but what it was she could not imagine. Kate's attitude to the baby was perplexing, it was so callous. Easie remembered her own mother, and she knew also what the ordinary, normal attitude of parents and children generally was ; so why was this woman so unkind to this child ? She looked old to be its mother, too, Easie thought : she must find out.

" I'm feared the bairn's no' weel the nicht," she ventured to say.

"She's aye the same," Kate answered. The child's horrid little whingeing cry seemed only to tease her, instead of causing her any anxiety. Easie felt that solicitude on behalf of the bairn was not approved of ; she stood by the chimney corner waiting for orders, but as Kate did not issue them, she made another venture :

" Ye look gey wearit, Grannie," she said. " Would ye no' like tae gang till yer bed ? "

"I wad that," said Grannie wistfully, " but I canna get up the stair my lane, an' Kate's no' ready for an 'oor an' mair—there's a' the kye tae milk noo." She looked round with that curiously timid air that Easie had noticed before.

" I'll tak' ye up the stair," said Easie confidently. In reality she was not so sure of her own powers, but she felt it was necessary to assert them.

" Ye've been sittin' ower lang," she said, with quite a professional manner. " It was the same way wi' an auld body lived near us at hame ; she aye got stiff in the jints."

23

The Bairn-Keeper

"Aye, that's it, my lassie," said Grannie, beginning to hoist herself up painfully out of the chair. Easie stood by her side, small but alert, ready to do her utmost. Once Grannie had got upon her feet, Easie felt less anxious ; she put her stick-like arm round the old woman's waist and began to guide her trembling steps across the uneven flags of the floor. When they reached the staircase and began to make a toilsome ascent, Easie caught hold of Grannie's elbow with an iron grip.

"I'll haud ye firm," she assured her, though her heart was really beating with trepidation. Nothing, as we are always being told, is so infectious as courage—or even a show of courage. Grannie knew nothing of Easie's fears, and gained the head of the steep little staircase in safety.

"Ye'll gie me a hand oot o' my claes, Easie ? " she said then.

"Aye, I can do that fine," said the little boaster again, and Grannie remarked contentedly that she was "a real good lassie."

During the process of undressing her old charge, Easie obtained some information about her young one : the baby did not belong to Kate. This bit of news was imparted to her in a whisper.

"Wha's aucht the bairn then ? " Easie asked.

"Wheesht, wheesht—it's Lizzie's bairn—Kate's dochter's bairn. Lizzie's a fine lassie tae ; this was jist a mistake like—it was Robert MacIntyre the pleughman. . . . "

Easie had not been brought up in cotton wool.

24

The Bairn-Keeper

At the Huts she heard of such mistakes before. Still, she was but a child herself, and her understanding of these subjects was necessarily incomplete ; but not for worlds would she have confessed to such childishness—her *rôle* was that of a capable woman of the world, so after a moment's pause she replied : " Sae that's the wye, is't ? " in a very sagacious tone.

" Aye ; an' William was that affronted he sent Lizzie aff til a place in Stirling when the bairn was a month old. Puir Lizzie didna wish tae gang an' leave the bairn ; but my William was aye a dour man. She's no seen it syne—I'm thinkin' she'll see an unco' change on it—it was a fine bairn the day she left it."

" It's no' verra fine noo," said Easie, pursing her lips as she considered this story.

Having got Grannie safely to bed, Easie had now to address herself to the more difficult task of getting the bairn ready for the night. She went down to the kitchen to receive her last instructions from Kate. These were not illuminating. A dirty feeding-bottle filled with sour-looking milk, and a medicine bottle containing a dark, sticky, sweet mixture were given into her hands.

" Gie her the bottle when she's wakefu', an' gin she cries ower muckle gie her a soop o' this," Kate said, vaguely indicating the dark bottle.

" Is't meedicine ? " Easie inquired.

" Aye," said Kate shortly. " Gang aff til yer bed, and tak' the bairn wi' ye."

25

The Bairn-Keeper

To Easie's entire ignorance of all the perils that might have befallen the baby thus thrust upon her care, may perhaps be attributed the measure of success that crowned her efforts. She would do her best—this was her fixed resolve, and her heart was filled with a burning pity for the baby—the baby that no one wanted apparently.

So with her mouth pursed, her brows knitted with determination, she fell to the awful task of putting the child to bed. It was crying to begin with, and Easie's unaccustomed fingers fumbling at its garments only made it cry the more. Perseverance, however, prevailed; the last dingy wrapping was got off, and the pitiful little limbs were disclosed.

" Losh me ! the bairn maun be washed ! " Easie exclaimed. She had frequently helped at the ablutions of the Donovan family ; but they were children of three and four ; she had yet to learn what it was to wash a baby. Giving no thought to possible difficulties, she laid the squalling child down between the blankets and dashed down to the kitchen in search of hot water. Kate was out, so, unhindered, Easie filled a large pail with hot water and hauled it upstairs, spilling it on each step of the painful ascent. Then, almost distraught by the baby's screams, she had to descend again in search of a tub. This time Fate was also kind ; a tub was found behind the back door. Easie caught it up and rushed, panting, through the kitchen and up the stair. By the time she reached her room,

The Bairn-Keeper

the baby's little face was almost black. " Lord save us ! What gin I've killed the bairn ! " she cried, catching it up in her arms. The touch of its little shivering naked body nearly moved her to tears, and the blind way it stretched its helpless claw-like hands up to her as if praying for love. The change of position soothed its cries for a minute, and Easie was able to lay it down again while she poured the water into the tub. Oh, careful nurses with bath thermometers, what would you have said to Easie's happy-go-lucky methods ? But her guardian angel must have been watching at this desperate moment, for the temperature of this first bath proved to be strangely right. Clumsily, cautiously, tremblingly, Easie lifted the bairn into the tub. As she splashed the warm water over its clammy little body, she saw the child's suffused face cool down to a more ordinary tint. A wan smile began to play over its features, and it gave a feeble kick or two that in a more healthy child would have been a splash of delight. The bath was a manifest success. But when it came to lifting the bairn out, that was quite another matter. It had been difficult enough to lift when clothed—naked and wet it felt as slippery as an eel. There were more cries, you may be sure, before the bairn, dry and clean, was at last put to bed, and Easie was at liberty to seek repose herself.

You would have imagined that sleep, long and profound, should, by all the laws of justice, have crowned such efforts as Easie had made that night. And indeed she had scarcely lain down (cautiously

The Bairn-Keeper

it is true, because the baby was at the back of the
bed) before she was sound asleep. But it could not
have been more than an hour later that a piercing
scream rang in her ears : the baby was awake,
and yelling again.

Poor Easie ! Drugged with sleep and fatigue, it
was a bitter moment for her. With a valiant
effort she rubbed the sleep from her eyes, and fell
to her appointed task once more. The idea that it
was a task beyond her powers was not entertained
for a moment. Most of us are half alive all through
life because our powers are so seldom called into
full play : the proud consciousness came to Easie
that night that her whole being was needed for what
she had to do—she was alive for the first time. Two
whole hours she fought away alone, then, daunted
at last, she crept across the passage to Grannie's
room, and roused the old woman.

"Will ye can help me, Grannie ? " she said
piteously. "The bairn's been greetin' these twa
'oors, and I'm that tired I dinna ken what tae dae."

She stood beside the bed, a small wearied creature
in an unbleached cotton nightgown, her feet red
with cold, her hair tangled about her eyes.

"Hae ye gien her her bottle ? " Grannie asked.

"Aye, a while syne, an' she's greetin' the mair."

"Lay her ower yer knee, lassie, wi' her face doon,
an' pat her on the back," Grannie suggested.

Having got this bit of nursery lore, Easie stole
back to her own room and sat down on the bed to
practise the newly learned lesson. Heaven was

The Bairn-Keeper

kind ; the cries gradually ceased, and at last the wearied bairn-keeper was able to lay her charge back into bed asleep, and creep in beside it for a little well-earned repose. Youth is a wonderful thing ; she woke fresh and strong again when the baby's first whingeing cry heralded the dawn.

After this awful night Easie's education as a nurse advanced by leaps and bounds. In a week's time you would have thought her the most experienced of bairn-keepers ; you should have seen her whipping the baby in and out of its clothes, dandling it on her knee, rocking it in her arms, washing, feeding, tending it as it had never been tended before. The change in its conditions brought about a corresponding change in the baby ; it screamed less, and was much easier to manage. Now and then it even smiled a faint little attempt at a smile when Easie tried to amuse it. Easie beamed with pride. Never had there been such a bairn, she thought.

.   .   .   .

The more pressing claims of the bairn having been looked to, Grannie's case now came into Easie's consideration, for they had become great friends before the week was over.

Poor Grannie had a sad time of it, sitting there stiff and blind by the fire ; it was a problem what to do for her. She was so stiff and frail that Easie had to help her whenever she rose from her chair. Yet in this glowing summer weather why should Grannie have to sit always in the ill-smelling kitchen when outside the sun was bright and the air

The Bairn-Keeper

warm ? Easie revolved the matter in her few quiet moments, and at last ventured to speak about it.

"Would ye no step oot intil the sun, Grannie ?" she said one day. "I'll pit the bairn in the cradle and gie ye my airm oot."

"I've no been ower the door this year an' mair," the old woman replied.

"Ye maun try," said Easie briskly. "It's fine and warm the day." She laid down the baby and took Grannie by the elbow, raising her out of the chair. Then together they made a slow pilgrimage across the kitchen and stood by the door. How bravely the sun was shining !

"I feel it's gey warm," she cried.

"Come oot by a wee bittie," Easie urged. Here's a cromach the maister had will help ye." She put the stick into the old woman's right hand and took a firm grip of her left arm. "Ye'll dae fine, Grannie," she said. "Ye mauna be feared ; there's an auld box out by the west barn door ye'll can tak' a seat on." Grannie was afraid to venture so far on her shaky old limbs ; but Easie mocked at these fears, and step by step guided her round to the end of the barn and set her down on the up-turned box to rest. Then Easie scooted off to the house to fetch the baby, and they had an hour of almost delirious enjoyment sitting together in the sunshine. It became a regular thing after this that Easie should lead her feeble little company out to the end of the barn every fine afternoon, and there she would entertain them for hours at

The Bairn-Keeper

a time. Sometimes Grannie held the bairn, sometimes Easie, and sometimes it was allowed to lie
and kick about on the short, sun-warmed sward.
Then Grannie had long, old stories to tell, and these
were of enthralling interest. Easie's own powers
as an entertainer were neither few nor small : on a
wet day, when it was impossible to take the old
woman out, she would always find something to
amuse her.

" I wonder is there onything in my bag would
divert ye, Grannie ? " she asked one day, when the
bird of time seemed long upon the wing.

Therewith she produced the bag, and handed
it to her to feel all over : " Aye, an' ye maun smell
it tae," she directed, " it's a fine smell ; an' see
til the clasp o't—nic, nic—d'ye hear the way it
gaes ?—in an' oot that cliver : and the inside is a'
lined wi' grand red stuff (pit yer hand intil't,
Grannie), an' there's a wee pooch tae the side (d'ye
feel it ?) and anither tae the ither. I wunner wha
aucht it aince ? My word, she maun hae missed
it awfae ! Did ye ever see siccan a bag, Grannie ? "

This eulogium quite kindled the listener's interest.
She sat up and fingered the wonderful article,
clasped and unclasped the fastening as directed,
and even obediently sniffed at the leather.

Then Easie began to catalogue all its various and
interesting contents. To another mind these had
been but worthless : Easie had powers of imagination and description that made her poor little
oddments into a most worthy collection.

The Bairn-Keeper

" There's three pirns here, Grannie—bide a wee
and I'll gie them intil yer hand—there, ye hae
them. Weel, thae pirns are awfu' bonnie gin ye
seed them. There's a blue yin—Mrs. Adams at
the shop had a dozen o' them frae Glasgow aince,
an' what for ye'll no guess ? " Grannie could not
imagine, so Easie went on :

" They was for a weddin' goon, nae less ! There's
ane a Mistress Clarke has a fairm doon Kippen way
had a dochter marrit twelve years ago—weel, thae
pirns was tae sew her weddin' goon. Ye'll ken
Mistress Clarke yersel' ? "

" Aye, I ken her fine, Easie," said Grannie, and
had to tell in her turn all the story of the marriage
for which the reels had been bought. This took up
quite half an hour, and then Easie had another
treasure to display : " The bonniest thing ye ever
saw ; the minister's leddy gied it tae me at the New
Year's pairty she had for the school. It's a wee
box, Grannie, shapit like an egg and pentit Stewart
tartan—feel what smooth it is ! but ye see the tap
screws like, an' there's a thimble in the inside. Did
ever ye hear o' sic a conceit ? "

Grannie unscrewed the top and duly admired the
thimble, before Easie went on to the next treasure.

" There's a set o' wires here wad be awfu' fine
gin they werena rustit. D'ye ken what's good for
rustit wires, Grannie ? "

" Aye, Easie, a bit rag wi' ile an' ashes is fine,"
the old woman replied. Then Easie found a bit
rag and even a drop or two of oil, and Grannie

The Bairn-Keeper

demanded that she should have the joy of cleaning the knitting needles. Easie sat close beside her, exclamatory, enthusiastic, supplying fresh ash or another drop of oil, and Grannie rubbed away at the needles as happy as a queen, forgetting the length of the afternoon altogether. By the time that the needles had a high polish on them, Easie began to make tea, and during the meal Grannie herself made a faltering proposition that she would like fine to knit a stocking again if Easie could set it on for her. "Aye and lift the stitches whiles tae," she added sorrowfully. "I was a grand knitter aince, but noo I let the stitches fa', and Kate hasna the time tae be aye liftin' them for me."

"I'll can dae it," said Easie. "I had the first prize at the school for knittin'."

Thus it came about that a sort of Penelope's web was set a-going for Grannie. She worked a few rows, and then Easie was called upon to pick up the stitches. This was generally an impossible task, so Easie would stealthily pull down the work and feverishly re-knit it to its former length before she returned it to Grannie. Those whose days are filled with interesting and important work may find it difficult to realise the flood of happiness that was brought into the old woman's life by these apparently trivial means. Easie's care of her, the little daily walk, the occasional charge of the bairn for ten minutes, the stocking knitting—what a revolution these things worked in her eventless days! Easie had brought her back to life—she felt herself

The Bairn-Keeper

of some account once more—was she not Easie's referee on all points about the bairn ? Indeed, it was her ancient wisdom that discovered what was making the bairn ill, by the simple expedient of smelling its feeding-bottle. " Losh me, Easie, the bottle's soor ! Did Kate no' tell ye aye tae scind it oot ? The bairn's poisoned a' this while."

" I didna ken. I aye jist pit in the milk," said poor Easie, abashed by her own carelessness as she regarded the evil-smelling bottle.

Thereafter her zeal as bottle-washer knew no bounds, and indeed ended in tragedy when, by an unwise application of boiling water, she broke the bottle in two. Then Kate's anger was kindled, and she docked Easie's pay for a week to repair the damage.

Still Easie persevered in her efforts after cleanliness, for the bairn prospered and was in health. Its little face was becoming daily more placid, and the strange old look was gradually passing off it. It was almost pretty.

Easie's cup of joy ran over when McCallum the baker, coming in with some loaves about six weeks after her arrival at Leeks, remarked upon the improvement in the bairn : " It's no' the same ava'," he said. So July and August slipped away, two months of strenuous labour for Easie, but labour not uncrowned with a measure of achievement. There had been weeks of wonderfully dry, warm weather ; but in September came signs of change— darkening skies, keener winds, and showers that

The Bairn-Keeper

came charging down the glens. Winter had begun to make his stealthy approach.

.   .   .   .

Kate seemed very strange one morning when Easie came downstairs. She was moving about the kitchen restlessly, trying to work, but getting nothing done. The place was in even greater confusion than usual, for no apparent reason.

" I'm tae send ye a message tae the Braes, Easie," she said abruptly, as they finished a very badly cooked dinner at midday.

" But I canna tak' the bairn a' that road, mistress. Will ye can mind her yersel a' the aifternoon ? " Easie objected, casting a jealous eye upon the cradle, where the bairn, clean and quiet, was lying asleep.

" Awa' wi' ye—I'll mind the bairn. Is there nane but yersel' can dae that ? " Kate asked sarcastically.

She produced from a cupboard the parcel which Easie was to carry to the Braes Farm, and without further preparation the bairn-keeper had to set off. Somehow or other, Easie started on this long walk with curious misgivings. Kate looked so queer— she could not understand her—and how would the household get on all afternoon under her charge ? Grannie would be stiffening in her chair, and the bairn crying in its cradle, she felt sure. But hurry as she might to get over the long miles to the Braes, Easie could not hope to arrive home before evening. The dusk was indeed falling before, tired and hungry,

The Bairn-Keeper

she came up to the door of Leeks on her return journey from the Braes.

As she supposed, dismal wails were penetrating out into the chill night air.

" My certy ! she's left the door aff the sneck on Grannie's back ! " Easie exclaimed, darting in through the open door. The fire was black upon the hearth ; from the cradle the bairn kept up a steady screaming, and Grannie sat miserably in her chair, shuddering as the cold air from the open door blew in upon her poor old back.

" Eh ! Easie, lassie ! I thocht ye wad niver be here ! " she cried, as the welcome sound of the bairn-keeper's brisk little footfall came across the floor.

" Whaur's the mistress ? " Easie demanded indignantly, shutting the door and darting to the cradle to lift the child and quiet its yells.

" She's no weel ; she's awa' til her bed," said Grannie. " Eh, Easie, ma dear, it's terrible cauld the nicht, an' I couldna rise tae get at the bairn, an' it yellin' a' the time ! "

With blazing eyes and an almost awful energy, Easie set about the task of comforting her two forlorn charges. The fire had to be lit first of all, and Grannie wrapped in a shawl. Then the bairn was pacified with a bottle, and Grannie was provided with a cup of hot tea.

" There noo, ye'll be warmer," she said, as she knelt on the hearth, blowing up the smouldering logs.

The Bairn-Keeper

" Eh, I've an awfu' groosin' on me, Easie," the old woman complained, drawing her shawl more tightly round her, " an awfu' groosin' doon my back."

Easie was too inexperienced to feel any alarm that an old person should feel an " awfu' groosin' " down the back ; so she cheerfully administered the cup of tea and inquired after Kate—how she was and what ailed her ? But Grannie was mysterious ; she would not commit herself to make any statements, only by strange contractions of the mouth and shakes of the head indicated that something was far wrong.

" Ye'd best try an' mak' the guidman's parritch," she said. " Kate'll no be doon the nicht."

So this task was added to Easie's other labours. She grappled with it undaunted, and, when McLeod came in, was able to present him with a bowl of quite eatable, if slightly over-salted, porridge.

" Whaur's the mistress ? " he demanded.

" She's no weel ; she's in her bed," Easie replied.

Silence fell for a minute, then Easie heard the man swear roundly to himself. She had never heard him do this before, and wondered why he did it now. Oaths, alas ! were not unfamiliar to Easie ; she had heard plenty of them at the Huts ; but there seemed no reason why McLeod should be angry just now—how could Kate help being ill ?

" Maybe I could tak' something up the stair til the mistress ? A drop tea's fine when a body's seek," Easie said timidly.

The Bairn-Keeper

"Let her be, lassie," McLeod said gruffly—"let her be ; she's best let alane." Then, seeing Easie's mystified expression, he added curtly, "She tak's drink."

Thus was Easie abruptly introduced to the family skeleton at Leeks Farm. She said not a word on receiving the information, but shivered deep down in her heart. Life at the Huts had shown her only too clearly the meaning of the phrase, and given her an almost morbid terror of drunkenness. Kate sober had been bad enough ; but Kate drunk ! For a moment Easie's courage almost failed ; she would have liked to turn and fly from the house—anywhere, even out into the darkness. But, then, if she ran away, what might not happen to Grannie and the bairn ? The thought rallied her wavering courage as the note of a trumpet will rally a flying host. No, she would never desert them—not if she had to face Kate alone and unaided in their defence ! But in the meantime McLeod was still here. She decided to appeal to him.

"Maybe ye wad stop in the nicht ? " she said wistfully.

"Stop in ? " the man asked, not taking in her meaning at first.

" Bide in the hoose—dinna gang oot," said Easie ; and in a shamed whisper she added : " I'm feared of folk in drink. I've seen them gey wild at the Huts."

The man looked at her, half-inclined to smile at her timidity, and yet touched by it too, for he was kindly enough at heart.

The Bairn-Keeper

" I'll bide in. Pit Grannie til her bed," he said curtly, as he lit his pipe and sat down by the fire.

But Easie found that she had to face this terror again the next day, and that it was impossible for her to keep her protector in the house all the time. For obviously McLeod had to go out to his work, and then Easie must be left alone. When Kate McLeod took one of her fits of drinking, she did not drink and get it over, but went on at it for days at a time. She would get up and begin her work in the morning, but by noon would be quite incapable again. Thus poor Easie found herself with all the work of the house on her hands in addition to her care of Grannie and the bairn. It never occurred to her to question the justice of this arrangement or to protest against it in any way; she simply fought blindly on, doing all she could as well as she knew how to do it.

One good of this was that she had scarcely time to be frightened. After midday Kate was fairly quiet—generally sunk, an inert mass, into a chair, or sometimes even lying on the floor. Easie got into the way of going about her work without regarding her. The mysteries of the culinary art had now to be attacked—and here I must own that Easie failed dismally ; so the household came down to a very simple diet of bread and milk, cheese and tea, and such-like fare, which needed little preparation. So things had gone on for three days, and then, to crown all Easie's misfortunes, Grannie fell

39

The Bairn-Keeper

ill. The shivering of which she had complained came on more severely, and then she felt a pain in her side and back. There was nothing for it but that Grannie should be put to bed.

Easie realised then that she was nearly coming to the end of her resources. She carried the bairn to Grannie's room, took up her post by the sick-bed, and renounced all thought of keeping anything in order downstairs. It was a sorry household indeed that day. Grannie lay groaning in bed, flushed and restless, and tormented by a cough that shook her all to bits ; downstairs, in the disordered kitchen, Kate had collapsed on to the floor, where she lay unheeded for hours.

The long day crept on. Towards evening Grannie got worse, and Easie was frightened ; she did not know what to do. McLeod was late of coming in, and Easie shrank from going down alone to the kitchen where Kate lay, snoring heavily now in her horrid drunken sleep. She stood at the head of the stair listening till she heard McLeod come in, then she ventured down to the kitchen.

"Grannie's gey bad," she said, her voice trembling. The room was dark, except for the light from the fire, and the man could not see how white and drawn Easie's little face had become. But the next minute she broke out into loud sobs which revealed the tension of her feelings. "Ye maun get a grown body ; I canna dae more for Grannie. I've wrocht a' the day wi' her, an' she's waur nor she was. I'm feared she's tae dee. Oh, I'm awfu' feared !" All the tense strain of the last three days was in her broken words, her frantic sobs. No longer the complete bairn-keeper, she had become a child again, afraid of she knew not what—of life and of death and of all the powers of darkness that seemed to be crowding in upon her in that black moment.

It would be hard to say which of them felt the more impotent—the big, lumpish man or the puny child who stood beside him.

"Wheesht, wheesht, lassie!" McLeod began, dismayed by the violence of Easie's sobs, and searching in his mind for any possible helper. Leeks was a lonely spot, miles away from the nearest neighbours, and it was already late in the evening. Easie, in her present distracted state, could obviously not be left alone in the house while he went to seek for assistance. McLeod glanced from the sobbing child beside him to where his wife lay on the floor, sleeping off her drunkenness. "Gosh me! it's an awfu' business," he cried.

It was at this desperate juncture that a very prosaic angel of deliverance appeared in the well-known form of McCallum the baker. His cart had drawn up at the gate, but his whistle had sounded on deaf ears, so absorbed were those in the house by their own desperate plight. Now a brisk step came up to the door, the latch was lifted, and a cheery voice called out to them :

"Hoo's a' wi' ye the nicht, mistress?" He stepped in out of the darkness, carrying his basket

The Bairn-Keeper

of loaves — a welcome sight — but stopped short on the threshold, amazed by the picture before him.

"Losh me! what's a' this?" he ejaculated, laying down the bread on the dresser and advancing to the table. The sight of his kind face only made Easie cry more bitterly, and she turned to him and sobbed out all her woes in one long incoherent sentence:

"Grannie's that ill, she's an awfu' hoast, an' noo she's gey queer like, I dinna ken what she's saying— an' aye she'll tak haud o' me and say things ower and ower that I canna unnerstan, an' I'm feared she's tae dee—an' I'm that hungert—an' I'm feared o' the mistress—an' I've been a' my lane a' the day —an'——"

The voice of the whilom valiant bairn-keeper ("bold and firm!") trailed off into another tempest of sobs, and Easie collapsed on a chair and hid her face in her hands.

The two men exchanged glances. Then McCallum, a practical philanthropist of the first rank, addressed himself briskly to the situation.

"Hoots, man, come awa'! I'll gie ye a hand an' we'll tak the mistress up the stair till her bed," he said, addressing McLeod. Together they raised Kate from the floor and hoisted her upstairs. That was something done. Easie listened to their heavy steps as they dragged Kate along, and shuddered; but the kitchen did not seem so ghastly after that horrid inert figure was gone from it. She looked

The Bairn-Keeper

up when McCallum returned, and tried to dry her swollen eyes with the corner of her apron.

"Noo, Easie," he began, "the mistress is awa' til her bed, and McLeod's up the stair wi' Grannie. Ye maun pit on the fire an' mak' the supper. Here's a fine new loaf, and I've some grand cookies oot by for ye, an' ye can bile a wheen eggs." He stood beside Easie and patted her thin shoulder with his great, warm, floury hand. She smiled a vague, tearful smile.

"I'm that wearit," she explained.

"Aye, tae be sure! Maybe I could pit on the fire for ye," McCallum suggested. He raked away the ashes, brought in an armful of wood from the stack at the door, and soon had a huge blaze roaring up the cold black chimney. Things looked very different then. Easie crept towards the fire and held out her cold, skinny little hands to the warmth.

"That's fine!" she vouchsafed to say, wiping a last tear from her cheek.

"I'll fill the kettle for ye," McCallum said. "An' whaur's the tea an' the eggs, lassie?"

Courage began to flicker up again in Easie's breast. She stirred about the kitchen, producing from cupboards and boxes the requisites of the meal, only now and then a little sound, half sob, half sigh, would burst from her lips to testify to the past storm.

"Noo, Easie, my wumman," said McCallum, artfully employing a style of address which he thought likely to call up all Easie's latent pride, "when

43

The Bairn-Keeper

ye've had yer tea ye'll feel fine an' strong again, and ye maun gang up tae Grannie an' bide there a wee. I'll tak' the cairt roond Kippen way, and send Janet Mackenzie tae ye. She's gey skilly in illness, is Janet. Dinna ye fear for Grannie the noo if she's a bit wandered ; auld bodies fever easy."

Thus admonished, Easie at last sat down to her much-needed meal. By the time she had eaten two eggs, a quantity of bread-and-butter, and some cheese, also drunk three cups of tea, her fighting spirit revived once more. Tears were forgotten; she was mighty to do battle again.

" I'm fine noo," she assured her helper, " I maun be aff til the bairn an' Grannie."

" Weel, guid nicht t' ye, Easie, and keep up yer hairt," McCallum exhorted her. It was not an unnecessary exhortation. In the long hours that followed Easie needed all her courage.

Grannie had begun to shiver again instead of being too hot, and had to be piled with clothing. Then the shivering passed off, and she was crying out again at the heat. As the night drew on she wandered more and more in speech, till Easie was terrified. But when she was at her very wits' end, the welcome sound of a knock came to the door, and Janet, the woman " skilly in illness," made her appearance in the sick-room.

Her knowledge, had Easie only known, was not great ; but at that moment she seemed an angel of light. She shook her head and compressed her lips at the sight of Grannie's flushed face ; but Easie

The Bairn-Keeper

did not notice this—she was giving her patient a sup of water at the moment. With a good deal of the importance of office, Janet set about getting all that was needful for the night. Easie had to provide her with meal for poultices, and cloths to put them in ; a kettle, too, and various shawls and pins. Not unwillingly, you may believe, the poor child at last retired to her own bed when Janet declared she had got everything she needed. It was perhaps more than could be expected of human nature that the bairn should get much attention that night ; its toilet was very brief, and Easie was just getting into bed herself when Janet appeared at the door.

"Grannie's cryin' on ye, lassie," she said.

Up Easie got and back to Grannie she went. The old woman was looking more comfortable now. The bed had been tidied, and she had been lifted up on the pillows.

"What is't, Grannie ? " Easie said, creeping up to the bedside, a funny little figure in her short nightgown.

"Dinna gang awa', Easie ; I canna dae wantin' ye," said Grannie.

"Eh, but Easie maun hae her rest," Janet remonstrated. "She's gey tired, puir lassie."

"I'm no tired," quoth Easie sturdily. "I'll bide."

"Aye, just bide a wee while, Easie," Grannie entreated, closing her eyes with a peaceful expression.

The Bairn-Keeper

Easie gathered her bare feet up under her on the chair and waited ; she was tired to death, but her heart bounded with pride and delight. For the first time in life she felt herself essential to someone.

Janet threw a shawl round her and whispered in her ear to stay till Grannie fell asleep, and then to slip away. The room was very quiet ; you could hear the ticking of the big clock in the kitchen and the soughing wind round the chimney. Easie, perched upon the chair, a queer frog-like little figure, nodded now and then, then wakened up with the cold, and again would fall into an uncomfortable doze. At last it seemed safe to go off to bed, and she slipped down from the chair and noiselessly crept out of the room.

Two golden hours of sleep were then granted to her, but only two ; by that time Grannie was " cryin' " on Easie again. And once more Easie tore herself out of bed, saying proudly to Janet :

" Ye see, Grannie leans awfu' on me ; she canna be long wantin' me."

So it went on every few hours till the day dawned. When it was time to get up in reality, Easie was tired out. But up she had to get, and the bairn had to be dressed and fed ; and then the terrifying moment came when she had to descend to the kitchen and encounter Kate McLeod. That good woman had slept off her drunkenness, and wakened sick and savage. She was blundering about the dirty kitchen, incapable of doing any work. Easie thought it best to assume that she knew about

The Bairn-Keeper

Grannie's illness, so she volunteered the information that Grannie had had an " awfae nicht, but was a wee thing better noo." Kate grunted, and did not seem to take in how serious matters were upstairs. She begged Easie to make her a cup of tea, and sat down by the fire to wait for it. Easie hastened with this task, gulped some tea herself, and then ran up again to Grannie's room. She met Janet at the door.

" Bide a minit here, Easie," she whispered. " I'm wantin' a word wi' ye."

" What is't ? Is she waur ? "

" Aye, she's waur ; she's no tae get ower it, lassie. She's up in years, ye ken."

Easie drew in her breath hard. For the second time a great fear took hold upon her. She had never seen death, and the approaching shadow appalled her. How could she endure to face it ?

" Eh, Janet, I'm feared ! " she cried instinctively.

" Hoots, lassie ! we maun a' see deith soon or late," said the older woman robustly. She was not unkind, but her excellent nervous system did not understand Easie's fears, that was all. " Wheesht ! there she's cryin' on ye again," she added. And sure enough Grannie's voice, with a new, strange sound in it, was heard repeating Easie's name.

" Easie—Easie, lassie, are ye no' there ? "

" Aye, Grannie, I'm here. I was awa' for my breakfast. I'll no gang awa' another time," Easie cried, pushing her terrors away into the background of her mind with a great effort.

The Bairn-Keeper

Grannie was white as a sheet of paper now. All the fever was gone for the time being; she lay there shrunken away, it seemed, almost to nothing, but quite collected.

"I'll no' get ower this, Easie," she said. "It's a sair brash."

"Maybe ye will," Easie assured her.

"Na, na; I ken fine my time's come tae get awa'." There was a silence then, for, child-like, Easie did not know what to say at such a solemn moment. Then the old woman spoke again:

"Ye'll bide wi' me, Easie?"

"Aye, Grannie."

"A' the time, lassie? I canna dae wantin' ye."

"Aye, a' the time."

"Aweel, I'll no fash mair aboot onything," said Grannie, in a satisfied voice.

Easie had taken her vow, but she had still to find how difficult it would be for her to perform it. Fate seemed to have willed that obstacles were to be put in her path.

Visitors were not a common sight at Leeks, so that afternoon Easie was surprised to see an unknown man come up to the door. He knocked twice; then Easie, suspecting that Kate was not fit to see visitors, ran down to open the door to him.

"Is Mrs. McLeod at home?" he asked rather gruffly, casting a quick glance at Easie while he put the question.

"The mistress is in by, sir; but she's no verra

The Bairn-Keeper

weel the day," said Easie, using the formula which was generally employed, she found, at Leeks.

"Oh, indeed! Are you sure she couldn't speak to me? I'm Mr. Boyd, the inspector, tell her, and I've special, very special, business with her." He paused, planted a broad foot inside the doorway, and added firmly: "In fact, I *will* see either Mrs. McLeod or William McLeod, her husband. So no more nonsense, my lassie; just go and find one or other of them at once!"

The colour rushed to Easie's white, pinched face. The inspector—name of portent! She stood rubbing her thin hands together in an agony of perplexity.

"The maister's oot on the fairm, sir," she said, "an'—an'—sure's deith, sir, ye canna see the mistress the day."

"Is she so very ill? What's the matter with her?" the inspector asked. He evidently was not a person to be easily "got over."

Easie once again tried a little genteel evasion of the truth, but the relentless official would not accept her excuses.

"Tut, tut! What's all this? I don't believe a word you say. Go and find Mrs. McLeod immediately."

"Oh! sir," Easie cried at last, goaded to desperation, "she takes drink! She's gey bad the day; she canna speak wi' onybody." The inspector whistled.

"Oh, ho! Takes drink, does she! And who does the work when she's drunk? You, I suppose."

"Aye," said Easie, with pardonable pride, "I

The Bairn-Keeper

dae maistly a' the work whiles, an' mind the bairn an' Grannie."

" And how long have you been here doing all the work and minding the bairn and Grannie ? "

" Three month," said Easie.

" And how old are you ?   No lies, now ! "

" I dinna tell lees ! " Easie exclaimed passionately. " I was thirteen on the second day o' Juiy."

" When were you in school last ? "

" In June, sir."

" And this is the end of September.   Um !   And what standard were you in when you left the school ? "

" The fifth, sir."

There was a short pause while the inspector wrote down all this information in a notebook. Then, speaking with awful distinctness, and fixing Easie at the same time with a terrifying glance, he addressed his victim thus :

" Now, Easie Dow—you see, I know your name —either you present yourself at school to-morrow morning at the usual hour, or I send a summons to William McLeod."

" But, sir, I canna come the morn—it's no' possible," Easie cried, in dismay.

" Possible or not, that's how the matter stands. You're under age ; you haven't passed the sixth standard ; and back to school you must go for another year."

" And wha's tae sort the bairn and Grannie ? " Easie exclaimed, her voice shrill and fierce.

The Bairn-Keeper

" I can't tell that, but *you* are not to sort them.
You've to go back to school and mind your books
for another year."

" I've no books, sir," she objected.

" Then McLeod must buy you books."

" I'll no' gang—no' for a' the inspectors in Scotland ! " Easie cried suddenly. Her hands were
clenched, her eyes gleamed ; she faced this Tyrant
of Education like a little tiger.

" Oh ! won't you ? We'll see about that. But
tell me, why don't you wish to go to school ? Do
you wish to grow up an ignorant girl, unable to read
or write or count ? " he asked, surprised by the
wild antagonism Easie displayed.

" It's no' that, sir—I'd like fine tae learn things
—but Grannie's deein', an' I'll no' leave her till she
dees. She canna dae wantin' me."

The inspector considered this statement gravely.
The tiny creature before him seemed a frail reed for
the dying to lean upon. Could her story be true ?
He began to doubt it.

" I'll need to have that story corroborated by
some older person, I'm afraid," he said. " Do you
mean that you are the only person in charge of a
dying woman ? "

" No, sir ; there's Janet Mackenzie, from Kippen,
wi' her ; but it's me Grannie's wantin' a' the time,"
said Easie, modest triumph in her voice.

" But if there is an older person to look after her,
why does she need you ? " the man insisted.

" I jist keep her cheery like," Easie explained.

51

The Bairn-Keeper

" She's used wi' me, ye see, and whiles she'll speak a wurd wi' me when her hoast's no' sae sair, and whiles I'll sing her a bit psalm—and I can gie her a soop o' watter noo an' again, and she took a drop tea frae me when Janet was doon the stair. Ye see, sir, I ken hoo tae dae wi' her fine."

Thus vaingloriously did Easie boast of her skill as a sick-nurse; and the inspector, amused, and perhaps a trifle touched by the story, listened in silence.

" Well, Easie," he said at last, " if I let you off till Grannie is better—or gone—have I your word to begin school attendance then ? "

" And what aboot the bairn ? " Easie cried. " Wha's tae mind the puir bairn when I'm at school ? "

At this the inspector's dignity fairly broke down, and he laughed aloud.

" Do you think there's no one else who can mind a bairn but yourself ? " he asked.

" There's no anither body *here*," said Easie significantly.

" Then they must get another body, that's all ; and I'll write a summons to William McLeod next week. I'll give you a week to see how things turn out, and if after that time you fail to put in an appearance at school, there will be something to pay, I can tell you."

He turned away, and Easie stood in the doorway to watch his departure. The whole structure of her life seemed at that moment to be collapsing round her, the structure she had raised with such terrible

52

The Bairn-Keeper

effort. No longer was she to be an independent wage-earner—no longer an important person able to manage the bairn, depended on by Grannie ; deprived of these dignities and glories she would just become again a child at school, unheeded, unnecessary to anyone, dependent, non-wage-earning, occupied with a futile pursuit of worthless knowledge ! And then that terrible suggestion that McLeod would need to supply the school books—what did that mean ? What would he say to that ?

Poor Easie ! It was a bitter moment of realisation to her. She climbed the stair slowly, and returned to her post in the sick-room. She must make the most of the precious hours of usefulness that remained to her. Too soon they would be gone, and she once more an inglorious child, shorn of her brief authorities !

" Whatna man was yon at the door, Easie ? " Janet asked. " He was weel put on."

" Oh, jist a man on business wi' the maister," Easie responded warily ; though her heart was bursting with dismay, she would not reveal sooner than was necessary the indignity that was about to be put upon her ; time enough when, a week hence, the blow really fell. Just now Janet recognised her as a person of importance, urgently needed by Grannie ; let that impression be retained as long as possible. So Easie hugged her secret to her heart and said nothing to anyone.

That day the parish doctor was summoned, but had not much hope to give of Grannie's recovery ;

The Bairn-Keeper

it was not probable that at such an advanced age she could pull through this illness. Next day Grannie was worse, and then an awful hush fell over the house. Kate, sobered at last, sat moodily by the kitchen fire. She would not enter the sick-room ; the impending shadow terrified her.

On tip-toe, her mouth pursed, her heart beating heavily with apprehension, Easie slipped about upstairs. The bairn, poor lamb, reverted to something of its former untendedness these days, for Easie could not leave Grannie's side for ten minutes without being summoned back. Fear was knocking at her heart all the time, but loyalty kept her firmly at her post—only when Janet went downstairs for her meals a panic would overcome the child. What if Grannie were to die while she was alone with her ? She could scarcely endure the torment of apprehension she felt till Janet, kindly, reassuring, afraid of nothing, returned to the room.

Thus fully five days went on. And the Inspector's limit had been a week—seven days. Then the end came.

Perhaps some inkling of what Easie felt had penetrated Janet's heart after all, for with kindly dissimulation she bade Easie go off to her bed, as Grannie seemed to be " real quiet "—maybe she would not be cryin' on her for a bit. Grannie was indeed getting real quiet—with a quiet the reality of which must have struck any person more ex-perienced than Easie. But she, poor child, took Janet's assurance in the utmost good faith, and,

The Bairn-Keeper

being half dead with fatigue, gladly crept away to bed. She lay down without undressing, and never stirred till the light came in. Then with a start she jumped up. Eh, what would Grannie have been doing without her all night? How treacherous, how selfish she had been; she who had promised to be there all the time! Stung with confusion, Easie ran across the little passage towards the sick-room, and would have opened the door, but Janet met her on the threshold, her finger on her lips.

"Eh, I'm awfae vexed I slept in. Hoo is she noo?" Easie exclaimed.

"Wheesht, lassie; Grannie's awa'," said Janet solemnly.

Easie drew back in horror.

"Awa'—is't deid ye mean?" she asked.

"Aye, lassie, she passed aboot ane in the mornin'."

"And I no' wi' her!" Easie cried. "Eh, Janet, maybe she wantit me, and I no' there! What for did ye no come for me?"

"Na, na; she didna ken onybody—jist slippit awa'. Ye need yer rest, Easie—ye've been sair wrocht this lang while." But Easie's tears were falling fast; she refused to be comforted.

"Come in by—come, lassie, and see her," said Janet kindly. She opened the door and they went in. There, standing by the bed where so lately she had seen Grannie tossing in weariness and weakness, Easie received her first impression of the great restfulness of death. Not a line of weariness was left on the old face, not a furrow of pain—a grand repose.

The Bairn-Keeper

Instead of being terrified, Easie was strangely attracted by the sight—awed indeed, but calmed and reassured.

" Eh, Janet, she's awfu' bonnie—and that *still !* " she exclaimed through her tears. She did not now weep for Grannie, if she had only known, but for herself—for the charge that had been taken out of her willing little hands for ever.

So Easie stood, gazing at the quiet face, for a long time ; and then suddenly she turned and ran out of the room without saying a word. She had remembered the charge that was still left to her. The bairn, rather crumpled and forlorn, lay awaiting her care. Easie caught it up in her arms, and fell to work washing and dressing it with tremendous energy.

.   .   .   .

Grannie died on Saturday, and her funeral was to be on Tuesday. Monday evening saw a new member added to the family party at Leeks. This was Lizzie, the mother of the bairn. When Easie heard that Lizzie was expected, she formed a mental picture of the sort of girl who would appear ; she would be shrinking and ashamed-looking, Easie concluded, for the mistaken bairn would probably have crushed all her self-respect.

But on Monday evening arrived a big, rollicking, red-cheeked, good-natured-looking young woman, about as different from Easie's idea of her as any-one could well have been. The death in the house made it necessary for her to enter it soberly ; but one could guess that on any other occasion her entrance would have been a noisy one.

The Bairn-Keeper

" Sae puir auld Grannie's awa' ? " she said.
" Weel, she was gettin' gey stiff and blind. I was
whiles sorry for her mysel', sittin' there "—she
paused, to glance at Grannie's empty chair. Then,
catching sight of Easie, who sat in the chimney
corner with the bairn on her knee, she ran across the
kitchen and caught the child up in her arms.

" Eh, my bonnie wee lamb, there ye are ! " she
cried, without a trace of shame or contrition in her
voice or manner. She danced the bairn about in
her strong arms till it crowed with delight. Easie
stood up, her eyes fixed jealously on her charge.
Lizzie in the meantime was exclaiming with genuine
admiration on the improvement in her child.

" She's a real fine lassie noo." she said. Then
she glanced at Easie. " Y're wee tae mind a
bairn," she said, with a sound of good-natured
contempt in her voice.

" Aye, I'm wee," said Easie. She did not try
to assert herself as in former days. Lizzie laughed
and dandled her baby in her arms.

" I'll be takin' her mysel' soon," she said mysteri-
ously. " D'ye hear what I'm sayin', mither ? "
she continued, addressing Kate, who was baking at
the window.

" What's yon ? " her mother grunted out.

" Weel, it's this," Lizzie began, depositing the
bairn again on Easie's knee, and going across to
where her mother stood, " it's this, mother—John
and me's tae be marrit this day fortnight."

" Nane too sune," said Kate darkly. Lizzie
tossed her head.

The Bairn-Keeper

"We've got a fine bit hoose oot Kippen way, and I'll tak' the bairn wi' me there."

"A good thing tae," said Kate, "sic a fash she's been sin' ever ye had her."

"She'll no' be a fash tae me," said Lizzie hotly, "an' gin John and me had got a hoose sooner, ye'd no' have had her a' this while."

At this point of the discussion William McLeod came in from the fields. He greeted his daughter very sternly, but the greeting did not seem to annoy her in the least. She began at once to tell him the news she had just given her mother. He received it without a word.

"And what aboot Easie there?" Kate said. "She's engaged wi' me for six months—gets a shillin' a week and her meat—an' noo Grannie's awa', an' gin the bairn gaes, what for wad I keep Easie?"

"Send her hame," Lizzie suggested.

"She hasna a hame."

"Weel, then, ye maun keep her tae work oot bye."

The discussion raged thus for fully ten minutes, while Easie sat silent, listening as these arbiters of her fate disputed over her future. Too well she knew that within a day or two quite another solution of the problem would be given. Still she kept silence—not a word of the Inspector; she held on grimly to what remained to her of the life of responsibility. Even now, however, it seemed that her kingdom was going to be taken from her bit by bit. Grannie was gone, and now Lizzie was claiming the bairn.

The Bairn-Keeper

" I'll tak' the bairn the nicht," Lizzie told her, and Easie had to renounce the child to its mother with as good grace as she could muster.

"She'll maybe cry a wee," she said. " Being used wi' me, she'll ken a difference."

Lizzie laughed. " She'll surely ken *me*," she said proudly, as she lifted the bairn from its cradle and carried it off upstairs. Easie felt inclined to cry. Here she was, thrust aside, not needed by anyone ; she slipped away to bed (pausing for a moment at the door of Grannie's room where so lately she had always been going in and out) and crept into her own cupboard-like little chamber. She was free to sleep now without fear of interruption. No longer would Grannie be crying on her. No longer would she be roused by the whimperings of the bairn. Yet by some strange freak of our human nature, Easie wept bitterly at the thought of this undisturbed repose. The bed felt cold and empty where the bairn used to lie, and once again she started up, dreaming that she heard Grannie's voice calling her name. Each time she fell asleep once more, but at last an unmistakably real voice sounded in her ear, and the next minute Lizzie came in with the bairn in her arms. It was screaming lustily.

" Here, Easie, tak' her. She's that strange wi' me I canna get a wink o' sleep," she said impatiently.

Then indeed was Easie's hour of triumph. Sitting up in bed, flushed with delight, she joyfully received the bairn back into her arms. And the child, recognising her well-known touch, hearing her familiar voice, ceased its screams as if by magic, and snuggled down to sleep.

"Did ever ye see the like o't!" Lizzie exclaimed.

Easie positively smirked with delight.

"She's that used wi' me this long time," she said.

"I'm thinkin' I'll hae a job wi' her yet," Lizzie said, in a rueful voice, "but if ye'll keep her the nicht, I'll get some rest."

Easie acquiesced condescendingly, and the discomfited mother went off to seek repose.

In this way Easie felt that her dignity had been a good deal vindicated, and she came down to the kitchen next morning, proudly carrying the bairn, and fully aware that she, not either of the elder women in the house, was able to manage it.

This was the funeral day, and from all the district round the neighbours had been invited to the "buryin'." By twelve o'clock they began to arrive in twos and threes, black-coated and solemn. Then the minister appeared—dreadfully solemn also, and in the darkened "best room" they spoke together in low tones.

Easie was much impressed—or rather oppressed; for somehow, she thought, in her childish way, they should not be so sad. If they knew as well as she did all the weakness and weariness that poor old Grannie had got away from, they would not look so gloomy. But then the neighbours perhaps didn't know about these long hours of sitting in her chair, stiff and weary and not able to help

The Bairn-Keeper

herself—or about the long, long afternoons with nothing to do—or the blindness. Well, all these things were passed away now, and Grannie rested ; surely it was well with her—they need not look sad about it at all.

So Easie questioned as she watched the solemn assembling of the mourners ; and yet after the plain little hearse, followed by the company of black-clad men, had disappeared round the turn of the road, tears began to trickle down her cheeks, and she gave a big gulping sob. She, if no one else in the house, missed Grannie.

" Hoots, Easie, dinna stand greetin' there—it's a' ower noo ; gang ben the hoose and lift the blinds, we maun get tae wurk," quoth Kate.

.   .   .   .

The next morning as they sat at breakfast the postman came up to the door—a most unusual event at Leeks. Easie was sent to bring in the letter, whatever it might be. She did so reluctantly.

" Thae taxes," William McLeod growled, as he opened a large, official-looking envelope.

He read over the contents of the letter twice, then broke out with, for him, unusual violence, as he brought his fist down heavily on the table :

" Weel, I'm damned——"

" What is't, Willum ? " Kate asked curiously.

" Tell us what it's aboot, father," cried Lizzie.

Only Easie kept silence. She knew.

Slowly, because he was not a scholar, William read aloud the summons. It was quite distinct,

The Bairn-Keeper

and accused him, William McLeod, of employing as a domestic servant one Isabella or "Easie" Dow, the said Isabella being under age. The summons directed that Easie be sent to school immediately on receipt of the letter, should be kept there until she had attained her fourteenth year, and that William McLeod should pay for the school books necessary for her education.

When the truth penetrated to Kate's brain, she turned upon poor Easie in a very tempest of wrath. In vain the child protested her innocence, telling even with tears that she had been ignorant of all offence, and that she only wanted to earn her living and be a burden to no one. Not a word would Kate listen to ; and just because the blame rested entirely with herself she was doubly angry.

Then William began to question the legality of the summons. Had Kate known Easie's age when she engaged her ? Kate was reluctantly forced to admit that she had. And, knowing this, she had taken the risk ? Aye, she never took a thocht. This, of course, was strictly untrue, for Kate had weighed the probabilities of the case well before she engaged Easie. Some bitter vituperation ensued between the husband and wife, while Easie sat dumb and scared in the corner. Then she came up to the table and stood there, resting her hand upon it to steady her trembling limbs.

" Please, maister—what for will ye no send me back til my uncle ? " she asked.

" Whaur's he gane a' this while ? " William asked.

The Bairn-Keeper

Easie shook her head. No letter had reached her from this relative, whose one wish had been to be rid of the charge of a helpless child.

" Div ye ken whaur he is ? " William inquired.

" Na—he had no wurd when he left here," Easie admitted. There was a short silence.

" Please, maister," Easie said then, " I'll wurk wi'oot pay between whiles. I'm no' wantin' tae be a burden on onybody."

" Losh me, father," Lizzie struck in suddenly, " y're makin' an awfae clash aboot a wheen buiks."

She was feeding the bairn at the moment, and as she looked up to make this remark, it contrived to jerk all the contents of the spoon down upon its pinafore. Easie, distracted as she was, made a dart at her charge, and deftly scraped up the porridge with a spoon. She could not bear to see the child's frock spotted.

Lizzie's comment on the parental stinginess went home, for William suddenly broke out into a laugh.

" Dod, Lizzie, y're richt ! " he said. " The buiks winna send me tae the poorshoose ; it's mair that I've been sic a gowk."

" Ye have that," Lizzie agreed. " Onybody could see the lassie was ower wee."

But though her husband had laughed, Kate was not willing to take such a light view of the situation. Money was money, and she told William that he was a fool to speak so easily of it. " Siller's none sae easy come by—buiks indeed !—me tae pay guid

The Bairn-Keeper

siller for buiks for Easie ! " Her indignation knew no bounds.

" Haud yer clash, wife," said William at last, as he rose from the table. He was not such a bad sort of man when all was said and done, and some idea of Easie's unusual capacities had penetrated his thick brain during the late household crisis. It must have been some feeling about this which made him speak now. " Easie's a handy wee body," he said, as he stood lighting his pipe by the fire, "and she was gey guid wi' Grannie, mind."

" Aye," Lizzie chimed in. " She's real handy wi' the bairn."

" And what's the use o' a handy lassie if she's tae be in the school a' the day ? " Kate demanded.

" Aweel," said William, " there's nae mair aboot it. See here, Easie, dinna fash aboot thae buiks—there's two-three shillin's for them, an' ye maun be off till the school the morn. I'm no' wantin' the pollisman after me." He fished out the coins from his pocket as he spoke, and handed them to Easie with a grin ; but Kate darted across towards her.

" Haud aff ! " she cried. " I'm no' sic a saftie as you, William. She'll can pay hersel'. She's had a shillin' a week these three month frae me—that's twelve shillins she's got—an' she'll pay thae buiks oot o't."

" I've no got twelve shillins, mistress," Easie urged piteously. " Ye mind I crackit the bairn's bottle, an' ane and saxpence came aff me for't—an' there's been a bawbee for the kirk on Sundays—

64

The Bairn-Keeper

sax o' them—that's a shillin' an' ninepence, and there was a shillin' for the patch tae my boots—that's twa and ninepence aff the twelve—it's nine and thruppence I've got."

"Weel, tak' yer nine and thruppence and buy thae books," Kate retorted. But McLeod turned upon his wife savagely.

"Think shame on yersel', Kate," he said. "Let the lassie keep her bit siller; she's wrocht for it, I'se warrant."

"Aye, has she, mother," Lizzie chimed in.

Kate, finding herself thus in a hopeless minority, banged out of the room, leaving Easie to settle the matter with her defenders.

Now that the first bitterness of the blow was past, McLeod was inclined to look upon the whole thing as something of a joke. Easie's bite and sup counted for nothing, and, when he came to think of it, the books were nothing either. He represented this to Easie quite good-naturedly, and she began to face the idea of returning to school with a little more courage. Still Kate's hint that she might herself pay for the books rankled in her soul, and when McLeod had gone off to his work, she approached the subject again with Lizzie.

Instead of listening to her, however, the young woman got up and went out of the kitchen without a word. In a few minutes she returned, carrying one and sixpence in the palm of her large red hand. "There, Easie," she said, "yon's for my bairn's bottle. I think shame that mother took it aff ye."

The Bairn-Keeper

" Eh, but I was real careless," Easie protested, holding back from this lavish repayment.

" Hoots, lassie, y're wee—tak' it an' dinna say anither wurd," said Lizzie. Easie looked up at her and was surprised to see that her eyes were full of tears. She took the money, and ran away upstairs, to add it to the little store in the bag.

.   .   .   .

Easie's first day at school !

In the excitements of life at Leeks Farm, she had forgotten all the hateful monotony of school routine. Here she found herself back again at the desk, adding up sums, writing out exercises—no longer a responsible being occupied with tasks of portentous human interest, but one of a foolish band of children engaged upon subjects which did not bear upon life in any one way. Easie did not express this thought ; it was formless in her mind, but she felt it quite distinctly.

The schoolroom was close, and Easie, accustomed to the activities of Leeks, nodded over her desk. Nothing interested her. Of what use were those questions the master was putting to them all ? It was her turn now.

" Easie Dow, what are the constituent parts of air ? "

Easie shook her head. Had he asked her how to wash and dress a baby, her answer would have come pat enough. But what to Easie were oxygen, nitrogen, and carbonic acid gas ? Names, names, names !

The Bairn-Keeper

The master passed her by contemptuously, and a glib child on the next bench gave the required answer.

Then came a series of questions on the circulation of the blood to the heart, illustrated by a diagram of that organ on the black-board. It was a " general knowledge " class ; but of course it seemed to Easie that all this information was supremely useless. She listened contemptuously to this prattle of red and white corpuscles, of valves, and what not. . . .

But when the recitation class was called, Easie's interest quickened a little. She could understand something of what was going on now. True, it was a ruthless murdering of the masterpieces of English literature, but then our heroine was not critical in these matters.

With stammering lips and an uncertain tongue, a big stupid boy was repeating Milton's sonnet : " On his Blindness." The effect was somewhat as follows :

"When—A—conseeder hoo—ma—light—is—spent,
    Ere hauf ma days in thus—dark—wurrld—and—wide,
    And that one taulent which—is—deith—to—hide,
  Lodged wi' me useless tho' ma—soul—more—bent
  To sairve ma —Maker—and—present,
  Ma—true—account. . . ."

The words, garbled indeed by their rendering, penetrated somehow into Easie's drowsy brain. She sat up, listening and wondering what they might mean. " A talent which 'twas death to hide "—what was that ? " Lodged with me useless."

The Bairn-Keeper

Ah, she had it now! A sudden illumination from the flashlight of experience came to her aid. Didn't she know what it was to be kept from the work she loved and be set to useless tasks? Had Easie known the language of melodrama, she would have cried, " Avaunt these books ! " But as she was happily ignorant of it, she contented herself with letting her new " Reader " fall off the desk on to the floor. There she administered a savage kick to its smooth new boards, thus giving expression to her sense of its worthlessness.

Wicked Easie, and foolish Easie too, despising in this way the sources of knowledge. But you must remember that, with all her practical capacity, she was only a child after all. And, as a child, she had now to begin again humbly, and acquire some more of this much-despised book-learning. She must lay aside her newly acquired lore of life, and take up these less exciting but quite as necessary studies. The short, vivid chapter of her life was closed, and from being a bairn-keeper she had turned again into a bairn.

But when schooldays are over for Easie, I fancy she will have little difficulty in finding another sphere for her talents—that Kingdom of Heaven " where the merciful man will find himself out of a job " not having yet arrived.

THE TATTIE-BOGLE

THE TATTIE-BOGLE[1]

HOUSES very often seem to express the character of their owners ; certainly Cairn Tullie Farm was a case in point. You would have gathered at once from the look of the place that its owner was good-natured, easy-going, and comfortable, and you would not have been mistaken. The house stood full in the eye of the sun, and hills to the north and east kept off the keener winds that bit and tore at less favoured dwellings. The loch below the house was generally calm too, because a long spit of land stood out into the water and sheltered it from the westerly winds.

Janet McNee, who lived here with her son Sandy the farmer, had a great reputation for good nature. A big, lazy woman, she stood half the day in the doorway in the sun, with a pleasant word and a smile for every passer-by on that little-frequented road. Well fed hens pecked comfortably about the doors, half a dozen sleek, milk-fattened cats slept in the sunshine and carried on an intermittent warfare with the two great yellow collies—nothing was very tidy at Cairn Tullie, but the place was a home. Men and women had been born there, and lived and died there under the low-thatched roof,

[1] *i.e.* scarecrow.

The Tattie-Bogle

in the small sunny rooms. It was not the mere tent of a night as so many houses are.

This evening, however, something had happened to disturb matters at the farm. Sandy had been working at the hay in the morning, and had " taken a bit brash wi' the heat," as his mother expressed it. One of the infrequent spells of hot weather that occur now and then in the Highlands had fallen over the land. The hills reflected back the heat like the walls of an oven, and in the valley not a breath stirred. Everyone far and near was busy with the hay. Sandy had failed to find an assistant of any kind for his labours, so he and his mother had set to the task by themselves and toiled in the fervent heat till they could toil no more. Then Sandy, overcome by immense exertion and the unusual heat, had collapsed under the shade of a tree, to his mother's great alarm. She ran back to the house for the whisky bottle, and a wet cloth to tie across his head, but in spite of these remedies it was some time before Sandy " came to " again. Then, very sick and dizzy, he staggered across the field to the house, and Janet got him to his bed with some difficulty.

Obviously there could be no more hay-making that day, unless some strong helper could be found. With the optimism that was characteristic of her, Janet decided that such help would shortly be forthcoming.

" Some likely body'll maybe be passin'," she said ; then, remembering the pre-occupation of all the

72

The Tattie-Bogle

neighbours with their own hay, she amended the thought into one more probable : " There's sometimes a going-body can do a turn for ye."

She laid a fresh wet rag on Sandy's flushed forehead, and went to the door to look out for some chance passer-by. Everything was quiet in the intense heat ; the collies lay in the shade of the barn, their tongues hanging out, panting—even the hens had gone under cover. Yet round the corner of the road, stumbling along in the full glare of the sunlight, came a man—no, it was only a boy—no, surely it was indeed a man or something nearly approaching to one !

As the figure came nearer, Janet took a step further out of the doorway to gaze at it in surprise. The man—if he was worthy of the name—was the strangest sight you could see on a day's march. His clothes were really falling off him ; here and there they were tied on him by bits of string, but so far had they advanced towards dissolution that they fell round him in tatters—veritable flags of distress they were. What had once been boots made pretence to cover his feet, but the uppers had been tied on to the soles, and at every step the two tried to part company.

" Gosh me, sic a Tattie-Bogle ! " cried Janet as she watched the approach of this living scarecrow. Then, her optimism asserting itself, she concluded that, rags or no rags, the Tattle-Bogle was Heaven-sent and not to be flouted at.

" Good-day tae ye, it's gey warm on the road

The Tattie-Bogle

the day," she said cheerfully, and the figure halted by the door.

"Hot," he said, lifting his eyes for the first time. Such eyes—blood-shot, pulled down at the corners in an inexpressible way, vacant, tired, hopeless.

"Gang intil the barn an' rest ye a wee," Janet said; "I'll gie ye a soop o' soor milk; it's fine on a hot day."

The dogs had rushed out like wolves at the first sight of the scarecrow; but now, threatened by their mistress, only growled their disapproval of such a visitor. Janet escorted him herself to the barn, and he stumbled into the welcome darkness and fell rather than sat down upon a heap of dried bracken in a corner.

This was a queer-like customer to deal with, thought Janet, but she was blessed with the most robust nervous system, and indeed would have been able to knock the poor Tattie-Bogle over with her little finger if it had come to that, so she went off to the dairy for the buttermilk without a qualm. The yellow dogs squatted themselves beside the man like two lions, ready to spring upon him if he stirred hand or foot. In a few mintues Janet returned with the milk.

"Y're gey farfauchin wi' the heat, I'm thinkin'," she said, looking compassionately at the bundle of rags before her.

"Yes," he said, putting his lips to the pitcher and drinking down to the last drop before he handed it back to Janet.

74

The Tattie-Bogle

" I'm wantin' a hand wi' the hay," she said then.
" Are ye for a job or no' ? There's some going-
bodies that dinna care tae wurk."

"Rest," said the Tattie-Bogle. He seemed not
to be able to speak more than one word at a time,
whether from exhaustion or imbecility Janet could
not well make out. She looked at him dubiously.
" Weel," she said, " we canna leave the hay ower
lang, it's a fine heavy crop, an' if a storm comes up
wi' this heat that'll be an awfae loss." The steady
blue overhead was reassuring however, so after a
moment she added : " Aweel, tak' a bit rest the noo,
an' when the sun's doon we'll gang east tae the
field."

The man did not wait to be told twice; he simply
rolled over on his side in the bracken and fell asleep
there and then. Janet returned to the house to
see after Sandy, and the yellow dogs kept up their
cautious unwinking watch over the sleeping man.

. . . .

Soft-heartedness almost amounted to a vice in
Janet, so when she went back to the house her
first action was to begin to hunt up some clothes
for the Tattie-Bogle. " There's some old castings
o' Sandy's in bye," she reflected, " I maun hae
them oot—it's no decent tae see a body want for
what ye can spare."

She went into " the back house "—a fusty-
smelling receptacle for everything not immediately
in use—and hauled out, from the depths of a big
box, some well-worn clothes of Sandy's. " They'll

75

be ower muckle for yon puir craeter," she thought,
so produced a huge needle, linen thread, and her
brass thimble, and fell to work to shorten the legs
of the trousers by several inches. There were some
patches to be made too, and by the time these were
executed, long evening shadows had begun to fall
across the fields.

" I maun wake the body noo," said Janet, marching off to the barn with the bundle of clothes tucked
under her arm.

" Hi, my man ! " she cried, " ye maun be stirrin'."

Then, as the waif sat up and rubbed his eyes, she
went on, " Yer claes are gey far through. Here's a
coat and trousers will maybe fit ye."

" Clothes ! " the man exclaimed. (It is impossible to express his intonation.) And again :
" Clothes ! "

Janet saw that he seemed always to employ this
monosyllabic style of speech, as if he had forgotten
most of the tricks of the tongue and could only
wring out one word at a time.

" Aye, they're claes. Pit them on an' come east
tae the hoose an' maybe I'll can find a pair o' boots
will fit ye."

" Boots ! " he cried, " boots ! "

" Aye, thae bauchles ye hae on are fair done,"
Janet said, looking down at those shameful coverings
that were somehow attached to his poor feet. " Tak'
them aff, an' throw them on the midden at the west
end o' the byre," she commanded, " an' when ye've
cast thae auld rags, jist tak' them oot bye an' put

a spunk tae them; the verra tinklers wadna touch them."

" No," the man admitted, " no."

Janet went off again, leaving him to his toilet, and ransacked the back house again for a pair of old boots. These were difficult to find, for her well-known good nature made Janet an easy prey to every beggar on the road. So as there was nothing else to be done, she went into Sandy's bed-room and removed from it a very excellent pair of boots indeed.

" Sandy's real easy-going," she told herself, to condone the theft.

Thus it was that as evening fell a wonderfully improved edition of the Tattie-Bogle appeared at the door of the farm.

" We maun be aff til the hay," Janet told him, wondering what sort of workman her protégé would turn out. " Gang awa' yer lane an' begin spreadin' —syne I'll follow ye and gie ye a hand wi' it."

She went with him to the corner of the house and pointed out the field to him, then returned to " sort " Sandy for the evening. Half an hour later she joined the Tattie-Bogle in the field. He was working with feverish energy—his newly acquired coat had been taken off, and he was fairly running about the field in his eagerness to do all he could. As he whirled the hay-rake from side to side, Janet noticed that it was the great length of his arms, out of all proportion to his low stature, which gave him such a strange look.

The Tattie-Bogle

Together they worked on through the long evening till the dusk fell and a great mild summer moon came swimming into the pale yellow sky. Now and then Janet made a remark to her fellow-worker, but he always replied in one word only, and made no effort to keep up conversation.

As the moon rose and its light glinted on the creature's awful eyes, even Janet began to feel a little eerie. She flung down her rake at last.

"I'm awa' til the hoose," she declared; "we canna dae a' thae cocks the nicht, we maun leave them till the morn—it's a fine clear nicht, the hay winna harm. Gin ye come west tae the farm I'll gie ye yer meat and ye can sleep in the barn."

The Tattie-Bogle nodded, gathered together a great swathe of hay with one swing of his rake, and prepared to follow Janet to the house.

. . . .

The sun shone as hotly as ever next morning. Sandy was a little better—able to talk and to drink a cup of tea—able also to be deeply distressed over the hay. For when he tried to sit up in bed his head went "roond an' roond" again, and he was forced to lie down and give up all thoughts of work.

"Hoots, Sandy, dinna fash yersel'; I've got a grand body oot bye in the barn can work twice as weel's yersel'," his mother told him, laughing. Then she described to him with some humour the appearance of the Tattie-Bogle and the evening they had spent together at the hay.

The Tattie-Bogle

"I'se warrant ye gied the body a suit o' claes, mither," said Sandy, who knew his mother's ways well.

"Weel, what o't? What for wad ye keep the hoose filled up wi' auld duds that's no' required?" she retorted.

"I wadna hae claes tae my back if ye had yer way," Sandy growled; "it's time Grace was here —a fine thrifty lass, Grace."

Grace was Sandy's betrothed, a brisk young woman in service with the laird's family. Janet knew well that her own reign at the farm, with all its easy-going ways, would come to an end when Grace arrived there—she was so very thrifty, already she had laid by a good sum in the bank, and every year added something to it. Janet did not quite approve of all this, and had once made bold to question the young woman as to the circumstances of her parents—were they well enough off, to do without help from her? Were they still young and hale? But Grace always made evasive replies on this point.

Sandy, who had a good deal of his mother's nature, was already clay in the hands of his young woman. He admired her thrifty ways and her power of laying by money—a faculty he did not himself possess. So to-day, when he heard of Janet's gift to the Tattie-Bogle, he consoled himself with the thought that after all he would soon have Grace to keep things together, for they were to be married next spring. In the meantime his mother must just be allowed (as he expressed it) to "gang her ain gait" as usual.

He watched her now, through the door of his room which opened off the kitchen, as she moved about her work. To a more subtle observer of character all Janet's little ways would have been very suggestive. She did things on such a generous scale. First she threw a great armful of sticks on to the fire that it might blaze up into a more cheerful flame —then she shifted the big porridge-pot up a joint higher on the chain it hung from, and, apparently afraid lest there should not be enough of porridge, added a huge handful of meal to the mass that already bubbled in the pot. She would kick the collies aside impatiently and the next minute fling each of them a bone to atone for the kick.

Then she singled out a particularly large bowl from the rack above the dresser and filled it to the brim with porridge, took up a mug of milk from the dresser, peered at its quality, found this too thin, added a dash of cream to it, and finally went off to the barn to feed the Tattie-Bogle on this royal fare. In a few minutes she returned, breathless, to give Sandy a piece of news.

"Saw ye ever siccan a thing, Sandy?" she cried. "The body's been up half the nicht, an' the hay's a' in grand cocks, an' noo he's muckin' the byre an' him wi'oot bite or sup!"

"Did ye ever!" Sandy exclaimed, "Dod, I niver heerd the like o't," he added admiringly; "he maun be a fine man tae wurk."

The Tattie-Bogle

" Aye is he, for a' he's that shauchlin' and queer,"
said Janet, " but he's no' athegither wise, Sandy ;
he winna speak, an' he's a gey queer look in the
eyes o' him."

" Hoots, it tak's a wise man tae mak' haycocks
weel. He canna be muckle wrang. See you if he
kens aboot a horse, mither—I'll no' be up the day,
and yon young beast's gey camsteerie whiles—
tell him tae mind himsel' when he gangs intil the
stall."

" Aye will I," said Janet. She was immensely
impressed by the unexpected capabilities the Tattie-
Bogle had shown, but her curiosity was piqued by
his silence and his strangeness. She went out to
the end of the barn, where he sat eating his porridge,
and tried a little direct questioning.

" What's yer name, my man ? " she asked. He
shook his head, gulping down a big spoonful.

" What do they ca' ye ? " she persisted, altering
the form of her question. But the man only shook
his head and shovelled in the porridge like a famished
wolf.

" Aweel, I'll jist ca' ye Tattie, then," Janet said,
with a grin. " Ae name's as guid's another tae
wurk wi'."

" Yes," he said—and held out the now empty
bowl to her like a child.

" D'ye ken aboot horses, Tattie ? " she asked
him next.

" Yes."

" Can ye manage a camsteerie beast ? "

The Tattie-Bogle

" Yes."

" Then gang intil the stable an' feed the colt, an'
syne I'll hae anither job fer ye—the maister's no'
weel—it'll be the end o' the week afore he's aboot
again.   Will ye bide here and wurk the place ? "

" Yes."

Janet stood at the door and watched the man
shamble off towards the stable. A little later she
heard the clatter of hoofs and saw that Tattie was
leading out the colt to the water-trough. It was
a fine, rampageous young animal, " ill to manage,"
as Sandy always said. When it came out through
the stable door into the sunlight, it took a spring
into the air that was not very canny. But the
poor little Tattie man held on to the halter like a
vice, though he was almost lifted off his feet for a
moment.

" Gosh me ! he'll no' manage the beast," Janet
thought. But she was quite mistaken. He seemed
already on the most excellent terms with the horse,
and led it capering along to the trough, where it
dipped its velvet nose into the water, looking slant-
wise at its new master while it drank. Tattie
scarcely came up to the horse's shoulder as he stood
beside it—a poor shambling wreck of a man he
appeared, contrasted with the fair, shining young
animal he led. Yet, as Janet watched them, she
saw him lean his face against the beast's neck as
if they had been old friends, and she noticed that
the caress was well received. The dogs, too, had
made up their minds to like Tattie. As he came

The Tattie-Bogle

across to the byre they followed him, wagging their tails and giving furtive licks at his hand.

" He's a' richt : the beasts ken," said Janet, and she went into her son's room to assure him that all was well.

" Dinna fash yersel' aboot onything, Sandy," she said. " Thon body'll manage fine—the beasts are a' freens wi' him, an' they ken mair nor we do. Lie still in yer bed till ye get ower this brash : ye'll find a' thing richt when ye rise."

.   .   .   .

This was how Tattie established himself at the farm. It took quite ten days for Sandy to recover his strength, and in these days Tattie was wonderfully useful. Only his annoying peculiarity of speech made him a tiresome servant ; he either could not or would not speak, though he generally understood any directions that were given to him. When Sandy was " aboot again " there was some question of sending Tattie about his business ; but Janet was unwilling to do this.

" Hoots, no ; let him be : he's a grand wurker and y're no' that strong yet, Sandy—let him bide a wee."

Sandy did not like to contradict his mother, and Tattie was undeniably useful now that the autumn work was coming on ; so it was agreed that as " orra man " he was to remain at the farm for a time.

The question of wages had been raised at the end of Tattie's first week of work. But in the matter

The Tattie-Bogle

of money, the creature seemed quite deficient—one coin had the same significance to him as another; if Sandy had proposed to pay him a penny a week it would have been the same to him as a pound. Seeing this, Janet and her son agreed that it was nonsense to pay Tattie regular wages. "The craeter's no' wise; he hasna ony use for siller—it's a hame he's needin'," Janet said, "jist a hame, an' somebody tae mind him."

In pursuance of this theory, she decided to do her best to increase his comforts. She bought yards of thick shirting and with her own hands manufactured a set of shirts for Tattie; she provided him with "a change of boots," and knitted him many a pair of woollen socks—altogether he was well looked after. Just as a child appeals to its mother, Tattie went to Janet for everything he wanted, and somehow or other she always managed to understand him. But as winter drew on, both Janet and Sandy noticed that Tattie seemed to be considering something. They could not get him to say what it was, till at last one day he drew Janet into the barn and pointed up the ladder that led to an empty loft. Janet, following the direction of his finger, went up to the loft and Tattie scrambled up after her. "Weel, what is't? what ails ye?" she asked kindly, trying to help out his difficult speech. He pointed round and round the loft silently, then at last with a great effort got out two words :—

"For myself?" he asked—"*A home.*"

The Tattie-Bogle

The world of longing he put into the words would have touched a far harder heart than Janet's.

" Eh, the puir craeter," she said, adding, " Sae y're wantin' a bit place for yersel', Tattie ? weel, I maun see what Sandy says—the loft's no' wantit the noo. I'll speir Sandy aboot it for ye."

Over their supper that evening she told her son how Tattie had asked for the loft for himself. " Ye maun gie it him, Sandy," she said. " He does an awfae wurk tae ye wi'oot ony siller ; ye maun let him hae the place—and there's an auld wooden bed oot bye he can hae. . . ."

" Aye, and a mattress and blankets nae doot, an' an auld chair there's nae use for, an' maybe a bit table and twa three rags o' carpet," sneered Sandy —he was in reality rather proud of his mother's generous nature, and it gave him an excuse to let his own kind impulses have their way, but he liked to pretend that he disapproved.

" There's a wurd in Scripter ye should mind," Janet said with severity, " ' There is that scattereth and yet increaseth '—mind that."

" Weel, weel, hae yer way, mither—gie the body the loft," said Sandy, rising from the table, and laughing his rather foolish good-natured laugh " ye'll hae me in the Puirshoose some day."

. . . .

If you had seen that little home Tattie made for himself, it would have lived long in your memory.

As a bird in spring-time begins to collect straws and twigs for its nest, thinking nothing beneath its

The Tattie-Bogle

notice, so the forlorn creature cast about him for objects wherewith to decorate his poor resting-place.

He would consider the possibilities of every old tin can or broken shard he could find, and often walked miles in pursuit of such treasures. In the evening he would sit by the kitchen fire scouring his old tins with a rag and Bath-brick till he got a high polish on them, when he displayed them triumphantly to Janet. These, however, were only the decorations of the loft. Furniture of a kind had been produced from sheds and byres and barns : a worm-eaten wooden bedstead, two broken chairs, a meal-kist—over these effects Tattie gloated amorously.

With a hammer and nails he mended the chairs and actually got them to stand quite steadily. Into the meal-kist were packed his new shirts and stockings, his extra suit of clothes, his new boots. Only one thing was lacking—a table. There did not seem to be anything like a table to be found anywhere.

Tattie was like a disappointed child.

" A table ! " he would say at intervals of a day or two, with the air of one who demands gifts from the Higher Powers. Janet longed to provide the table, but in that region, far from shops, it was not easily done, and moreover Sandy jeered at the suggestion.

" Dinna be gi'en him a' he asks for, mither," he said. " It's fair ridickles." (Grace had been down spending the evening before with her sweetheart, and his judgment was tempered by her counsels.)

" Eh, the puir craeter, it's little he gets frae us an' muckle he daes," said Janet ; but in the face of her son's opposition she dared not buy a table. As the next best thing, she supplied Tattie with a box to act as table in the meantime—covered with a moth-eaten red cloth, the casual observer would scarcely have noticed that it had no legs.

As winter drew on, the loft became terribly cold. Janet turned the problem over and over in her kindly mind and finally approached her son on the matter.

" We maun pit a grate in for Tattie," she told him. " Ye canna let the body bide oot yonder in sic cauld—what wad ye say yersel' tae be sleepin' in the loft thae nichts ? "

Sandy grunted, thinking of Grace's thrifty advice, nor could Janet get any further answer from him at the time. But a few days later, much to her surprise, Sandy told her he had sent for the mason to put in a grate to the loft.

" I was talkin' it ower wi' Grace," he said. " And for a' ye think her near, she's no' sae hard as ye mak' her ; says she, ' Pit a grate in, Sandy ; it'll maybe no' be lost siller in the end.' And says I, ' Na, Grace, a body doesna lose in the end daein' the richt, says I ' ; sae ye see, mither, ye dinna dae Grace justice."

Thus rebuked, Janet was fain to believe in the generosity of her daughter-in-law-to-be. She was delighted, moreover, to have got the grate for Tattie by any means.

Highland workmen are, if such a thing is possible, slower than any other workmen under the sun. So it was well on to Christmas before the grate was got into the loft. When it was at last in its place, however, it proved that Sandy had not scrimped upon it ; for the grate was large and there was a fine hob for a kettle at one side, and—wonder of wonders—a little oven at the other side ! Altogether the grate was on a generous scale.

"What'll Tattie want wi' an oven ? " Janet asked, but Tattie found no fault with it. To see him carry up an armful of sticks and pile them up in the grate and then set a light to them was a sight to warm the heart. He would stand gazing at the leaping flames, and, when a shower of sparks flew up from the logs, would rub his hands together and grin. Then how cosy the loft looked in the firelight ! Tattie had swept down the cobwebs which had once festooned the rafters, and whitewashed the dingy walls. Above the fireplace he nailed up a shelf, and on it he lovingly arranged all his bright polished tins, his cracked plates and chipped teacups. Someone, humouring the creature, had given him an old brass candlestick ; and the very summit of his ambition was reached when he was given a " farthing dip " to stick into the socket. The cats were pleased to share Tattie's fire : three of them were generally to be found sitting in a row before the blaze. Tattie made them very welcome, and

The Tattie-Bogle

when he came in would stoop down and very carefully stroke each cat in turn ; thus no bad feeling was created among them. It became a habit with him to follow Janet to the dairy and get three of his cracked plates filled with warm milk; these he carried with much difficulty up the ladder, and deposited them before the three cats. Then he stood to watch them licking up the milk, and a slow smile would spread over his face the while. He had been so hungry himself, it seemed, that he loved to feed even the cats. The dogs found themselves in difficulties on the ladder, or they too would have been made welcome to Tattie's hearth.

There was something pitiable in his joy and pride in this poor kingdom into which he had come : that so poor a kingdom should fill any heart ! Janet and Sandy laughed and shook their heads over it. " The puir body—he's unco' pleased," they said. It did not strike them as pitiful, however ; they thought it rather a good joke.

. . . .

Spring was coming on apace after the long, long winter, and Sandy and Grace began to make arrangements for their marriage. You would have supposed that these would not be very complicated ; but it appeared that Grace had some ideas of her own upon the subject which were not entirely easy to carry out. She had, it seemed, decided to have some alterations made at the farm before she became mistress there.

" Really, Sandy," she told her sweetheart, " you

must smarten up the house a bit for me ; put out
a window or two, and have a stove in the kitchen
instead of yon horrid open fire. And then I want
a sink to wash the dishes in. I'm not used to such
rough ways."

Sandy looked a little ruefully round the cheerful
old kitchen he had known from his boyhood. He
did not relish the thought of a dismal iron stove
where the great roaring open fire was wont to be.
Nor would a sink adorn the sunny window where
Janet's chair always stood.

" Maybe the windy micht be a wee thing lairger,"
he admitted.

" And the stove, Sandy ? I must have a stove.
I'm that used to having things convenient," Grace
persisited.

" It'll cost a deal o' siller," Sandy said, bringing
forward an argument he thought likely to tell with
his bride.

" Not in the end ; these open fires waste a heap
o' fuel," said Grace.

So, after a little more arguing, it was decided
that the alterations were to be made. A jaunty
young tradesman from Glasgow came and measured
the window for the sink, whisking about with a
footrule and a notebook, telling Janet how necessary
it was to be " up to date " nowadays (an assertion
the good woman did not in the least understand),
and assuring her that a cheap cooking-range would
entirely supersede the open fire in her affections
before a week had gone. " No' it," said Janet

The Tattie-Bogle

with decision. " I canna be doin' wi' thae cauld,
black, dour things ; but my good dochter that's tae
be, she canna bide the fire, an' the auld maun gie
up til the new, ye ken."

"Yes, yes, we must march with the times," the
young tradesman said, jotting down a measurement
and whistling a music-hall air the while.

So the old order began to change. You would
scarcely have recognised the farm kitchen in two
months' time. A big window, out of all proportion
to the size of the room, admitted a glare of light
through panes of thin, very bad plate glass. The
window seat was replaced by a sink, warranted to
smell detestably in about six months ; the floor was
covered with linoleum having a chrysanthemum
design, and where once the great fire had blazed
and crackled, stood a sulky-looking stove which
smoked badly whenever the wind blew from the
east. So much for marching with the times. Janet
felt strangely at sea among these new surroundings.
The old home seemed to have disappeared ; she
was restless and unhappy. For this, after all, was
only the beginning of the end. She was no longer
to be the mistress here : a new order had begun.
Unknown to her son, Janet wrote a long letter to
her married daughter in Glen Tullie, telling her
the state of the case. By and by a letter came in
reply, begging Janet to come to Glen Tullie to end
her days there. Not that the good woman was
thinking of ending her days ; but this was how her
dutiful daughter expressed herself. There were

The Tattie-Bogle

six grandchildren at Glen Tullie, and much work they entailed. Surely Janet would be happier there than living on at the farm deposed by Grace, and not getting on very well with her ?

"Aye will I—I'll be better awa'. Grace and me'll never 'gree," Janet admitted. She was sorry to leave the farm—the home of a lifetime ; but there was nothing else to be done ; so she wisely decided to look only on the bright side of the situation. Her daughter and the grandchildren would amply make up for Sandy ; she was " gey fond of bairns " and they of her ; all would be well. On one point only Janet was a little disturbed—would Grace be good to Tattie ? Some warning inner voice told her that it was unlikely. For, alas ! poor Tattie was rather a burden just now, and Grace had not a patient nature. This was how it happened: Working late out in the stable, Tattie had managed to tear his hand on a rusty nail, an accident which did not seem at all alarming. But some poison must have got into the wound, for the hand was all swollen up next day, and Tattie was in great pain. It was a weary business after that, and many a poultice Janet had to make and apply. This was weeks ago, and still Tattie was useless. He sat in his loft, crouched together like a sick animal, nursing his sore arm and giving a grunt of pain every now and then. Not "a hand's turn " could he do about the place ; indeed, he was little likely to be able to work for some time to come. All this Janet realised as the date of Sandy's marriage

The Tattie-Bogle

drew near. She was practically certain that Grace would make herself disagreeable if Tattie still needed nursing after a little.

"I hope Grace'll be guid tae Tattie, the puir body," she ventured to say to her son one day just before the marriage.

"Hoots, mither, y're aye thinkin' ill o' Grace," said Sandy roughly. It was scarcely to be wondered at that he disliked his mother's attitude towards his betrothed.

"Weel, weel, I'm maybe wrang," Janet sighed. But the day before she left the farm she decided to give Tattie a great "speaking to."

"I'm awa' the morn, Tattie," she told him, "and ye maun mind yer manners wi' the new mistress when she comes hame. She's awfae genteel is Grace. She's pit a bit mattie at the door, sae look that ye wipe yer shoon on it afore ye gang intil the kitchen ; yon grand linoleum mauna be a' cover't wi' glaur. Try and do a bit turn for her wi' yer left hand, my mannie—carry in a bit wood tae her, and maybe ye could drive oot the kye noo ? Yer hand's a wee thing better, is't no' ? Ye mauna jist aye be sit-sittin' in the loft noo. Are ye heedin' what I'm sayin' ? "

"Yes," said Tattie. But it is doubtful whether he at all took in the subtleties of Janet's counsels or in the least understood that his best friend was about to leave the farm.

. . . .

When Grace began her reign at Cairn Tullie

everything was put upon a new basis. All the easy, untidy ways of the household were altered, and an extreme orderliness and punctuality took the place of the old happy-go-lucky system that Janet had pursued for so many years. Sandy's meals were always well cooked, and he was sure to find them on the table at the right hour; the braw new kitchen was speckless, and Grace as neat as the proverbial new pin. Yet surely the house had lost some of its old welcoming air—there was a sense of restraint and gentility about it.

For the first few weeks after her marriage Grace was occupied in that pursuit vulgarly known as "getting her husband under her thumb." Very cleverly she did it ; by little, imperceptible tugs this way and that, the knots were drawn tighter and tighter in the cords of his slavery. It is generally the case that one will gains ascendency over another in this way rather than by any gigantic tussle, and the ascendency thus established is always the surest in the end. Whenever Grace saw that she had a chance to break her husband's will on some small point she broke it—quite pleasantly, but it was done all the same. She knew that if this system were consistently carried out she would in time be able to do whatever she chose with him. Sandy was essentially weak-natured; he would do almost anything to avoid a row, so he saw no reason why he should ever oppose Grace about trifles— they didn't matter, he told himself; of course it

The Tattie-Bogle

would be different if it came to any big thing—
then he would be firm. He was quite unaware that
every trifle he gave in to added a tiny link to his
chain. Then at last he began to say with a laugh,
" Hoots, the wife aye has her way," and accepted
the position. This point gained, Grace began to
suggest larger reforms.

" It's time we were beginning to lay by a bit
money," she said.

" That's no' sae easy done," said Sandy.

"Well, I don't know. Why don't we let the
house for the summer ? " Grace suggested.

Sandy was astonished. The house had never
been let before.

" We canna let the hoose, lassie ; there's no' a
place for oursel's," he told her.

" Oh, aye, there's the loft," Grace said lightly.
" Tattie's room. A good room it is, Sandy, with
an oven and a window. It would do fine in the
summer, and see what a gain we'd have."

" But Tattie has the loft for his ain—ye canna
disturb the puir body."

" Dear me ! What's to hinder him sleeping in
the barn for a month or two ? " said Grace. She
had made up her mind that Tattie was to go altogether, but this must be worked up to ; it would
not do to turn him out suddenly. Sandy, with his
ridiculously kind heart, would not allow that.
But now that Tattie did nothing and ate a great
deal, and occupied the loft, Grace saw clearly that

she must get rid of him at all costs. She began with the thin end of the wedge.

" That's a fine hay crop you have, Sandy," she said. " You must mind and engage a man to get it in with you. I'm not used to outfield work, and Tattie won't be fit for it, I'm sure."

" Maybe he'll mend afore the hay's ready," said Sandy, shifting from one foot to another uneasily.

" Not him. I doubt if he'll ever do a day's work again. I had a look at his hand to-day ; it's all out of shape." She sighed expressively, adding : " He makes a good deal extra work to me—not that I'm grudgin' it."

" Eh, the craeter ! He'll get ower it yet, nae fear," said Sandy.

" Well, I'm sure I hope so ; there's an awful lot of work about a farm after you're used to being in genteel service, and Tattie's just one more to cook for and wash up after—oh, but I'm not grudgin' it."

Sandy went off to the field musing ; but he decided, after the fashion of the weak-minded, to do nothing at present and let things take their own way. He was sorry that Grace should have anything to complain of, and he was sorry for Tattie, too. Hoots, it would all come right—a man must give things time . . . he shouldered his hoe and whistled to the dogs, telling dull care to begone.

But next day Grace was at it again. She had had an offer for the house—some likely people from Glasgow—and she had told them to return next day

The Tattie-Bogle

for an answer. They offered a good rent. Surely
Sandy could see what an advantage it would be to
have a sum like that to put by in the bank?

" We'll do very well in the loft for a couple of
months," she insinuated.

" And Tattie in the barn? " Sandy asked.

" Oh, he'll do fine there. I spoke to him myself
this morning. He was quite pleasant like," said
Grace quickly. She had not said a word to Tattie,
but it made things sound easier to pretend that she
had.

" He's awfae set on his bit hoose an' a' his things,"
said Sandy, reluctant to give his assent, yet morally
unequal to resist the stronger will that governed him.

" Oh, we'll not disturb his bits of things," said
Grace.

" Weel, weel, have yer way, wife—but dinna vex
the puir body."

" Just you leave him to me," said Grace confidently, her face aglow with the prospect of money-
making. She cared no more for Tattie than she
would have heeded a fly under her duster. No
sooner was Sandy off to the fields than she set to
her task. That it was painful never occurred to
her. Out to the barn she swept, and up she went
to the loft.

Tattie crouched as usual by the window, nursing
his sore hand as if it were a baby, and crooning over
some old tag of a song to himself. He rose and
touched his cap to the new mistress, mindful of
Janet's words.

The Tattie-Bogle

"Good morning, Tattie," said Grace briskly. "I've come to give a look round the loft. We're letting the house ye see, and we'll need the loft for ourselves."

Tattie looked mystified.

"My house?" he said stupidly, twice over. "My house?"

"It's not *your* house at all. It never was," said Grace, getting quite angry. "Here," she added, "I've just had enough of you. Me and Sandy have been talking it over and you're to go."

"Go?" Tattie repeated.

"Yes, *go!* We can't be looking after you for ever—now you can't work. The harvest's coming on, and lots of work to do ; you're to go."

Tattie stood at gaze, apparently quite uncomprehending. Then he touched his arm. "Sore," he said, "can't work."

"No more you can, so you won't stay here eating off your head," said the pitiless young woman. Her eyes, blinded by self-aggrandisement, saw none of that almost divine quality in weakness and suffering that most people recognise there ; she only felt provoked by the half-witted weakling who stood mumbling before her. Every moment her resolution became more inflexible. She would make short work of the matter before Sandy came in again. Feeling in her pocket, she drew out one or two coins and laid them in Tattie's left hand.

"There's for you from Sandy, and you're to be off now ; pack up your bits of things and be off with you," she said.

The Tattie-Bogle

"Sandy!" the creature cried out, taking in all the misery of his own case at last. "Where's Sandy?"

"He's gone away for a week," said Grace quickly. "I was to give you this and send you off."

Tattie stood and pointed from one of his treasures to the other—the old wooden bed, the chairs, the polished tins.

"All mine," he said, and then shook his foolish head, and a tear trickled down from his poor bleared eyes.

"Don't stand blubbering there. See, I'll roll up your things for you," said Grace, anxious to put an end to this scene. She opened the chest in the corner and turned out its contents : the change of clothes, the shirts Janet had made, the new socks—all these she folded dexterously up into a bundle, pinned it together with a pin or two, and handed the bundle to Tattie.

"There, be off, or I'll have the polissman after you!" she said.

This parting thrust sent Tattie quickly down the ladder. He had the vagrant's terror of the law. Across the yard he slouched towards the open door of the farm. Grace, her heart beating a little faster from this encounter, stood to watch him go. He paused on the doorstone and peered into the empty kitchen.

"Sandy! Mistress!" she heard him call, and again "Sandy! Mistress!" with a curiously pleading intonation. Then, when no one answered, he shambled away down the road, his head sunk forward on his breast, looking neither to the right nor

The Tattie-Bogle

the left, and vanished as he had appeared just a
year ago round the distant corner.

. . . .

Sandy came in for dinner and suspected nothing,
because Grace, with far-seeing craftiness, took out
a portion for Tattie to the barn, and returned with
an empty plate, the dogs having had an excellent
dinner. But towards sundown he inquired where
was Tattie ? " I havena sichted him the day ;
hoo's the body's hand, I wonder ? It's gey sore
whiles, I'm thinkin'. I'll gang up til the loft an'
speir hoo he is."

Grace said nothing, and Sandy went off to the
barn. In a few minutes he returned, a strange
look on his face.

" Gosh, Grace, he's awa' ! no' a scrape o' him
left ! A' his claes gane frae the kist. Whaur's
the puir body ava ? "

Grace feigned as great surprise as her husband,
and was able to declare truthfully that she had no
idea where Tattie was. Questioned more closely,
she had to confess that she had spoken to him in
the morning of the possibility of their needing his
room ; but her account of the interview was far
away from the truth.

" He's maybe taken a huff ; these queer bodies
often do, Sandy. I wouldn't heed him," she said.
" He'll come back to-morrow, when he feels hungry,
no doubt."

" He had a fine dinner the day, too," said simple
Sandy. " Did he speak then ? "

"Not a word," said Grace, congratulating her-

The Tattie-Bogle

self, as liars generally do, on being able in this instance to speak the exact truth.

" He maun hae slippit awa' after his diet," mused Sandy. " Queer ye didna see him go by the windy, Grace."

" I've more to do than look every time Tattie passes," she said, tossing her head.

" I'll awa' tae the village and see if onybody has wurd o' him," said Sandy, stretching up for his cap that hung on a nail above the fireplace.

" You're a fool to fash yourself about him, I'm sure ! " said Grace. " Just leave him alone."

Sandy for once was of another opinion, however. It was getting dark now—that velvety dark of the Highland night, with flittering bats, and the hills showing black against a faint yellow sky.

Sandy loped along the three miles to the village at a great pace, his big nailed boots leaving patterns in the thick white dust that covered the road. He smoked as he went, and stopped to have a crack with every neighbour he met, invariably asking if they had by any chance seen Tattie.

Yes, one man told him at last, Tattie had passed early in the morning, carrying a bundle.

" Na, na, no' in the mornin' ; y're wrang there," Sandy corrected him, " for he was west at the farm for his diet at noon."

" That may be, MacNee ; but he passed me at ten o'clock the morn," his neighbour insisted ; " and awfae queer he lookit."

Sandy could not grapple with this disparity of hours, but, assured now of Tattie's direction, he

The Tattie-Bogle

forged on towards the village, sure of getting the information he desired. Rumour with her thousand tongues indeed waited him there : Tattie had been seen ; Tattie had gone into the inn ; Tattie had got drunk; Tattie had come out; Tattie had gone west the road, very drunk—there the stories ended. Sandy was a little annoyed, but not much. In his eyes " takin' a glass " was a venial offence.

" Hoots, I maun get him hame, puir body ; a wee thing wad gang til his heid," he said, biting more firmly on his pipe as he started off in search of Tattie. It was a thickly wooded road, and all under the trees now was as black as night. Sandy went slowly, searching as best he could, along the road-sides and in the ditches wherever a drunken man would be likely to have fallen ; but nowhere was Tattie to be found. In the darkness the owls came out and hooted wildly ; one of them flew right at Sandy and beat its wings in his face. He swore roundly, not liking either the darkness or the owls, and began to feel cross with the missing Tattie.

" Aweel, I canna dae mair ; he maun jist sleep it aff as many anither decent man has done," he said to himself. " I canna be oot a' the nicht seekin' him. Grace was richt—she's aye richt ; I shouldna hae fashed mysel' wi' him."

With this consoling thought Sandy " turned him right and round about " and made for home again, trying to argue down the pricks of conscience. After all, the loft was his, not Tattie's, and it was absurd of the creature to take offence and go off in this way after all they had done for him. Sandy

The Tattie-Bogle

even tried to lash himself into a state of righteous indignation with the absentee, but somehow the piteous, humble face of Tattie would always rise up in his memory; it was no good trying to be angry with the creature, whatever he had done.

"Hoots, I'll find him the morn an' get him hame. It doesna dae tae be angered wi' the likes o' him," he told himself.

.   .   .   .

The next morning was Sunday, so everything was very quiet at the farm. Breakfast had been a little later, as a concession to the day of rest, and Sandy, in his best clothes, stood smoking at the door. He had his mother's habit of standing there in any odd minutes of time, to speak a pleasant word to any neighbour who went by, to hear a bit of news, and "pass the time of day." He looked rather dull this morning; he was thinking about Tattie, and had decided that it was his duty to go off again immediately in search of him.

"I'm a wee thing vexed aboot Tattie," he called across his shoulder to Grace.

"Tuts! You and Tattie!" she answered contemptuously. So Sandy, ashamed of his tenderheartedness, walked off to the barn to escape further ridicule. There, coming round the corner of the house, whom should he meet but the village policeman—an unusual sight on a Sunday. He was a young, stout man, unaccustomed as yet either to his duties or his tight new uniform, and exceedingly anxious to adorn his profession. Sandy was delighted to see him; he was the very man he

The Tattie-Bogle

wanted. He questioned him eagerly as to whether he came with news of Tattie.

" I ken he took a drop yesterday ; but surely ye knew better than tae pit him in the lock-up, sergeant ? " he said.

The policeman pursed his lips, full of the importance of office.

" Can ye give me some particlers, Mr. MacNee ? " he said, bringing out a little black book and a pencil. " I'm wantin' some particlers."

" Hoots ! I've nae particlers for ye. He's jist a puir silly body that bides here wi' us, an' ye ken that as weel's mysel', sergeant."

But your born policeman is not to be balked of those doubtful joys which sometimes fall to him in the exercise of his profession.

" I must have particlers," the man insisted.

" Weel, come in bye, then, an' tak' a chair," Sandy said ; and together they stalked into the kitchen, much to the surprise of Grace.

" Here's the polissman wantin' particlers aboot Tattie," Sandy explained, a trace of sarcasm in his voice. The policeman sat down by the table, grasped his pencil in unaccustomed fingers, and turned over the leaves of the virgin notebook that had never yet held notes of any conviction. Tattie was evidently going to be the first case. Then, as Sandy stood smiling ironically at this fussiness, the policeman spoke these startling words :

" If ye can't give me particlers, then, Mr. MacNee, I must enter it under the heading ' *Death of person or persons unknown*,' I suppose." The phrase

The Tattie-Bogle

pleased him mightily ; he rolled it under his tongue, repeating, " Person or persons unknown," and watching with solemn relish the effect of this announcement upon his hearers.

" Deith ! Wha spoke o' deith ? Tattie's no deid ! " Sandy cried.

" Aye is he," said the policeman, forgetting his fine speech for a moment ; then, correcting himself and searching in his mind for some more dignified phrase, he added : " Life was extinc', as ye may say, when I found him this morning. Yes, that was it, life was extinc'."

Sandy was knocked perfectly stupid by the news. He sat down by the table, his big hand flung out across it, and repeated over and over again, " Eh, puir Tattie—puir Tattie ! " Grace, more self-possessed, drew near the policeman and questioned him as to the details of the case.

" I jist found him in the ditch, Mistress MacNee, a bit down through the wood," the man told her, " jist in the ditch, face down. Being in liquor, ye see, and his sore hand, he couldn't raise himself— jist fair choked, poor body ! I'll put down, ' Cause of death : Suffocation.' " He bent over his notebook again, entering the words laboriously into it. Sandy in the meantime had collected himself a little.

" What for did they gie the puir body sae muckle drink ? " he demanded. " Onybody could see a wee drap wad harm him. An' whaur got he the siller for't ? He didna get siller frae me."

Grace turned away to jerk a pan about on the stove.

The Tattie-Bogle

" I missed three shillings," she said in a low voice.

The policeman pricked his ears, and added a note into his book, regretfully, however, for even his intelligence could see the futility of convicting a corpse. But at this Sandy jumped up from his seat with an angry exclamation.

" Haud yer tongue, Grace ! Dinna ye ever say that wurd again ! Mind, sergeant, no' a wurd tae ony ither body o' that. Tattie was aye a good servant tae me ; I've naething against him."

" But three shillings—" the man of law and order protested.

" Damn ye, man ! Haud yer tongue aboot thae shillings ! " cried Sandy so furiously that the constable shrank before him.

" Well, then, Mr. MacNee, since y're so kind, we won't prosecute," he said grandly. " Is it yer wish to bury this man at yer own costs ? "

" Aye is it ! Wha wad dae it else ? "

" There's the parish," Grace suggested. Sandy turned and looked her full in the eyes. Then he took her by the shoulders and pushed her before him into the little room off the kitchen and closed the door upon her.

" Bide you there, Grace," he said ; " me and the constable'll arrange a' thing thegither."

.   .   .   .

So Tattie came into undisputed possession of six feet of earth—a resting-place from which no man would turn him out, which might really be called his own at last.

OWER YOUNG TO MARRY YET

OWER YOUNG TO MARRY YET

" NICHOLSON's Orphanage and Training Home for Young Servants " : you may visit it any day, inspect its spotless dormitories and class-rooms, pry into its inmost workings, examine personally each of its fifty inmates, and yet be unable to find the slightest fault with anything.

Except—but here a very big except comes in—that a chill will creep round your heart at the thought of fifty young lives growing up in the terrible iron precision of the place. Not a tendril of individuality allowed to escape the shears of system ; each little budding character relentlessly pruned down to the regulation shape and kept to it.

But no such sentimental reflections overcame good Mrs. Gilchrist, of Sandyhill Farm, in the county of Fife, when she arrived one day to interview Miss Martin, the matron of Nicholson's, about a young servant.

Mrs. Gilchrist had gone over the whole institution in company with the matron, and they had prosed, as such women will, on the (to them) exhaustless subject of domestic servants. In the class-rooms she had been shown the fifty little orphans, all dressed alike in peculiarly hideous frocks of speckled brown and white cotton, with their hair dragged back from their foreheads by crop combs. When they stood up it was exactly as if a set of nine-pins had come to life, so precisely similar was each child to the other. The fifty were divided by age into different classes, so that even their height was in most cases identical—the younger girls in two classes, the older ones in three others, for the orphans ranged from four to fifteen, at which age they were supposed to go out into the world to seek their desperate little fortunes as best they might. They were equipped, it is true, with a good knowledge of household work, a fair education, and even an outfit of simple clothes—all these they had; but of love, the one thing that is most needful in a young life, they were cruelly destitute.

To return to our story. Mrs. Gilchrist had told Miss Martin just what she wanted: " A nice young general servant; not perfection, Miss Martin, for you won't get it nowadays, but one I can make something of." (Women of this type will quite invariably make this remark and agree upon it with portentous headshakings, though it is much to be questioned whether perfection was at all easier to find in olden times than it is in the twentieth century.)

" No more you will," Miss Martin agreed. " I don't know one among all my girls that I could call perfect in her work." (Poor mites, it would have been sad if they had been, at their age !)

" Well, as I say, I don't expect perfection ; but I must have a good worker, and I hate a lazy girl."

Ower Young to Marry Yet

Miss Martin dubitated, her thick underlip thrust out in an ugly expression of intense consideration. She was an excellent woman, kind and capable, made for the position she occupied—but the gods had denied her beauty.

" I wonder now would Divina Binning suit you ? " she exclaimed suddenly.

" Tell me about her," said Mrs. Gilchrist.

" Well, Divina's the oldest girl I have just now ; she's home from a place where she's been for a while. Divina's sixteen and more now, and a well-grown, healthy girl."

" Why did she leave her place ? " the intending mistress asked ; and again Miss Martin fell into her ugly grimace of deliberation.

" Well, I don't mind telling you that I took Divina away myself. The fact of the matter was, I found they were not very desirable people. They gave almost no wages either. I didn't mind that as a beginning, however ; no, it was other things I found out convinced me it wasn't the place I wanted for one of my girls, so I advised Divina to come back here for a week or two while I looked out another place for her, and she's here now. I have to be careful the sort of places I send my girls to." The two women looked at each other and nodded sagely.

" Indeed you do. Well, what about Divina's work ? " Mrs. Gilchrist said.

Miss Martin paused, apparently summing up the character of the absent Divina before she spoke.

Ower Young to Marry Yet

" Divina can work when she likes, Mrs. Gilchrist. She's a good riser, a fair cook, and honest and respectable ; but she's careless—very. It wouldn't be right of me not to warn you of it. But there's one thing about Divina—everyone that has to do with her likes her. I like her myself, though I was never done reproving her all the years she was here. She came to me a child of six, and so I've a good knowledge of her. Divina's full of faults ; but I advise you to take her, Mrs. Gilchrist ; you might get many worse."

It was not a rose-coloured character sketch, but it was an honest one. Mrs. Gilchrist finally asked to see the girl, and Miss Martin bustled off in search of her.

Divina appeared : one of the regulation Nicholson type, only taller ; gowned in hideous speckled print, aproned in white, an image of decorum and tidiness. Her curly red hair had been remorselessly treated with a wet brush, which had almost managed to flatten it down—only her eyes defied all the powers of Nicholson's to change their congenital sparkle.

" This is Divina," said Miss Martin, by way of effecting an introduction between mistress and maid. " And, Divina, Mrs. Gilchrist here is wanting a general servant."

Divina bobbed an old-fashioned courtesy, as she had been taught to do, and kept silence.

" I've a farm in Fife," Mrs. Gilchrist said, " and I think you may suit me for a general servant. There's not much work, for there's only myself in the house. You get good food, and can get early to bed if you like ; but I like a girl that will rise early, and a willing girl, and one that can take a telling."

" Yes, m'am," said Divina.

" I think you're always willing to do your best, are you not, Divina ? " said Miss Martin anxiously —it was like pressing a pair of reluctant lovers to come to the point.

" Yes, m'am," said Divina again.

" And many a telling you've taken from me," said Miss Martin, with a smile that roused an answering sparkle in Divina's eyes, while she made answer once more :

" Oh yes, m'am."

" Well, then, Divina, I think you may suit me quite well," said Mrs. Gilchrist. " Do you wish to try the place ? "

" Yes, m'am, thank you ; I'd like to try the place, please."

Thus the bargain was come to, and then Miss Martin and Mrs. Gilchrist fell to discussing the question of wages. Finally Divina was engaged to go to Sandyhill Farm on the first of the following month at the rate of one pound a month.

" And you may count yourself a very fortunate girl," Miss Martin told her, " to get a good place, a kind mistress, and twelve pounds a year. You couldn't get a better start in life ; see that you make the best of it ; it's not every girl who is so lucky."

Ower Young to Marry Yet

Divina was quite of the same opinion, and set off blithely to seek her fortunes in the kingdom of Fife.

. . . .

In the next six months Divina made about as many mistakes as it would have been possible for one girl to make in the given time ; yet, strange to say, at the end of these six months, Mrs. Gilchrist decided to ask her to stay on for the summer. There was certainly "something," as Miss Martin had said, about Divina which made one like her in spite of countless faults. She was so intensely willing, so impetuously obliging, that, although these qualities often led her into the most provoking mistakes, it was impossible to be angry with her for more than a minute. "I must try to make something out of her yet," Mrs. Gilchrist thought. The fine, caller air of Fife, the healthy work, and the good food she got were in the meantime making something of Divina physically. She was developing into a very pretty young woman indeed, rather to the dismay of her mistress, who had a slight distrust of too much beauty. "She'll need looking after," the good woman thought ; "there are so many lads about the place." Divina, therefore, had a tolerably strict watch kept upon her—a watch she did not resent in the least ; it was as nothing compared with the stringent discipline of Nicholson's. The girl went about her work gaily, singing, as she scrubbed the floor or peeled potatoes, in a shrill soprano voice that made Mrs. Gilchrist clap her

hands to her ears and command her to be silent.
Then Divina would chirp out, "Oh, I'm sorry,
m'am," in the most pleasant way, but ten minutes
later would be at it again. One might as well have
commanded a canary in a sunny room to be mute.

Still, whenever Mrs. Gilchrist thought of sending
Divina away, it seemed as if the house would be
intolerably dull without her; so she decided to keep
the girl and put up with her many shortcomings for
the sake of her pleasant nature.

"Are you willing to stay on here, Divina?" she
asked her one morning.

"Yes, m'am, quite willant," said Divina, who had
retained some of her native idioms in spite of all
the educational advantages of Nicholson's; "I like
fine to be here."

"I'm glad of that; I thought you were looking
well and bright lately," said Mrs. Gilchrist, rather
flattered, naturally, to find that her place was considered such a happy one. Divina grinned, and
fell to work scrubbing the kitchen table with great
energy.

"I'm sure it's a comfort to see a girl so contented
in these days," said Mrs. Gilchrist; "most of them
fly from one situation to another every six months
in search of excitement. I'm glad to see you have
more sense." Had she known the true reason of
Divina's present contentment, her mind might not
have been quite so easy; happily for herself, however, she was not omniscient, and the girl kept her
own counsel. This was the secret, such as it was:

Ower Young to Marry Yet

One fine evening, some weeks before, Divina had been sent across the yard to the dairy for a jug of cream. She carried in her hand Mrs. Gilchrist's most precious old china cream jug—a manifestly absurd thing to do. As she crossed the yard, John Thompson the ploughman came through the gate, leading his horses to the water-trough.

John was a handsome, well set up man, but of a taciturn, unfriendly nature, very unlike that of our young friend Divina. With a nod and a smile she passed the time of day with him, but John gave only the most surly response, and tramped on across the yard, the great, thirsty horses hastening their laggard steps as they smelt the water.

Divina was angry; what had she done to be treated like this? All her budding feminine instincts were roused to life; she determined that John must be the captive of her bow and spear. But in her anger she did not look where she was going, and stumbled on the step at the dairy door. The jug fell from her hand and cracked across on the stones. For a moment Divina stood perfectly still, gazing at the broken jug; then she sat down and burst into tears. Her simple grief over what she had done would have melted a heart of stone, and John, turning to see what was the matter, left his horses at the trough and came across to where she sat weeping among the fragments of broken china.

" It's the best chiny—the very best," she sobbed. " And Mrs. Grant from the Mains coming over for her tea and all." She wept aloud.

Ower Young to Marry Yet

Even John was melted to pity, and sought for some consolation to offer her.

"The mistress'll no' be hard on a bonnie lassie like you," he assured her, taking certainly the surest way he could have taken to erase all thought of her fault from Divina's mind. It was the first time in her life that she had heard herself called bonnie —no wonder the sudden compliment went to her head like wine. Of course her chief thought from that time onward was to make herself look bonnier still in the eyes of the man who had first apprised her of the fact of her own good looks.

Like a smouldering fire that will suddenly leap up into flame, all the dormant vanity of Divina's nature sprang to life. She examined her face in the tiny square of cheap looking-glass which served her for a mirror, and began to see latent possibilities in herself. Not every girl had such fine curly hair: that was one thing certain ; she had heaps of it if it wasn't brushed back flat with a wet brush. Then Divina realised with a throb of delight that she was now a free agent—no longer under the yoke of Nicholson's, so why should she not do her hair as she chose ? She shook out the tumble of curly red hair and began to adjust it on more fashionable lines. In church last Sunday she had noticed that all the young women in the choir had their hair frizzed out to the sides ; hers would now be the same. A few minutes had changed the unimpeach-able Nicholson plaits into something that nearly resembled the head-dress of a savage queen. On this erection Divina pinned a cap, and then, feeling a little conscious but on the whole very proud of her appearance, she went down to the kitchen. Alas ! Mrs. Gilchrist pounced upon her in a moment.

"Whatever do you mean coming down with your hair like that, Divina ? " she said quite sharply. " Go upstairs at once and put it right."

" Please, m'am, I saw the girls in the choir," Divina said, a note of pleading in her voice, putting up both her hands to her head as if to protect it from an injury.

" Yes, of course ; silly things that should know better. They're a sight to be seen, with their hats and their chinongs," said Mrs. Gilchrist pitilessly. She had not the imagination that was necessary to divine the universal note which underlies even the most grotesque efforts at fashionable dressing. She did not see that one of the great primitive instincts prompts it ; something " not to be put by," like that Presence of which the poet sings. Failing to see this note of universality in Divina's striving after fashion, Mrs. Gilchrist saw only individual silliness in it ; she decided to check this in the bud. But being a kind and sensible woman, she reasoned with the girl about it, instead of giving her harsh commands.

" Believe me, Divina, a girl just spoils herself by aping unsuitable fashions. They're silly enough for ladies who can sit all day doing nothing, but they're downright folly for girls that have to work ; look at the coal-dust and carpet-sweepings you'll get into your hair if you wear it all frizzed that way like a mop! If you're a sensible girl, you'll go upstairs and smooth it out again."

Divina's eyes filled with tears; she had liked her own appearance so much with puffed-out hair. She hesitated for a moment, almost meditating rebellion, then slowly turned away, mounted the stair to her room, and with great difficulty subdued the Zulu head-dress to smaller proportions. "I'll no' make it *quite* flat," she said to herself, pulling out a becoming little ripple under the frill of her cap. Its appearance comforted her, and she gazed at herself again with some complacency. "I wonder would Mrs. Gilchrist no' like me in a pink wrapper?" she mused; the hideous speckled brown and white Nicholson fabric, with its horrible wear-resisting qualities, was fit only for ugly girls. She, whom John the ploughman called bonnie, should wear pink print. Divina held a pink flannelette duster under her chin at this point, and thought the effect was exquisite. Then she descended once more to the kitchen.

"There, now, Divina, you look more like yourself," said Mrs. Gilchrist heartily. "And I must say you're a good-natured girl as ever lived. I've known some that would have been disagreeable over less."

Divina laughed in her pleasant way, and no more was said about the matter. But the incident had set Mrs. Gilchrist thinking. Without any doubt Divina was growing up rapidly; she looked almost

a woman now, and these first dawnings of vanity
would be sure to develop, and then there would be
all manner of love affairs to contend with . . . the
girl was certainly pretty, and was just beginning
to find it out, and no doubt the young men about
the farm would begin to pay their addresses to
her ere long. . . .

"Dear me, I wish I'd engaged that cross old
body Mrs. Grant recommended ; it wouldn't have
given me all this responsibility," the good creature
thought.

But all unconscious of the anxiety she was giving
her mistress, Divina advanced gaily upon life ; it
had absolutely no terrors for her, and just now
seemed very bright indeed. For she had begun to
lay siege to the reluctant heart of John Thompson,
and found this the greatest fun possible. John
was so silent, so unapproachable, that the element
of sport was not wanting in her attempted conquest.

Divina cared not a rap about the man; she only
wanted to have him admire her, and was determined that he should do so.

Under the stern eye of Mrs. Gilchrist it was not
easy to have many interviews with John, but it
is wonderful what determination will do in these
affairs. Divina seemed generally to be at the back
door as John came across the yard, and she always
had a smile and a word for him : once or twice she
even managed to extract a slow smile from John,
and that was a great achievement. He was a curious
man, dour and difficult, the product of a Scotland

that is almost extinct in these degenerate but happier days. His whole view of life was joyless and stern ; he "kept himself to himself," the neighbours said, and in all his thirty years had never been known to pay his addresses to any woman. Indeed, there was an almost aristocratic aloofness in the man : he would not associate with any of the village people. Alone he lived with his old mother, going and coming to his work with the regularity of a machine, toiling early and late, with apparently no thought of amusement or relaxation of any kind. A strange target this for Divina to aim at with her careless arrows !

It is well known that fortune favours the brave, so this must have been why Divina was sent along one afternoon with a message from her mistress to old Mrs. Thompson. Always glad of a diversion from the routine of her work, Divina was doubly pleased to have this opportunity of seeing John's house and John's mother. She would have liked to change into her Sunday merino, but Mrs. Gilchrist's command to " go as she was " could not be disobeyed, and, accordingly, Divina stepped across the field in her demure speckled print gown, her white apron, and little cap, as prim as a young Quaker.

The cottage door stood open, for the day was warm, and, looking in, Divina could see that John and his mother sat at tea in the kitchen. John rose at the sound of her knock and came to the door, silent, but, as Divina was quick to notice, with a lurking smile on his lips.

Ower Young to Marry Yet

" Come in bye," he said curtly, standing aside to let her pass in, for his great figure almost filled up the doorway.

" Oh, I'll not be comin' in the day, thank you," said Divina primly, though she was dying to enter the house. " The mistress sent me over wi' a message for Mrs. Thompson."

" Come in bye, lassie ; what for are ye standin' there ? " called the old woman insistently from the kitchen. Divina hesitated, relented, and then found herself in the cottage at last.

" The mistress says, could ye kindly spare her a pair o' ducklings, Mrs. Thompson, please ; she's wishful to keep hers for the market, and she's expectin' friends to their dinner come Friday ? " Divina said, repeating off her message as a child says its school lesson.

The old woman, however, did not apparently wish to be hurried into this bargain.

" Sit ye doon, sit ye doon till I think, lassie ; it's no' easy to say a' at aince. Ye'll hae a cup o' tea wi' us ? " She looked sharply at the girl as she spoke ; but Divina, with down-dropped eyelids, made the most modest reply :

" Thank ye kindly, Mrs. Thompson, but we're thrang at the farm the day. I'll not stop the day, thank ye."

" Hoots, a cup'll no' hinder ye long," said John suddenly. He drew forward a chair for Divina, and reached across to the dresser for another cup and plate. It was impossible to refuse such pressing hospitality, and Divina accepted the chair and the tea without any further show of reluctance.

She might not have been so willing to do so if she had realised the intense scrutiny she was undergoing from the eyes of Mrs. Thompson. Every woman undergoes it from the mother of the man who has the temerity to let his admiration be evident—under heaven there is no searchlight to equal that maternal eye.

But, all unconscious of this, Divina sipped her tea and made herself most agreeable, answering the old woman's questions quite frankly.

" Yes, she had been trained at Nicholson's ; yes, you got a fine training there ; no, her parents were both dead ; yes, she was very happy at the farm ; no, she didn't find the work heavy." . . . So the catechism ran. John had finished his tea, lighted his pipe, and now puffed away at it, listening in silence to everything that passed between Divina and his mother. What it was that attracted him in the girl he scarcely knew. It wasn't altogether her pretty face—John rather despised these allurements ; nor altogether her way of making a man laugh in spite of himself. No, he thought it must be something in the way she had been brought up. She seemed to have none of the nonsense of most girls : just look at her, how sensible-like she was, always tidy and quiet in her dark print and her white apron ! Perhaps, though John did not admit it to himself, some hidden instinct of chivalry also moved deep down in his heart ; the girl was young and unprotected, without father or mother, kith or kin of her own. She needed a man to care for her if ever a woman did.

But John was horribly prudent; nothing was farther from his thoughts than any hasty revelation of his feelings ; he decided to wait and see more of Divina.

In order to do this satisfactorily, however, it would be necessary to take one decided step : he must ask her to walk out with him. In this way only could he see more of Divina, and without knowing her better John could not make up his mind to make her an offer of marriage.

All this and more passed through his thoughts as Divina sat there drinking her tea and talking with his mother. Finally, when she rose to go, John offered to go as far as the farm with her : " It was time to see to his horses," he said. But Divina knew better.

They set off together across the field, walking slowly by a little footpath that led through the now yellowing corn, John very silent, Divina very talkative, till they reached the stile leading over into the farmyard. Here they came to a standstill, and John became aware that the awful moment for speech had arrived.

" Yer oot on Sundays whiles ? " he asked bluntly. " What would ye say if I cam' wi' ye ? "

Divina had been expecting this advance, yet she feigned surprise and even hesitation. " It was very kind," she said, " but then she went to the minister's Bible-class on Sunday afternoons." . . .

Ower Young to Marry Yet

"What o' that? Y're no' at the class a' the aifternoon?"

"No more I am," Divina admitted.

"Weel, then, I'll be at the cross-roads at five," said John with great finality, giving Divina no time to hesitate more, for he leaped over the stile and went off to the stable without waiting to hear another word that she might have to say.

As for Divina, she was in a state bordering on ecstasy. For unnumbered Sabbaths now she had trudged along the dismal Fifeshire roads, high-walled and dusty, to attend the Bible-class which Mrs. Gilchrist fondly hoped would be for her soul's good. And on the way, how many loitering couples she had met—couples who seemed contented with all things here below, while she, sorely against her will, went on her unattended way to Mr. Ferguson's Bible-class!

Now everything was to be changed. No more would she take her dismal unattended trudge, but in company with John, the best-looking young man in the village, would proudly loiter along like other girls. That John should be her cavalier was a special joy; he who was known to be impervious to all female charms, that he had capitulated to hers. This was a triumph worth having! Divina hurried back to her work, smiling and demure, but with a kindling eye.

. . . .

Sunday, of course, was wet. Such red-letter days in a girl's calendar often are; and Mrs. Gilchrist

did not suppose that Divina would be anxious to
go out.

"You're better quietly in the house with your
book," she told the girl. "I've a nice set of addresses,
written for the Young Women's Christian Associa-
tion, I'll lend you to read." But, to her surprise,
this alluring offer did not seem to tempt Divina;
the pages of the book of life were in truth what
she longed to turn that afternoon, if Mrs. Gilchrist
had only known!

"Oh, m'am, I don't mind the rain. I'm sweir
to give up the class. I wasn't at the church either
the day," said Divina eagerly.

"I'm sure I'm glad you are so thoughtful," said
her mistress, innocent soul that she was. "Well,
see that you put on your thick boots and your
waterproof. Mr. Ferguson will be very pleased
to see you make the effort to go in all this
rain."

Divina laughed in her sleeve. She was not in
the least a hypocritical girl, but youth is youth, and
nothing on earth will ever alter that fact. She was
dull, and saw a prospect of amusing herself. You
cannot blame the child.

So, bible in hand, Divina sped along the muddy
roads towards the Manse. Never had the way
seemed shorter; but, alas, never had good Mr.
Ferguson's exhortations seemed longer. Again and
again Divina's eyes sought the clock: a quarter to
four; four; a quarter past four; half past four;
the hands stole along, and the minister's patient

old voice droned on, explaining the journeys of St. Paul.

Of what significance, alas! was one word that she heard to Divina, who sat there watching the hands of the clock and thinking about John the ploughman? As well might the minister have spoken to the wind: it would have paid as much heed to his teachings.

This was to be a day of triumph to Divina, for as she came out of the Manse gate, along with a little band of her fellow class-mates, she saw John waiting for her under the shelter of the trees at the church door. Here, indeed, was an open declaration in the face of the world! The girls nudged each other and giggled, asking in whispers who John Thompson was after. (Far from their thoughts already were the journeys of St. Paul!) And Divina, knowing the answer to their question, fell behind so that John might have no difficulty in distinguishing her from among the group.

Who can tell the throb of gratified vanity that her young heart gave as John came forward and joined her? The other girls looked back at them and laughed loudly; but John minded them not a whit.

" We'll gang roond by the ither road," was all the comment he made upon their laughter.

Divina was in a twitter of excitement; but if she expected that John would put his arm round her waist and kiss her, she was much mistaken. John was far too prudent to commit himself in any such way. What he did do, was to saunter along in the pouring rain (apparently quite oblivious to it, as any self-respecting ploughman should be) while he talked gravely to Divina about Mr. Ferguson's Bible-class. Divina would have preferred almost any other subject ; but she had enough of tact to allow her adorer to choose his own topics of conversation.

John was incurably theological, with that deep, worrying, questioning mind that belongs more inherently to a certain type of Scot than to the native of any other country under the wide arch of heaven. He could not keep off religious subjects—they fascinated him as horses and cards fascinate some men. His sombre imagination played round the problems of this bewildering world of ours unceasingly.

And here he seemed to be going to choose Divina for his life's partner—Divina, careless as the wind, and unthinking as a kitten : in truth the attraction of opposites. She did not in any way try to deceive him ; but she certainly tried hard to please him. The method she adopted was a very old one, but one which is in most cases entirely efficacious—she merely listened with rapt attention to every word that fell from the man's lips, and said little herself.

When the walk came to an end, therefore, John was under the impression that Divina and he were absolutely one in thought, so cleverly had she listened, so little had she said, so much had she looked. He might have been a little hurt and surprised if he had stood beside Divina in the farm porch while she shook out her wet umbrella. For, with a great sigh of mingled relief and disappointment, she exclaimed to herself :

" Losh me, is yon courtin' ? "

.   .   .   .

This was only the first of many walks. Mrs. Gilchrist, of course, found out very soon that Divina and John were " keeping company," and though a little sorry that the girl should begin to think of matrimony so early, she was thankful that such an exemplary young man should be her choice.

" You're far too young to marry yet, Divina," she told her ; " John must wait a year or two for you, then you can lay by some money, and you'll have learned many a thing before then."

" Oh, I'm no' thinkin' about gettin' married, m'am," said Divina ; " I'm only walkin' out with John."

" Well, I'm sure I don't understand you girls," said the older woman. " What does walking out with a man mean, but just that you're thinking of marrying him ? It's nonsense to speak that way, Divina, and I hope you're not trifling with John ? "

" No' me, m'am—maybe John's triflin' wi' me," said Divina, laughing.

She laughed ; but there was in reality a nip of truth in her words, for in spite of all their walking and talking, John had never yet made her a definite offer of marriage. This fact Divina could not hide from herself, nor could she deny that such an offer would be extremely gratifying to her vanity.

" I'm no' quite sure that I'll tak' him," she said to herself, judicially weighing the situation ; " but I'd like him to offer."

Things then were in this parlous condition, when Divina had a sudden inspiration, and set to work to carry it out at once. John must somehow or other be brought to the point : her vanity could not bear his silence any longer—speak he must. Having come to this decision, Divina began to act upon it.

" If you please, m'am," she said one day, " I'm wantin' to go to Edinbury if you don't objec'."

" To Edinburgh, Divina ? Have you friends to see there, or what is it ? "

" No, m'am ; it's things I want to buy."

" Why, Divina, haven't you all you need ? I'm sure your things are all very good."

" I want a hat," said the girl.

" The one you have is quite neat and nice—what would you be spending your money on a new one for ? " Mrs. Gilchrist remonstrated. " Especially if you think of getting married some day, Divina, you should be laying by for that."

" Oh, I'm no' thinkin' o' it," Divina said evasively. " But, if you please, m'am, I'd like the day in Edinbury."

" Well, of course you can have it—but, Divina, do you know your way about the town, and what shops to go to and all ? "

Ower Young to Marry Yet

" I'll manage fine," said the girl. " There's a shop they call Lyons—I've heard tell of it."

" Yes, it's a good shop ; but when you go there, be sure you know what you want, for you'll be so confused by the number of things they offer you, that as likely as not you'll end by buying what you don't want."

Unfortunately for herself, Divina had a great deal of self-confidence ; she did not believe these words of wisdom in the least.

" I know fine what I'm to buy," she assured Mrs. Gilchrist, who, with the wisdom of age, shook her head over this announcement.

" I suppose girls will never learn except by experience," she said, " but let me give you one bit of advice : beware of bargains—there's not such a thing as a bargain. When a shopman tells you he's giving you one, he's really getting rid of the goods for some reason or other—I've found that out long ago."

Divina listened, of course ; but she was quite sure that she knew better. Had she not been reading the advertisements in the *Weekly Scotsman?* That powerful organ of public opinion surely knew more than Mrs. Gilchrist, and it spoke of " Phenomenal Bargains " ; of " Things going under cost price " ; of " Summer hats being given away." Certainly, if this was the case, she would easily get what she wanted ! It was arranged, therefore, that Divina should go to Edinburgh on Friday for her day of shopping. Bright visions of hats visited her pillow all the night before. In dreams she saw an endless perspective of pegs, hung with hats of every shape and shade, and she, with the exhaustless purse of the fable, strayed among them buying, buying, buying. . . .

Divina, you must remember, looked upon herself by this time almost in the light of a capitalist. In the six months since she came to Sandyhill Farm, she had been able to lay by five dirty one-pound notes, and this, almost the first money she had earned, seemed to her an enormous sum, with illimitable spending capacities. Divina had none of the spirit of the miser in her—she thought that money was there to be spent, not to be hoarded—a philosophy that has a good deal of sound sense in it.

On her way to the station on Friday morning Divina had the good luck to meet John going to his work. He stopped to ask her where she was off to ?

" To Edinbury, for the day," she answered, her face glowing with soap and pleasure. " I've things to buy."

" Y're lucky that have siller tae buy wi'," said John grimly. " It tak's a man all his time to live these days—let alone buyin'."

Divina laughed gaily, and assured him he had risen on the wrong side that morning, to be taking such dark views of life. Then she hurried on to the station, and John stood looking after her admiringly.

" She's a sight for sair e'en—none of the fal-lalls some lassies wear—yon's a sensible bit thing, would make a man a good wife," he meditated as he plodded on to his work. His thoughts were full of the trim little figure that had flitted across his path : " None o' your dressed up huzzies for me," he added aloud.

. . . .

Those who have had occasion to go a-shopping in Edinburgh must have observed that pleasant note of intimacy which prevails in most of the shops. Trading is here carried on under genial conditions ; and, except where the intolerable " young lady" from London has intruded, the saleswomen take an almost passionate personal interest in their customers.

Impossible to convey the welcoming intonation of the Edinburgh saleswoman as she presses her wares : " This now I can really recommend, for I've tried it myself—it'll be the verra thing y're wantin' : or stop a minit, I've a cheaper line I'd like to show you—no, it's no trouble at all. . . . now, to my mind that becomes ye better than the dearer one."
. . . Surely in no other known capital do the salespeople so earnestly consider how to spare the purses of their clients. But this may be only a deeper depth of subtilty, for it is so disarming that the purse-strings fly open before it in a wonderful way.

When Divina then entered that genial emporium known as Lyons, she was immediately made welcome by one of these redoubtable saleswomen. Our heroine scarcely needed to voice her wants ; they were understood almost without speech on her part by this omniscient creature.

" I perfectly understand : what you're wantin'

is a dressy hat that'll look well at the church and yet do fine for your afternoon out. Yes, we've got just the thing here—but maybe that's too dear— it's nonsense spending too much on a hat, I always say, that'll be out of fashion next year. Here's another exactly half the price—it's real stylish too —I sold one to an officer's daughter half an hour ago. I believe it's the very thing for you. Just you try it on, please—let me put it on for you—a wee bit to the one side—that's it—now, if you ask me, I think that's the exact thing you've been look-ing for. It's a cheap hat for the money, really— the feather's a beauty."

Thus cajoled, Divina assumed the hat, and then gazed at her own reflection in the glass and wondered at the awful power of dress. For this hat trans-formed her in one moment from a Nicholson girl into a fine lady—or so she fondly imagined. It was a gigantic structure of emerald green velvet, turned up sweepingly at one side. A long white ostrich (whalebone) feather depended from it, and fell bewitchingly across her shoulder.

"Take a look at yourself in the hand-glass," the saleswoman recommended.

Divina did not understand the uses of the hand-glass, but these were quickly explained to her : the back view proved even more striking than the front had been—Divina drew in a long breath.

"What's the price ? " she asked.

"Fifteen and six—very cheap that for the style," said the woman.

Ower Young to Marry Yet

Divina had never heard of anyone paying 15s. 6d. for a hat—the idea took her breath away. She looked again at herself and hesitated—then suddenly made up her mind.

" I'll tak' it," she said curtly.

" Very good ; then where'll I send it to ? the saleswoman asked, licking her pencil.

" I'll tak' it ; it won't be ill to carry," said Divina.

" Not a bit. I'll put it up in a nice box for you— and now what's the next thing ? " was the brisk reply.

Divina put her finger into the corner of her mouth, a childish habit she still retained when in doubt.

" I'm wantin' a dress," she said a little shyly. Again her wants were comprehended almost before they had been spoken.

" That'll be in the next department—but I'll come through with you and bring the hat—it'll be better for you to see them together ; just come this way, please."

Divina stepped " through" into the enchanted region of the ready-made costumes ; it was her dream come true—pegs and pegs and pegs hung with wonderful garments, and she wandering among them, purse in hand. The genial saleswoman escorted her until they met another lady of the warehouse.

" Here's Miss Campbell," she said, as if there was but one Miss Campbell in the world, then addressing the other woman : " Where are these nice serge costumes " (the emphasis was, of course, on the last syllable—"cos*tumes*") "you were showing me yesterday ? This young lady wants one to go with this hat—a bit of trimming on it, and good value for her money ; see what you can do for her."

The two had got Divina now ; she was clay in their hands. The serge costumes with bits of trimming were quickly produced, and it was then evident that Divina had set her heart's affections on a rather bright shade of green to suit the hat. Her choice was applauded by the two saleswomen : " It's the one I would have chosen myself," said Divina's first friend ; " I'm glad you're to have that—well, now you're suited, I'll leave you with Miss Campbell," and she swept away.

Divina found herself thus committed to pay £2, 10s. for the costume, and her conscience began to prick ; but the redoubtable Miss Campbell had decided that her victim was to make still further purchases.

" I call that a very nice showy costume," she said, holding it out temptingly ; " but what blouse are you to wear with it ? We've a very cheap line of white silk ones here would look well with this green." She swept Divina along to another counter where blouses of all degrees of vulgarity were displayed : " It's really difficult to choose where they're all so choice," she said.

But Divina had a wonderfully quick eye for what she admired—in two minutes she had singled out a particularly showy trifle made up almost entirely of cheap lace medallions and sarsenet.

Ower Young to Marry Yet

" This'll be very dear, isn't it ? " she asked long-ingly.

" Dear ?   Oh no, I call that quite a bargain—and I daresay I could let it down a shilling to meet your price : we're selling off this line at five eleven three. Let me think now—I daresay I might let you have it at four eleven three, if that would suit, and there's a bargain for you."

" Four eleven three ? " Divina interrogated, not having yet caught up the lingo of the cheap shop. Miss Campbell smiled, and explained the enormous reduction that the term conveyed, so, of course, Divina bought the blouse.

" These make a nice finish to a costume," the temptress remarked casually, as they passed along where a bunch of feather boas waved in the draught from the staircase. Mental arithmetic had been tolerably well taught at Nicholson's, so Divina was quite aware that she had already spent the tremendous sum of £3, 10s. $5\frac{3}{4}d$. ; yet pass these boas she could not. She was as awfully in their toils as if they had been the monsters they derived their name from. There was in Divina some of the reckless spirit of the true dissipator—she would have a good spend while she was at it.

" What'll they be ? " she asked firmly.

" Oh, they're a cheap line too—six eleven three these : how would you like this white coque ? it's real showy."

Divina laid down her six eleven three like a man, and received a farthing's worth of pins to salve her conscience and make her believe that the boa too had been cheap. Miss Campbell was now carrying the hat in one hand, the costume over one arm, the blouse laid across it, and now she whisked up the boa and carried off the whole lot in triumph to the fitting-room where Divina was to try on the dress. Fitting was rather too precise a word for the perfunctory tug here and ruck there that were given to the jacket; but Divina was assured that it would be " quite all right " and that Miss Campbell " saw what it wanted " exactly.

Divina would have liked to carry away all these beautiful purchases with her; but this, of course, was impossible, so she had to content herself with the assurance that the parcels would meet her at the station in the evening. Then feeling wonderfully rich (for was she not the possessor of all these splendid garments?), yet strangely poor (because her purse was half empty), Divina took a walk along Princes Street, ate a bun and drank a cup of tea in a confectioner's, and got to the station an hour too soon. There she looked out anxiously for the messenger from Lyons, fearing terribly that he would be late for the Fife train. When at last he came in sight, laden with big cardboard boxes, Divina nearly clapped her hands for joy. She bundled the boxes into the carriage, and waited impatiently for the train to start, that she might take a peep into them. Then prudence forbade this—prudence and the thought that the parcels had to be conveyed along the mile of road between

the station and Sandyhill Farm. She contented
herself with breaking a corner off the lid of the hat-
box that she might get one glimpse of the emerald
velvet hat. How beautiful it was! and how it
would " become her!" Divina laughed aloud in
the empty carriage.

" He'll speak this week," she said gleefully.

.   .   .   .

Sunday dawned without a cloud. All round and
round the great arch of sky was brilliantly blue,
smiling down upon the green earth and the valleys
thick with corn. Could death and grief reign in
this splendid world that seemed quick only with
life and joy ? . . .

Divina certainly was finding it a joyous place.
Her light Sunday duties were over, and now at
three o'clock, she was free to don her new clothes.

Of course she had already held a hurried dress-
rehearsal late at night by the flickering light of a
candle; but that had scarcely counted. Now in
the full blaze of day, with her door securely locked
against intrusion, Divina began her toilet. It was a
tremendous occasion—how tremendous you will only
be able to realise when you remember the repressive
influences under which the girl had been brought
up, and the great natural law that was working
now in her young nature like a ferment.

First of all, Divina arranged her curly locks in a
huge halo round her face, as she had done once
before. Then she put on her skirt and blouse, but
was rather perplexed by the discovery that the

blouse was transparent and showed her tidy pink
flannelette under-bodice almost down to the waist.
Could this be right ? " Transparencies are all the
rage," Miss Campbell had said when showing her
the garment—this must have been what she meant ;
but why display one's underclothing ? Divina
pondered the question, then compromised by pin-
ning a clean pocket-handkerchief across her bosom
—that seemed better, and she went on with her
toilet. The length of the skirt was rather dismaying to one who knew nothing of the art of lifting a skirt elegantly ; Divina tried to grasp it in
each hand alternately, then gathered it all up in
one immense bunch to one side, and wondered
how it would be possible to walk when so hampered.
The coat was too big ; it was also badly cut ; but
its owner was mercifully unaware of these deficiencies—she thought it perfect.

Divina then crowned her brows with the great
green hat which sat more jauntily than before upon
her puffed-out hair. Last of all, she flung the white
coque boa round her shoulders, and fell back from
the glass to gaze at her own reflection with a feeling
that was akin to awe. The Nicholson orphan had
completely disappeared—" gone as if never she
had breathed or been," as Christina Rossetti sings,
and in the orphan's place stood a vision of fashion,
dazzling to the eye of the beholder.

" My word but I'm braw ! " Divina cried, pirouet-
ting before the glass, moving it up and down in a
vain effort to get a full-length view of herself in its

six-inch surface. She felt a little shy at the thought of facing people in such an altered guise; but it was a proud shyness—surely everyone must see that the change was for the better ? Yet a lurking fear oppressed her. " I wonder would Mrs. Gilchrist like them," she thought—" them " being, of course, the new clothes. Mrs. Gilchrist, however, was comfortably asleep behind the pages of the *British Weekly* in the parlour, so Divina was able to slip downstairs and get across the yard unobserved. Out upon the high road she was safe, but Divina had now to learn the truth of that severe little proverb, " Pride must suffer pain."

For it was a windy afternoon, and her great hat swayed perilously on her head, secured only by one pin. Before she had gone many yards the hat blew off altogether. Divina clutched at her new treasure, pinned it on again—awry—struggling at the same time with her unfamiliarly long skirt. For a few minutes she felt perfectly desperate, then coming to a more sheltered bit of road, she stood still and endeavoured to get herself more in hand. The hat was skewered on squintly but firmly; she gathered up her skirt in an iron grip, rearranged the ruffled plumage of the boa, and then walked slowly on towards the cross-roads, her usual trysting-place with John.

This fight with fashion and the elements had made Divina a little later than usual, and as she drew near the cross-roads she saw that John was coming to meet her.

Ower Young to Marry Yet

" Eh me, what'll he say ?—he'll be a prood man the day ! " thought Divina, strutting along exactly like a peacock. She even let go her grasp of the skirt, and let it trail behind her in the dust.

John came nearer and nearer, yet made no sign of recognition. At last, as they came actually face to face with each other, he halted, staring at her in a bewildered way.

" This is a real fine afternoon," said Divina, simpering, by way of opening conversation. But still John uttered not a word. It is true that he took his pipe from his mouth as if preparing for speech, yet no words came from his lips. He simply stood there and gazed at Divina, with a long, disgusted, contemptuous stare. Then very deliberately he turned away and walked off in the opposite direction, without having exchanged a single word with her. She, stupid girl that she was, did not take in the situation—or refused, perhaps, to admit it to herself. A wave of colour rushed over her face at this " affront " that had been " put upon her " ; then she decided that it must be a mistake.

" Hi, John ! it's me—d'ye no' recognise me ? " she called after him. He halted at the sound of her voice and looked round. Divina came towards him ; she stood close beside him, her face flushed with vexation under the great green hat.

" Did ye no' ken me ? " she asked again. His answer came slow and unmistakable :

" Fine that, Divina ; but I'm fair scunnert at ye."

Ower Young to Marry Yet

" What for ? " she asked defiantly, though she knew perfectly well.

" Y're ower braw for me," said John sarcastically, indicating by a wave of his hand the green hat, the white boa, the trailing skirt, all the bravery her young soul adored.

" What ails ye at the hat ? " she asked, trying to put in a feeble defence.

" It's no' the hat ; it's the lassie that could buy it ; I thought more o' ye, Divina; it seems I was mistaken."

It was Divina's turn now to mount her high horse. No girl of spirit could have done otherwise. She tossed her feathered head and made stiff reply. " Oh weel, Mr. Thompson, if that's the way of it I'll wish ye good evening."

" Good evenin'," John responded, and they turned away from each other, Divina gulping down tears of mortified vanity and intense disappointment.

" Mistaken indeed ! I'll mistake him ! " she muttered, employing that vague and awful kitchen threat at which many a brave heart has quailed.

It was no good to walk on alone in her fine clothes —where would the pleasure be ?—better go home and tell Mrs. Gilchrist that she found it too hot for walking. . . . She floundered along in the dust and wind and hot sunshine, her heart bursting with rage and vindictive feeling, longing only to get in again and be able to tear off the finery that had brought this humiliation upon her.

John meantime, trudging steadily away from his Divina, experienced equally bitter feelings.

Ower Young to Marry Yet

" A Jezebel, just a fair Jezebel ! " he told himself.
" And I that took her for the quietest lassie in the
countryside . . . did ever a man see the like o'
yon hat ? . . . she's made a fool o' me athegither."

Now a man can face up to most griefs, to almost
every sorrow, but to be made a fool of is more than
he can bear : this is the ultimate bitterness. John
bit upon the thought after the fashion of some
natures, telling himself over and over again what a
fool he had been to imagine Divina a sensible, quiet
girl of his own way of thinking, when in reality she
was a good-for-nothing huzzie of the usual sort.
She was not the wife for him ; he must cast her out
of his thoughts, forget her entirely, never see her
again. All the harsh Calvinistic side of the man's
nature came uppermost at this moment, effacing the
normal human feeling that had begun to spring up
in his heart.

So the two went their separate ways, as unhappy
a man and woman as you can well imagine.

Mrs. Gilchrist being apparently still asleep,
Divina had the good luck to gain the shelter of
her own room without encountering her mistress.
Once having attained this haven, she gave way at
last to the pent-up feelings of the afternoon. Taking off the unlucky green hat, she flung herself down
on the bed and burst into noisy passionate sobs,
like the child she still was at heart. Do not suppose
that Divina wept the tragic tears of wounded love
—no, they were only tears of bitter mortification.
But then, as the Bible truly asks, " A wounded

spirit who can bear? "—certainly extreme youth cannot endure it, and Divina wept on until she had made herself quite sick, and her eyes were all swollen up. Then when the storm had a little worked itself out, she rose, changed the green costume for her black merino gown, smoothed out her puffed hair, bathed her eyes, and went down to prepare supper. Mrs. Gilchrist was quick to notice that something was wrong; but with a fineness of feeling that is often wanting in elderly people, she took no notice of Divina's swollen eyelids, and contented herself with sending the girl early to bed. So ended this disastrous Sunday for Divina.

John, too, had gone home; but not being able to relieve his feelings by a burst of tears, he sat glumly smoking by the kitchen fire all the evening. In vain his mother tried to get him to talk: he remained doggedly silent. Things had, indeed, gone far deeper with John than with Divina, and the events of the afternoon had made him profoundly unhappy. For the first time in his thirty healthful years, John could not sleep that night. From side to side he tossed, counting the slow hours as they went by, and struggling with something that was too strong for him. At last, as morning dawned, he gave up the struggle. With a great sigh he turned over on his pillow :—

" The worst o't is—*I maun hae her—hat and a'*," he confessed to himself.

.   .   .   .

A few days later, Mrs. Gilchrist thought it necessary to question Divina plainly on the subject of her relations with John Thompson. The young man made so many excuses for coming to the back door, and managed to hold such long conversations there with Divina, that there seemed little doubt about his intentions. But the good woman did not get any very definite information out of Divina.

With a toss of her head, and a smile of quite infinite satisfaction, she gave the following enigmatic reply :

" It's true John's wantin' me ; but I'm no' so sure that I'll tak' him."

CHARLIE OVER THE WATER

CHARLIE OVER THE WATER

I

Of all the children that she had brought forth, there now remained to the Widow MacKay only one, her son Charlie, and he was " over the water " —that great water which stretched away from the shores of the Island till it reached those of the New World.

The Widow would sit by the door of the cottage on summer days and count over on her fingers the tale of her grief : John—he died in '75 in Australia ; Andrew was killed in the war ; Jessie married and died " on her first " (as the Widow expressed it), and Charlie had gone over the water.

In her age and increasing frailty the one stay left to the Widow was Hector, Jessie's child, now grown to be a big lad of sixteen. Even in his childhood Hector had been a little warrior worthy of the classic name he bore : to see him advance in single combat against the cow was a brave sight, and the utter rout of the pig when attacked by Hector with " the graap " [1] was memorable. The grandmother and grandson lived in a tiny cottage that seemed to

[1] *i.e.* fork.

cling to the edge of the cliff as a barnacle clings to a ship's side. Just a patch of turf in front of the door, where two or three hens pecketted about, and then rocks and heather sheer down to the sea below. A curious and precarious spot it seemed for man to have set his foot and built his tent of a day, yet here the MacKays had been born and reared, and from this rude shelter they had gone out to all corners of the world, after the traditional usage of Scotsmen, carrying with them always an image of the little home clinging to the side of the cliff, with the waves churning down below it. Dreams of the shieling had visited John as he lay a-dying in the parched Australian night. Poor Andrew's last flicker of consciousness, after the bullet passed through him at Tel-el-Kebir, recalled just the cottage on the cliff wind-swept and rain-washed, and his mother standing in the doorway. Jessie, as she gave up the ghost in a back room of a Glasgow slum, seemed in fancy to breathe again the authentic air of her Western home, and prayed that Hector, the baby, should be sent there with all speed. And this same vision, you may be sure, visited Charlie over the water—the prosperous member of the family—just as persistently as it had haunted his brothers and sisters. Late and early, as he toiled over there in the rich new world, Charlie dreamed of the old home. Fat as grease was this splendid virgin soil : you might drive a spade down through it as you might cut butter, and no stone would turn the edge ; yet Charlie would sigh, remembering the croft on the hillside at home where there seemed more stones than soil, and a thin hungry-looking crop of corn was all your reward for the long labours of the spring. . . .

But I wander from the Widow and Hector, the real subjects of my story.

Hector, as you must know, was now sixteen years of age, and had long ago finished his education at the Balneish school. A good memory, great quickness of apprehension, and not a little ambition had turned him out an excellent scholar, yet now behold the poor lad settled down for life, as it seemed, on the parcel of stony ground that formed his grandmother's croft. He knew well enough that the croft must be worked if they were to live ; but he could not feel the same enthusiasm for the place which his uncles had felt. Hector's character had taken its bent from that stirring Glasgow artisan his father, and as time went on the paternal strain developed more strongly than the maternal ; Hector longed exceedingly to leave the Island and the croft, and seek his fortunes in Glasgow, where his father had worked in the shipbuilding yards, and a prosperous uncle, Neil MacLean, was working still.

Yet here was his grandmother rooted in the soil like a tree : nothing would make her leave the Island where her five-and-seventy years had been passed ; and how could Hector even dream of leaving her ? For she was the only mother he had ever known—he always called her by that name,

Charlie over the Water

and looked upon her in that light. Now, as he laboured in the stony croft month after month, Hector revolved the position in his own mind. He was growing stronger and more able to face the world every day—how would it be possible for him to live this sort of life much longer ? The compulsory idleness of crofters on a poor croft during the interminable winter months is something that is difficult to realise unless you have seen it. No work to speak of out of doors ; no work at all indoors; rain and wind and darkness compassing about those Islands that seem so enchanting to admiring visitors in the short Hebridean summer !

All this Hector knew ; he had watched the other crofters, his neighbours—these tall, languid looking men, who stood about at the doors of their wretched hovels all the winter through, idle and for the most part unhappy. Hector, I say, had watched them with his quick young eyes, and decided that this was not the life for hi n . . . he was like a rat caught in a trap, running round and round, biting at the wires of the cage, restless and angry—from whence could help come ?

It was October, sometimes the most perfect month of the year, and the Islands seemed to sleep an enchanted sleep, the purple sea lapping gently against the cliffs. If you rowed out from the shore this deep colour died away, and you might have been rowing on a sea of milk. The very gulls seemed half asleep rocking on the gentle swell of the tides, and if you looked down into the water you would see great translucent jelly-fish drifting far down below—an enchanted world indeed, where it seemed impossible that storms and darkness would ever come again. Surely that drowsy sea would go on for ever lap-lapping against the rocks, and the sleepy gulls would rock on unendingly on the placid tides.

It was a season that favoured daydreams, and the Widow took out her three legged stool to the door, and sat there, her hands idle on her knees, gazing out across the sea. She had not been very well of late—the work of the croft was getting too much for her, and she had left it all to her grandson. But there was more than that wrong. " I have taken a longing for Charlie," she told the boy.

" Is it for to see him you are ? " Hector asked sympathetically. He had come down from the croft, where he had moiled away alone all the afternoon, and now, stopping by the door where his grandmother sat, he leant upon the hoe he carried as if it had been a staff.

The Widow shook her head. " I will never be seeing him again ; that is why the thought is on me."

" Perhaps he will be for coming home some day," Hector suggested ; but again the old woman shook her head. She drew out from under her shawl a bundle of letters, tied together with a leather boot-lace, and bade Hector sit down beside her and " read out " the last of the letters aloud. Her eyesight was so bad now, that these precious documents were illegible to her ; so it was well that Hector's excellent schooling made him amply able to read them.

"He says never a word of coming over," she said wistfully. "If you will be reading the letter again, Hector, you will be seeing that."

(All this conversation, you must remember, was carried on in Gaelic, of which this story can only give a transcript.)

Again and again Hector had read aloud the letter. With his quick memory he knew it almost off by heart; yet he complied with his grandmother's request kindly enough : he was sorry for her that afternoon. The letter was long and not very well written. It was dated from Cypress Creek, Memphis, Tennessee, U.S.A.; but, as is often the case with well educated letter writers, this uneducated writer quite failed to convey through the unfamiliar medium of pen and ink any impression at all of the life he wrote about. They had had heavy crops, the heat had been great, he was short of help to get in the crops—such items had not very much interest. Then he came to more personal themes. He had his health wonderful, and so had the wife, and a son had been born to them in June and they had named him Donald. This was more exciting.

"He will be going four months now," the grandmother said thoughtfully. "Och! but I would be liking to see Charlie's son!" Then she seemed lost in reverie till she woke up to say, "And are you sure that is all the letter is saying, Hector?"

At that moment a thought darted through

Charlie over the Water

Hector's brain like an arrow from the bow—sudden, sharp, arresting. He held his breath hard, swallowed quickly, fumbled with the letter, turned it round. . . .

"There is a bit of writing I had not been noticing," he said, leaning down as if to read more easily the rather illegible words.

The old woman sat forward, her face lighted up with joyful interest.

"Maybe he will be coming himself," she suggested. But Hector shook his head. "That is not the word," he replied; then, as if spelling out the message with great difficulty, he read out:

"What would you be saying, mother, to come over to me? Now that Hector must be grown to a big lad and able to look after you on the road."

"Och! Och!" the old woman cried. "Eh, he wrote that to me four months past, and I to have no knowledge of it; what for did you not read that word before, laddie? Read it out again."

Hector was more glib this time—he remembered the exact words of the imaginary postscript. With fine enunciation he now cried out:

"What would you be saying, mother, to come over to me? Now that Hector must be grown to a big lad and able to look after you on the road."

"That will be all, Hector?"

"That will be all, mother," he answered, wisely anxious to keep his invention within manageable bounds.

And now they sat down to the discussion of this

fearful and wonderful proposal. To Hector, as you may imagine, the prospect was one of unmixed delight. His imagination leapt up at the thought of adventure, and as for fear, he did not know the meaning of the word. But for the old woman it was a very different matter. She had never left the Island in all her seventy-five years, and of the world that lay beyond her home she was as ignorant as a baby. It is true that in this way she had no idea of distances, and five thousand miles were to her much the same as five, because she simply could form no conception of the difficulties involved in crossing that extent of land or sea.

In this, I say, she was happier than those who know a little of the hardships of travel; but then the timidity of age was upon her, and a good deal of its frailty. A dozen perplexities presented themselves to her mind, and, as is generally the case with those who are not much accustomed to leave home, the unessential obstacles bulked larger with her than the real ones.

What would become of the cow? Who would look after the hens? Would they need to put a new lock on the door? she queried; for as they talked over this wonderful adventure it never occurred to the Widow that they would be leaving the Island for ever.

It was far otherwise with Hector; but he would not have suggested any doubt of their return to his grandmother. On the contrary, he smoothed away every obstacle as it was presented to him. The

Charlie over the Water

rent was paid for a year to come (did not Charlie over the water send it to the Factor every year?), so what would hinder that they should turn the key in the lock? Mrs. Matheson would look after the cow too, and they themselves would kill and eat the hens before they started on their travels. ("Och! the poor hens" from the Widow at this.) Almost in a breath Hector urged it all; he was bewildered himself by the cogency of his arguments—they sprang to his lips as he talked, a fresh one rising every minute; and as his grandmother brought forward each timid objection, he found that he could beat it down with some convincing negative.

"If you had your sight, mother, you would be seeing what a short way it will be to Uncle Charlie," he told her. Getting out his school atlas, he spread it on her knees in the sunshine, and pointed to the map of America. The old woman shaded her eyes from the glare and peered at the map. The lettering was invisible to her, but she could make out the masses of light and shade that signified land and water. Hector explained to her how a map was a picture of the world just as it is. Here they were (he put down his stubby finger on the Hebrides as he spoke), and this white thing she saw was the Atlantic, and this dark thing was America, and she couldn't see, but he could, the word Tennessee written in big letters just *here* (again the finger went down), and Cypress Creek was not very far from Tennessee, so that was all—nothing of a journey! It certainly did not look so bad on paper; but then,

Charlie over the Water

the Widow objected very sensibly, if it was so easy
why had Charlie not come over himself all these
years ?   Again Hector's arguments leapt out :

What about Uncle Charlie's farm ?—look to the
crops he was having—how could he be leaving them ?
—and it wasn't one cow he would be having, but
ten perhaps, and horses too—oh, it wouldn't be
easy to leave them !

This doubt laid to rest, the Widow produced
another.   How much would it cost ?   and how would
they find this out ?   Here, indeed, Hector found
himself a little at fault.   Such a simple helper as a
daily newspaper was, of course, unknown to them ;
but after a moment's reflection light dawned.   The
mail steamer from Glasgow passed once a week in
summer, and Hector never allowed a week to pass
without seeing it.   Wet or dry, he was always
down on the pier at Balneish when " the steambote "
(as he called it) came in ;   gazing hungrily at the big
steamer that went and came to Glasgow, that city
of unknown delights, where he had been born, and
where, above all things, he longed to go.

Hector's regular appearance on the quay had
become a matter of comment to the sailors, and
they would chaff the boy, asking him when he was
coming on to Glasgow with them ?

Hector had made special friends with one of the
stewards ;   the man was not very busy at the hour
the boat came in, and would often step ashore and
stroll along the quay in all the bravery of his blue
coat and brass buttons, while the tourists were getting

Charlie over the Water

off or on as the case might be. Then Hector, falling
into step with him, would question him eagerly
about Glasgow, and life on board ship. Here,
then, was the very helper he wanted now—who
should know more about how to get to America
than the steward of MacBrayne's steamer ?

"I'll be finding out from Mr. MacGregor, the
steward, mother," Hector said confidently. "The
steambote will be in to-morrow."

Assuredly Hector had food enough for thought
that night. As he lay down his mind was seething
with the possibilities of this great scheme which
he had himself set on foot. It opened out in a
wonderful way as he thought it over. Wouldn't
Uncle Neil, his father's brother in the shipbuilding
yard in Glasgow, help them ? The uncle had come
on a trip from Glasgow two years ago, and had been
very kind, and gave Hector a shilling because he
said he "favoured his father." Hector had his
address on a bit of paper in the cracked teapot on
the shelf—it would be easy to write to him. . . . At
this moment, however, sleep overcame Hector, and
off he went into the land of dreams.

But next morning he sprang out of bed, conscious
that much depended on his exertions. The boat
might come in early, it was such a calm morning ;
he must be early at the quay.

Food had little savour for Hector that day. He
gulped down his porridge, seized a bannock from
the pile, and ran off down the rough hill road eating
as he went. A finer lad you could scarcely have

Charlie over the Water

seen : his curly black hair grew thick and strong, his skin was tanned and flushed with health, and he ran down the road on his bare brown feet as swiftly as a deer, jumping from stone to stone, whistling and singing in the joy of his heart and the freshness of morning. There are no obstacles to such youth and health—the whole world bows down before them; even his grandmother's frailty was about to be caught up and whirled along in the wake of this exuberant vitality, this abounding life.

Far off on the horizon a trail of smoke appeared —the steamer was in sight. Leaping, running, almost flying along the road Hector went, till he had left the cottage far behind, and the village appeared—a handful of houses—and the quay.

In general Hector paid great heed to the tourists who stepped ashore from the steamer, laden with wraps and cameras ; but to-day he cared nothing about them—his one thought was to find Mac-Gregor the steward. At last he descried him, sauntering along the pier, smoking his pipe. With a run Hector was alongside of him, breathless, pouring out his story incoherently, hunting for English words, losing them, supplementing now and again with Gaelic, yet so desperately in earnest that MacGregor could not laugh, and lent a willing ear.

" Tut, tut, take your time, laddie," he said kindly. " What's all this ? You're going to America—you and your grannie ? What takes you off on such a long road ? "

Charlie over the Water

"It will be my Uncle Charlie that is wanting us," Hector explained. He had by this time quite made himself believe in the truth of this statement—it seemed so entirely the right thing for his uncle to have done.

"Well, it's a fine country; maybe he's right: you're the stamp for the Colonies, no doubt," MacGregor said. "And what is it you're wanting to find out?—the fares, is it?"

"Yes," Hector said; but when confronted by the question as to whether it would be second or third on a liner, or "emigrant," that they would go— there the boy was utterly at sea and had to confess his ignorance.

MacGregor then sat down on the edge of the quay and gave a long and very practical discourse to Hector upon the different ways of getting across the ocean. The boy became more and more confused; he shook his head and repeated in a bewildered way: "I just want to get over—how am I to *get?*"

"Well, amn't I telling you?—you must go in a liner, second or third, or you can go emigrant; but mind, if your granny's up in years there's no great comfort going emigrant."

The inexorable steamer-bell sounded. "There, we're off," MacGregor cried, starting up. "Come down next week; I'll find out more for you by then."

He ran off up the quay and jumped on board, leaving Hector dazed but determined, the possessor of a quantity of half assimilated information on the subject of ocean-steamer fares.

It really seemed as if the following week would never end. Hector lost all interest in his work, and could talk and think of nothing but the proposed journey to America. When he came to think over things, Hector was amazed by the simplicity of the method by which, apparently, he was going to get away from the Island. Why had it never occurred to him before ?

Now and then, when he glanced at his grandmother's thin bowed old shoulders, he was visited by a spasm of reproach, and wondered if she was quite fit for the journey ?—but then he would comfort himself by the assurance that she was fretting herself to death over her son Charlie, and nothing would cure her but the sight of him. Hector was very fond of his grandmother and anxious to be a good son to her ; but the hot, adventurous young blood in him leapt up at the thought of change, of seeing the world, of getting away from the Island—and the still small voice was silenced.

As they sat together round the peat fire at night, Hector tried to inspire the Widow with his thirst for adventure ; but he soon saw that this was no good : the old heart refused to beat more quickly at the thought of the New World—it seemed more likely to stand still in dismay. Then Hector struck another note, and began to picture the meeting with Uncle Charlie after all these years—would he

Charlie over the Water

be changed, did she think? What would "the wife" be like? And wouldn't she be wanting to see little Donald? Ah, this was another story altogether, and to Hector's huge surprise the old woman broke down and wept bitterly. He, who had gone such a short way on the road of life, could not understand that the thought of meeting again after long absence may have a heartbreaking poignancy, a quality of pain all its own.

"Will you not be wanting to see them?" Hector asked in surprise.

"Och, Hector, I will be wanting it too much," his grandmother told him—a statement which mystified the boy still more.

Then they began to discuss the all-important subject of ways and means—would their funds be sufficient for this great enterprise? Hector was directed by his grandmother to draw out from under the thatch an old tin biscuit box, which had been the Widow's savings bank for many and many a year. Together they counted over the long hoarded money, the price of many a stirk and sheep, each pound rolled carefully up in a little screw of paper. Money is not rife in the Islands, but the Widow had always been careful, and Charlie over the water had paid her rent for so many years, that somehow or other the little hoard had grown and grown till it amounted to nearly £50.

"Mother! mother! we can be going!" Hector cried, when he had counted out the last coin and realised what millionaires they were.

Charlie over the Water

It certainly seemed a princely sum to those two who had never entered a shop other than that of the "general merchant" at Balneish, and were therefore mercifully ignorant of the short way that money really goes. But the Widow still held back. "If I will die on the road, what will pay for the burying if we will have used all the money?" she asked. Hector brushed aside this dark thought.

"Uncle Charlie would be paying for the burying," he assured her. "And you will not be dying on the road," he added.

* * * * * * *

At last the mail-day came round again, and with a beating heart Hector stood on the quay to watch for his friend the steward. Ah, there he was at last, and he carried a little bundle of papers, too!

"Here you are, youngster," he cried; "here's reading will keep you going for a bit." He thrust into Hector's hand the advertisements of half a dozen rival lines of steamers as he spoke. "I'm busy today," he added; "I can't stop to explain them to ye; but y're a good scholar I dare say, and can make them out yourself."

Hector clutched the papers as a miser might have clutched a bag of gold. He did not wait, as his custom was, to watch the passengers on the steamer —he was far too much preoccupied with his own important affairs. But he did not begin to read the precious papers till he was well out of the village and some way on the homeward road. Then he sat down on the heather and opened out his bundle

Charlie over the Water

of advertisements. The rival claims of the different lines were very confusing at first ; but after reading them all over several times, Hector was pleased to find a certain unanimity in the prices that were mentioned. It was evident that he and his grandmother could, if they would, cross the Atlantic for about £5 apiece. But then Hector remembered MacGregor's warning that one " up in years " should be taken a little more comfortably across the sea. So he scanned the prices again, and weighed the difference between second and third class cabin fares. It was very perplexing—and more perplexing still this new feeling of responsibility that he felt growing within him. He, and he alone, would be responsible for the safe convoy of his grandmother to Uncle Charlie—it was imperative that he make no mistakes.

Alas ! Hector realised it would be impossible to start on their journey immediately. He began to see quite a number of difficulties ahead. First of all his Uncle Charlie must be written to and told that they were coming ; and then they must wait for his answer, which would give them directions as to how to get to Cypress Creek from New York. All this Hector revolved slowly in his mind as he lay on the heather and gazed at the flaunting pictures of giant ships dashing through emerald seas which adorned the steamer advertisements.

Now the moralising poet has told us that we weave a tangled web when first we practise to deceive ; and Hector, whose nature was really as honest as

Charlie over the Water

daylight, began to see this. He had deceived his grandmother, and now he wanted to do the rest of this business honestly. How was this to be managed ?

He got up, gathered the papers together, and climbed slowly up the road to the cottage. As he climbed, he revolved this question in his mind—would he confess his fraud to Uncle Charlie, or would he not ? He made a quick decision not to ; but, he added, he would tell no more lies—it would be quite easy to write a perfectly truthful letter.

Hector's handwriting was excellent, though his English left a good deal to be desired. He decided that the evening was to be devoted to the labours of correspondence. Writing paper was, of course, an unknown luxury in the cottage, but he had some sheets of exercise paper, saved from schooldays, and these were to be used for the momentous letter to Cypress Creek.

The Widow sat knitting beside the fire : there was not a sound in the house except the click of her knitting-needles and the grumble of the waves on the shore below when Hector sat down to write his letter.

"What are you after, Hector ? " the old woman asked, as she saw him bring out the exercise paper, the penny bottle of ink, and the one pen of the establishment.

"I'm after writing to my Uncle Charlie," he answered.

She laid down her knitting with a cry.

Charlie over the Water

"Ochone, Hector! What will you be saying to him?"

"That you will have taken a longing to see him, mother, and that you are thinking to come over the water to him," said Mr. Valiant-for-the-Truth ; surely no statements could be more entirely veracious than these.

"It's a true word you're saying, Hector ; but the Lord preserve us from the sea!"

As it was obvious that the sea could not be avoided if they were to reach Uncle Charlie, Hector wisely took no notice of this ejaculation, and began his letter forthwith :

"DEAR UNCLE CHARLIE,—I will be writing to tell you that my grandmother is not getting her health this long time. She has taken a longing for to see you once more, and now I am for taking her across the ocean to you.

"I am grown very tall and strong, and I will look after grandmother on the sea. Grandmother has laid by enough money in the box under the thatch that will be taking us across. We will be waiting for your reply to this at once. When we leave the ship, please to say where we go next ?— will we be taking a railway to Tennessee ?

"We will be going to Glasgow to my Uncle Neil MacLean, to sail from there. We will be leaving the cow with Janet Matheson, and eating the hens before we leave. If you please to write at once to your

"Dutiful Nephew,

"HECTOR MACLEAN."

167

Charlie over the Water

The dutiful nephew drew a long breath as he finished this effort. A weight fell off his heart : there was not a word of falsehood in the letter, only a plain statement of two undeniable facts— his grandmother's wish to see her son once more, and the proposal that she should take the journey to Tennessee !

He read the letter aloud to the Widow, who was not entirely satisfied with it.

" You have not been saying to Charlie that we were not finding the piece in the letter till last week," she said. Hector blushed, and answered " No " rather shortly. At the same time he slipped the letter into the one dirty envelope in his possession, licked it, and told the Widow that it could not be opened now.

" There, there, it will be a hard job the writing," she said sympathetically. Her own schooling had not amounted to much ; letter-writing was an impossibility to her, and she watched Hector's achievements almost with awe.

" It will be long till we're getting an answer," Hector said, with an involuntary sigh. His labours over, he sat back in his chair and gazed at the fateful envelope that lay on the table, all addressed now and only waiting for its stamp. He wondered how he could possibly wait until that letter had travelled out to Uncle Charlie, and then until an answer had travelled back from him. At the shortest computation it must be a month, he knew, and whatever would he be doing with himself all that time " at

all at all " ? Hitherto, Hector had taken some
interest in the croft, and an intense pride in the
amount of work he was able to do upon it without
the help of any grown man ; now all at once he ceased
to feel any interest in it. As he realised this, Hector
looked across at his grandmother with a sudden
feeling of guilt. *Why* had he ceased to care about the
croft ? Wasn't it simply that he hoped never to
see it again ? Did he wish to come back ? Did
he expect to do so ? Not he ! When first the
dazzling scheme had burst upon him, Hector had
been confused by its magnitude ; but since then
he had had time to examine it, and now it stood fully
confessed to his mind. He was taking his grandmother away from the Island for ever and ever, and
he himself meant to stay in the fine New World
when once he got there. This was the truth at last ;
and why all this foolish talk they had of leaving the
cow with the Mathesons and taking the key of the
door with them ? They would never come back
to the Island ; the cow would stay with the Mathesons for ever, and other hands than theirs would
unlock the door.

But as Hector came to this knowledge of his own
heart, he decided that he must keep it to himself.
The Widow would never leave the Island if she
thought they were not going to return to it ; and
now every energy of Hector's nature was bent on
getting her persuaded to start on their journey.
Somehow or other it must be managed—he would
die of disappointment if the scheme was given up

now ; he could not, would not, live another year
cooped up on the Island when the whole great world
was lying just beyond it. . . .

The Widow had fallen asleep ; the knitting had
dropped from her relaxed fingers and lay on her
knee. In repose her face looked very weary, for
she had had a hard life as well as a long one.

Hector sat and gazed at her. He felt almost
provoked with her for looking so tired : how was
he ever going to get her to America ?

His intent gaze perhaps wakened the old woman ;
she stirred, and took up her knitting again with a
sigh.

" I'm after dreaming that Charlie came in through
the door, and ' Mother,' he says, ' I'm come so that
you will not need to be crossing over to me.' "

Hector got up almost impatiently and lifted the
ink-bottle and pen on to the shelf.

" I will be going to my bed," he told her.

In the waiting-time that followed the despatch of
the letter to Tennessee, Hector occupied himself in
a good deal of correspondence with his Glasgow
uncle. Without going into detail, he told of the
proposed journey to America, and asked his uncle's
help about it. In reply, Uncle Neil at once offered
to put them up for a few days before they sailed, and
promised to find out about their passages when
they had finally decided to go

All this arranged, there was nothing left for
Hector but the exercise of unlimited patience.

Charlie over the Water

Week after week passed, month after month; autumn passed into winter, and still no answer came. Hector was sick with hope deferred, desperate from inaction. He would roam about the shore, gazing out across the sea, marvelling at the long silence of Uncle Charlie to his urgent letter. The Widow, too, was fretting. Uncertainty is as bad for old as for young people, and Hector's incessant talk of their proposed journey made it impossible for her to banish the thought of it from her mind. Then she began to " take a fear " that all was not well with Charlie ; she had a dream that she saw him lying with his head wrapped in a white bandage. This terrified her, and now she began to fancy that her son was dead.

But at last, towards the end of January, the letter came. Hector was out when it arrived, but the Widow was told by the boy who brought it that the letter was from America. It was a bitter day of wind and rain, yet the old woman flung a shawl over her head and hurried off down the road in search of Hector, the precious letter held firmly under her shawl. She met him coming up the hill, and almost ran towards him.

" Hector, Hector ! the letter is come ! " she cried out.

They were far too impatient to wait till they had regained the shelter of the cottage, so Hector drew his grandmother to the side of a big boulder, and there, slightly screened from the wind and rain, he tore open the envelope. What a study of expression

they made standing there together ! The old woman's
face was strained with a passion of anxiety ; she
pressed forward, her grey hair blown across her
brow in wisps, her dim eyes searching Hector's face
for the news she dreaded to hear.

" Is it himself is writing ? " she cried.

" Yes, yes," Hector said, half impatiently, as his
eyes ran down the page. His own face was tense
with feeling of another sort—with terror that his
scheme was going to be frustrated, with determination to carry it through, come what might.

" It's himself that's writing," he said at last ;
" but he has been sick these two months back with
the fever and ague."

" Wasn't it me that knew ! " the Widow exclaimed ; but Hector read on hurriedly.

" Surely," the letter ran—" surely, the Lord
Himself had put it into his mother's heart to be
coming over to Tennessee. The sight of her face
would be curing him—it would be like home again,
he thought. But was she able for the long journey ?
She wouldn't be knowing how long it was, surely ?
It's true Hector must be a big lad now, able to look
after her, but there was the sea to cross, and two
days in the train after that."

Then Charlie went into practical details. If they
really decided to come, they were to send him the
name of the steamer they were coming by and the
date of her sailing, and he would write to his wife's
sister in New York and tell her to meet them and
see them safe into the train. (" What need ? "

Charlie over the Water

Hector interpellated indignantly, as if he couldn't see himself and his grandmother into a train !) The same excellent person was to change their money for them (Hector puzzled a little over this), buy their railway tickets, and help them in every way. Her name was MacDonald, which had a reassuringly Scottish sound. Finally Charlie concluded the letter by the recommendation that they should not start until the month of April at least : let the storms and cruel frosts of winter be over before they arrived in America—his mother was too old to face them.

The length and particularity of this letter must have cost its writer (who was evidently no great scholar) infinite pains. Hector was provoked by it : why should they not start immediately ? What was all this about cold and storms ?—they had storms enough at home surely, when on winter nights it seemed as if the shieling would be blown off into the sea sometimes. But the Widow quite agreed with Charlie's view of things. " Och, Hector, we will be needing all our time," she told him. Then they toiled up the road to the cottage together, the rain and wind beating on their faces, came into the kitchen, fastened the door " against the wind," sat down by the fire, and told each other that it was settled now—they were going to Charlie over the water.

Yes, the decision had been come to at last. Hector's face shone with joy—he felt a man all at once, and rejoiced in his strength. But the Widow in her age and feebleness trembled as she crouched there by the fire of smouldering peats, stretching out her withered hands towards the warmth. A thousand fears rushed over her—a thousand regrets; only the thought of Charlie lured her on.

Now that their minds were made up, Hector found himself launched upon a veritable sea of correspondence. Both uncles had to be written to at great length, and the Glasgow uncle, on whom the responsible task of taking their passages was to devolve, had to be written to several times.

Letters only arrived once a week at the Island in winter, so several weeks passed before the final arrangements were made. At last, somewhere towards the end of March, Hector found himself the possessor of a letter which stated that the *Caledonia* sailed from Glasgow on 7th April, and that second-class cabins had been taken on her for himself and his grandmother. This extravagance had been urged upon them by Uncle Neil. As Hector stared at the letter he knew that it must be true, yet it was quite impossible for him to realise that they were really going. For in the meantime they rose and went about their daily work, and ate and slept and rose again, just as if the tremendous 7th of April was not coming nearer and nearer— the day that was to separate them for ever from the life they knew so well.

Thus the time crept on. They were to sail for Glasgow on Monday the 4th of April, arriving there late on Tuesday night. This would give them one

Charlie over the Water

day in Glasgow before the *Caledonia* sailed on the 7th.
What tongue can tell the dreary little preparations
that were made by our travellers during their last
week at home ? The Widow had, when it came to
the point, refused to kill and eat her cherished hens,
so they had to be carried off, cackling, to the Matheson's croft in baskets.

On Saturday the cow was taken away : Hector
drove her down the road, lowing as she went, and
the Widow stood and wept at the byre door the while.
Late that afternoon she packed her own and Hector's
few belongings in a battered tin trunk (the same
that Hector's mother had taken with her to Glasgow when she married), and a few extra garments
were rolled into a bundle to be carried in the hand.

All this being done, and the next day being
Sunday, a solemn hush fell over the place. The
Widow and Hector both wore their best clothes all
day, as their working clothes were packed, and this
in itself added solemnity to the occasion. Then, the
cow and the hens being gone, there was no work to
do out of doors, while indoors everything was swept
and garnished. "We will be leaving everything in
good order for when we come home," the old woman
said. . . . Something drove like a stab through
Hector's heart ; he turned away and kicked at
the peats on the hearth, saying never a word.

Long before the sun had risen on Monday morning
the Widow was up and moving about the cottage,
though there was nothing for her to do. Then she
wandered out in the darkness to take a last look
round : how quiet it was—the earth seemed to be

asleep, the very sea asleep. Right above the cottage the morning star hung like a great lamp in the dark sky, and far away in the east a long thread of light heralded the coming day. . . . She came back into the house and blew at the peats on the hearth till they sprang into flame. Hector's voice called from his bed : " Will it be time for me to be rising, mother ? Is it morning ? " and the Widow, anxious to be in good time for the steamer, assured him that it was.

The sun had risen by the time the kettle boiled, and things looked more familiar and cheerful ; but there was not much breakfast eaten in the cottage that last morning. The kind fates had luckily decreed that Hector and the Widow were to have a travelling companion to Glasgow, in the shape of Margaret Matheson, their neighbour's daughter, who happened to be returning to her " place " in Glasgow. Her advice had been invaluable to the Widow on many points. She it was who had insisted that the old woman should take two shawls with her " against the cold on the steamboat." By her counsel, too, a basket of food had been provided, and a little tin kettle was taken to make tea by the way, as is the comfortable habit of steerage passengers on the steamers between the Islands and Glasgow. No such luxury as a cabin passage had been suggested for this short voyage.

The Widow had just packed up the basket of food when John Matheson appeared at the door to give Hector " a hand with the box " down the path to where the Matheson's cart waited for them. So the last moment had really come. Hector sprang up and seized one handle of the tin box, while Matheson took the other. With scarcely one backward look he set off down the rocky path, calling to his grandmother to follow.

But she had more to do. Standing by the door, she looked round and round the little room to make sure that everything was in order. Then she lifted the smouldering peats apart, that the fire might die out, ranged the three chairs in a row against the wall, and turned away—there was no more to see to.

" Mother, mother ! it will be losing the steamboat you'll be ! " Hector called loudly.

The Widow drew to the door, locked it, and slipped the heavy old key into the pocket of her gown.

.   .   .   .

The steerage deck presented quite a lively scene when they got on board. Little groups of passengers sat about, talking together in Gaelic ; mothers walked up and down with their babies ; and children tumbled about in everyone's way. A little stove under the awning was the great centre of attraction, for there the women were making themselves libations of tea, black as ink, in little panni-kins, and distributing it to their husbands and children. It was cold in the sea wind at that early season, and most of the women had taken off their hats and bonnets and tied little tartan shawls ("shawleys" they called them) over their heads like hoods. As yet no one was sick, for the sea was calm ; so a good deal of cheerfulness prevailed.

I suppose no happier creature breathed than Hector that morning. The first quivers and snorts of the steamer as it got under way sent thrills and shivers of pure delight through every inch of him. He stood bareheaded in the sea wind and waved his cap in farewell to the Mathesons on the quay, then raced off up the deck, wild with pleasure.

Had not his friend MacGregor the steward volunteered to take him over every corner of the ship ? Had he not left the Island at last ? Wasn't life almost too exciting and splendid altogether ?

He hung over the ship's side that he might realise how quickly he was being carried away from the tiresome old life into the new one. The wind freshened, and the ship seemed to dash right at the waves as they rose up to meet her. Hector laughed with delight, and raced down the deck again to ask his grandmother if it wasn't fine ? But, lo ! huddled all together under her two shawls, she sat gazing backwards at the fast vanishing outline of the Island—and slow tears crept one by one down her withered cheeks.

.   .   .   .

It was Tuesday night when they put in to Glasgow—a dark wet night with buffets of wind. The preceding twenty-four hours had not been unmixed joy, even to Hector, and if it had not been for Margaret Matheson he did not know what would have happened to his grandmother.

Charlie over the Water

What a long, long night it had seemed. How cold it was, and then the straining noises of the ship, the rush of the waves, the howling of the wind! Overcome with sleep, Hector had nodded uncomfortably for hours, wedged into a corner; but the widow and Margaret had seen the livelong night out together with whispered colloquies in Gaelic. Towards morning Margaret had made strong tea for them, which warmed them up; and the other women were moving about more or less all night attending to their children. Some of the men lay on the deck and slept; but most of them sat up, grumbling, swearing, and nodding by turns till the daylight came.

With the light things had mended—there was solid food to be partaken of, and one could walk about and look round; but take it all in all, that steerage journey was not very pleasant, and the lights of Glasgow in the distance were hailed with joy.

" There now, Mistress MacKay, you will be getting to your bed," Margaret told the Widow, who only shook her head dolefully, sceptical that such bliss could ever be hers again in this world.

. . . .

Hector drank deep of the joys of living in the one day they spent in Glasgow before they sailed. To tread the paved streets of a large town for the first time; to see shops, and cars and railway-trains, and cabs and motors—it was a heady draught indeed, and by nightfall Hector was almost drunk

with pleasure. There was no room left in his heart
for pity of that strange timidity which made his
grandmother cower by the fire in Uncle Neil's
kitchen, instead of coming out to see the wonders
of Glasgow. " I am wanting to stay in the town,"
he told Uncle Neil ; " I am not wanting to leave
to-morrow."

" Hoots, laddie, ye'll see far finer places nor
Glasgow where you're going," the older man assured
him ; but Hector doubted the assertion. Nothing
could be more exciting than this city where he found
himself. In the short time at his disposal he
managed to take several rides in the electric cars,
spend an hour in railway-trains, and have what his
uncle very expressively called "a hurl" in a motor
'bus. When you consider that each of these experiences was entirely novel, you can form some
idea of the seething excitement in the boy's brain
at the close of day. And there the Widow sat by
the fire, her thoughts turned back always to the
Island. . . . Would the cow be happy in the
Matheson's byre ? Would the hens be roosting in
the unaccustomed barn ? She wondered was it a
soft day on the Island, or was the sun shining ?
If it was raining, the rain would be running in under
the door, and no one to wipe it up . . . and och,
dear, they had been forgetting to mend the thatch
—the same that the big gale blew off in March—
the water would be coming down the wall again. . . .
Uncle Neil's wife listened kindly to all these specu-
lations, and plied her aged relative with potent cups

of tea at least four times during the day, as the only form of comfort she could offer to her. Thus the time went past—slowly for the Widow, quickly for Hector, and the day of departure arrived.

Thursday at noon the *Caledonia* sailed. Uncle Neil had been at great trouble to get the most comfortable quarters he could for the travellers ; he felt anxious about their welfare. Under his escort they got safely on board ; but then there ensued a terrible hour when the Widow and Hector, and even sturdy Uncle Neil, were swept about the decks like leaves before the wind. Hundreds of passengers—steerage for the most part—were pouring on to the ship, bewildered, staring, weeping, and cursing, according to their nature. Among this crowd, stewards pushed their way, by turns persuasive and abusive, working like demons to get things in order. There seemed no one to appeal to ; everyone was too busy to answer questions ; it was all one vast confusion. And then came the clang of a great bell, the signal that friends must go ashore—Uncle Neil must withdraw his much-needed protection.

For a moment Hector felt a childish wave of something like terror sweep over him : he was to be left in this crowd to look after his grandmother —she that was crying like a baby now with fear and excitement. But he managed to conquer this disagreeable and unmanly sensation, and held out his hand to Uncle Neil with an appearance of the greatest composure.

Charlie over the Water

" I'm thinking we will be off now," he said.

" Aye, y're off—good luck to ye," said Uncle Neil.
" Things'll quiet down once y're off—good-bye to
you, Mistress MacKay, and a good voyage."

Our travellers indeed were in want of all the good
wishes they could get, at that desolate moment
when they pressed to the side of the ship and saw
the last of Uncle Neil's stout figure, as he stood
among the crowd on shore waving a red-and-white
pocket-handkerchief to them in farewell.

A mighty quiver passed through the ship—as if a
heart had begun to beat inside her iron ribs—the
people on the quay sent up a great shout, and they
were off.

Finding that no one was likely to attend to them
at present, Hector guided the Widow to a sheltered
corner, and suggested that they should just sit
there till things were more in order.

" Och, Hector, what were we thinking on to
leave the Island ! " the old woman cried ; and at
that moment the same thought had sprung into
Hector's mind also, though he repulsed it with all
his might.

" We will not be saying that when we see Uncle
Charlie," he told her.

" We'll never be reaching him," she sobbed, and
clung to his arm in an agony of fear at their unfamiliar surroundings. But just as matters had
reached this sad pass a steward accosted them.

" Now then, let's see where you belong," he
said.

Charlie over the Water

" We will be coming from Balneish," Hector replied with dignity, and wondered why the man laughed.

" From Balneish, are you ? Well, let's see your tickets, and I'll show you your quarters."

These, when found, were not, strictly speaking, palatial, but Hector and the Widow were not accustomed to much luxury, and would have meekly accepted far worse accommodation than they got. The Widow was to share a cabin with two other women and a baby ; Hector also had two room-mates ; while all round them on every side the cabins seemed bursting with passengers. A stewardess, fat and very cross, was elbowing her way among the women.

" Come along now ; get your bits of things un-done, I advise you, before we get out of the river—don't wait till you're all sick to get whatever you want . . . then we'll have a pretty time of it."

She shoved the Widow into her cabin with this not very encouraging prophecy, and began to scold the mother of the baby because she let the child cry. The mother, a meek white-faced woman, said nothing ; but the third inmate of the cabin, a stout loud-voiced person, took up her stand in the doorway and confronted the stewardess.

" None of your cheek here," she began ; " I'm no green one : I've crossed the ocean 'bout as often as yourself, maybe, so just keep a civil tongue in your head, or I'll report you."

" Report away," the stewardess retorted, as she

183

banged off down the passage-way. The fat woman turned back into the cabin with a chuckle.

" It's just as well to show them at once the stuff you're made of," she told her amazed companions. " She had no right to be at you about the kid there. Either of you crossed before ? " she added, nodding first to the Widow, then to the white-faced woman, in an interrogative way. Both shook their heads. " Well, I have," she pursued ; " I've crossed the Atlantic more times than I remember. I'm Scotch born, but I married in the States five-and-twenty years ago—Mrs. Koster I am—and I'm more nor half Yankee now. Oh, I know what's what, I tell you. I come across mostly every second year to see the old people." . . .

She glanced contemptuously at the two in-experienced voyagers before her ; then, stirred with some feeling of pity, she turned to the Widow :

" You're old to be crossing for the first time. Haven't you got anyone with you ? "

" I have Hector with me," the old woman said, " and we will be going across the water to my son —him that has been fifteen years across."

" It's a good thing you've some one with you. Well, the ship's beginning to rock a bit—you take my advice and lie down—here, I'll help you off with your bonnet. . . . Can't you get into the berth ? Tut, tut . . . try again ; there you are. I'm off to get my tea."

She bounced away, and the Widow with a groan adjusted herself in her narrow berth. " Och, it's many a broader chest (coffin) I've seen in my day ! " she murmured to herself.

She was fated, poor soul, not to rise from the narrow couch for many a day. Over her sufferings it is kinder to draw a veil—they were not romantic, though real enough in all certainty.

One strange fact might have been revealed to her if she had been a student of human nature—namely, the sterling qualities that lurk in the most unexpected persons. For how the Widow would have survived her week at sea without the ministrations of her truculent neighbour Mrs. Koster, it is difficult to imagine. The stewardess was far from attentive ; but Mrs. Koster was always willing to do what she could for the sufferer. Many a battle she fought for her with the stewardess too. Whenever that lady entered the cabin Mrs. Koster had what she called " a set to " with her, and she always came off the victor. The Widow was to have this or that, she needed it, and if the stewardess wouldn't get it, she (Mrs. Koster) would complain . . . " so just off with you, and get it, and no more about it."

" It's not customary for second-class passengers to want so much attention—them that wants luxuries should pay for them," the stewardess retorted ; but Mrs. Koster always managed to have the last word :

" And them that are paid to work should see that they do it," she screamed after the stewardess down the passage-way, so that everyone round about heard the taunt and laughed. Then, turning back

into the cabin, she fell to her task of cheering the
Widow once more—no easy task, for she, poor
creature, was quite under the impression that she
would never reach the shore. The burden of her
lament was all for the Island—just home, home,
home, that was all she wanted. Sure the sea was
a wicked cruel way to be travelling, and whatever
had made her start to cross it she did not know. . . .
Then a storm came on, and things were worse and
worse. The slapping of the waves against the sides
of the ship all night long, the frantic grinding of the
screw below, the straining of the timbers above, the
trampling and yelling on the decks—never a moment
of quiet night or day, and plunging up and down,
rolling from side to side, the whole world reeling
round. . . .

But through this scene of terror (as it seemed to
the poor Widow) Mrs. Koster moved with no sign
of perturbation. . . . " Yes, it's a storm, as dirty
a storm as you'd get—a beam sea on—makes a row
would waken the dead. . . . A plague upon that
rolling, I can't fasten my stays." . . . Her ejacu-
lations, so unemotional, so calmly prosaic, had a
strangely comforting effect upon the distracted
nerves of the Widow. When she, poor woman,
was saying her prayers and commending her soul
to her Maker, Mrs. Koster would break in with some
abuse of her enemy the stewardess that in its earthly
vindictiveness was supremely reassuring :

" Drat the woman ! Can't she bring a cup of
soup when she's told to ? She's too busy carrying

Charlie over the Water

on with the head steward to attend to her business
. . . dirty huzzie that she is."

Such animadversions really comforted the Widow
far more than if Mrs. Koster had joined in her
terrified petitions. She did not understand why
this should be ; but so it was.

As the Widow's sea-sickness lessened, she was
able to appreciate more fully Mrs. Koster's powers
as a *raconteuse*. Days at sea are long ; but not so
long as were Mrs. Koster's tales. These included
the story of her first marriage, of the illness and death
of this first husband, of her second courtship, her
second marriage, her seven confinements, the ill-
nesses of each of the seven children, the deaths of
three, the placing in business of two, the marriage
of one, and the education of the last and cleverest
olive-branch, Miss Cassie Koster. All this, and more,
the Widow was regaled with during her convales-
cence in the half darkness of a stuffy cabin. By
the side of these thrilling narratives her poor life
history would have cut a sorry figure ; but she was
far too simple to wish to mention her own affairs,
and listened with reverence to her fellow-traveller's
talk, saying never a word of her humble experiences
of life and death and birth.

Hector in the meantime was having a week
of the most extraordinary enjoyment. It never
occurred to him to be sick, bred as he had been all
his childhood in boats ; and even the sight of his
grandmother's misery could not damp his pleasure
for more than a few moments. He was taking a

plunge into life, indeed—life as it may be studied in the saloons of an ocean steamer. I will not say that everything his young curious eyes saw was desirable, that everything his young sharp ears heard was profitable ; but " all was grist that came to his mill " and he found no fault with anything. So the week passed very differently for Hector and his grandmother. About this time Mrs. Koster began to bestir herself on the Widow's account.

" We're off the Banks now," she told her, " and the swell's gone down wonderfully ; it's time you got on to your legs—you're much better to-day. You must get up."

" Och, no, my dear ! I cannot be leaving the bed," the old woman cried.

" Come, come, you mustn't give in like that—a breath of fresh air is what you want," Mrs. Koster persisted.

With groans and sighs the Widow allowed herself to be hoisted out of the berth, and somehow or other got into her clothes and up on deck. There, leaning heavily on Hector's arm, she staggered along, dizzy and weary, yet thankful to breathe the air of heaven again—to look up into a blue sky and down upon a placid sea, to hear above all the blessed assurance that the land was nearly gained at last. Poor old soul ! she walked thus along the deck for a few yards, and then subsided on to a bench quite worn out. " Hector, Hector ! " she cried, " it's a terrible long road you've taken me ! "

Charlie over the Water

He could not deny it—a long road, indeed; but Mrs. Koster would not encourage sentiment.

"Tuts," she said. "Not a bit of it—it'll do you good; there's nothing better for the stomach than a week's sea-sickness. I've often said to Koster, 'I wish I wasn't such a good sailor, for what with the good living on board, I do get stout, and no mistake.' Now, a week like you've had would thin me down capital; but there—I relish my food better on sea than on land."

Hector was quite comforted by this panegyric of sea-sickness, for he had been not a little concerned by the Widow's white face and trembling gait. He too adopted the cheerful key, and began to tell his grandmother that they were now within measureable distance of Uncle Charlie.

"Just the two days after we land, mother," he said. "Think on that—how soon you will be seeing him."

The fresh air, this cheerful conversation, and a cup of Bovril administered in a timely manner by Mrs. Koster, began to put some heart into the Widow again. She took another turn along the deck, felt less shaky, and looked about her with some interest.

Mrs. Koster was triumphant. "Didn't I tell you? You'll be all right to-morrow, I reckon," she said, proud of her own powers as a sick nurse, and glad at the bottom of her kind vulgar heart to see her old charge revive a little.

They were standing close together, this strange

Charlie over the Water

trio, when the ship came into the dock at New York.

" You look out sharp, Hector, for that Mrs. MacDonald," Mrs. Koster admonished the lad; " I tell you it'll take you all your time to find out some one you don't know in that crowd." She pointed down as she spoke at the mass of yelling, laughing, weeping, handkerchief-waving people who always await the incoming of a big ocean steamer. " How're you to find her out ? " she inquired.

" Her name will be MacDonald," Hector answered slowly.

" MacDonald ! And are you to ask every woman in that crowd what her name is ? Great Scot ! you'll never find her ! "

" She will be looking for us," Hector said—he did not like to be considered foolish.

" Well, don't you lose sight of me all at once— maybe you'll find you want some help yet, young man," Mrs. Koster said, laughing; she detected Hector's wounded pride. " I'll have a tussle with the Customs—there's nothing I like better. You wait and see if I don't get a rise out of them."

As the Widow's foot first touched the shores of the New World, she called down a blessing on the " good ground " : glad she was, indeed, to feel it once again solid beneath her; but she was given no further time for reflection. The crowd surged round them like the billows of the sea they had crossed, and she clung terrified to Hector's arm. On every side were sharp-faced men and women, alert and practical, gesticulating and exclamatory, meeting friends, laughing and excited. And side by side with this happy crowd stood groups of poorer passengers as helpless and bewildered as were our travellers. No friends hailed them ; they did not know what to do or where to go, and were hustled this way and that—poor terrified sheep that had come so far in search of greener pastures.

Hector wandered on among the crowd, scanning every face which seemed likely, and now and then even timidly asking, "Will you be Mrs. MacDonald, if you please ? " Always to be met with the same blank looks and shakes of the head. The Widow hung heavily on his arm, and every few minutes she would groan and ejaculate, " It's lost altogether we are, Hector ! " At last, overcome with fatigue, she sank down upon an upturned packing-case, and let the crowd drift past, while Hector stood by her side looking eagerly round in search of the mythical Mrs. MacDonald. Alas ! no one appeared to answer to the name, and at last Hector became ashamed to repeat his question—so often it had been repulsed. He would have gone through the crowd and searched it more thoroughly, but the Widow would not let him out of her sight for a moment. " No, no, Hector, do not be leaving me," she cried, almost like a child—so stay he must. Gradually the crowd thinned away, and now Hector's hopes began to revive. Mrs. MacDonald must appear now—she would surely distinguish them in the comparative solitude of the quay. But as time went on his hopes faded again—he could not see anyone who seemed to be looking for anyone else ; the people who were left now were merely waiting to get their boxes through the Customs.

In spite of his manly spirit, Hector confessed to a feeling of relief when he caught sight of Mrs. Koster's well known figure not very far off, and heard her familiar voice raised in shrill vituperation at the Customs officer. She had been met by a small, meek looking man, probably Mr. Koster ; but it was she, not he, who was attending to everything. As usual, she was getting the best of it in her battle with the Customs.

" I told you so ! Didn't I tell you not a blessed thing would you find in my box, you silly ? " she was calling out, as she stuffed back heaps of crushed looking garments into her trunk. She turned and waved her hand to Hector as a signal that they were not forgotten, and went on cramming things into the trunk, and talking all the time as hard as she could.

At last she came along to where the Widow sat, bringing the meek little man along with her.

" Here's Koster come to meet me," she said by way of introduction. " And, Koster, this is Mrs. MacKay that crossed in the same cabin with me, and Hector MacLean, her grandson. There was a friend going to meet them, but she ain't turned up apparently. Well, I never ! Say, now, Hector, what are you to do ? She won't come *now*, you bet. Where does she live again ? "

Charlie over the Water

" In New York, please," Hector answered. Mrs. Koster laughed aloud.

" That's a wide word! What's the street, I mean ? "

" I will not be knowing," Hector had to confess.

" Well, here's a fix! And you've never been in an hotel in your blessed lives. . . . Say, Koster, they'll have to come right home with us, there's no two ways about it—the old woman wants a night's rest before she starts off in the cars."

This was undeniable. To start the Widow on her long journey that night would have been sheer cruelty.

Mr. Koster nodded acquiescence. " That's it, Maggie," he assented ; " it ain't possible the old lady goes on to-night."

Our voyagers were too innocent to be quite aware of the obligation they thus accepted from strangers. In truth, they could scarcely have refused this kind hospitality, so deep was their ignorance of the ways of towns, so pressing was their need.

Mrs. Koster drew her husband aside for a moment and whispered into his ear ; he nodded, and went off to find a vehicle to convey them and their boxes from the harbour. Then off they set through the badly paved streets, at that desperate lunging pace which the New York cab-horse generally affects. Hector and the Widow were happily unaware that they were the sole reason of this extravagance— they had not heard Mrs. Koster's whisper : " Never in *this* world we'd get them into the Elevated—the

old woman would have a fit, sure's death ! " So
they accepted the drive as a matter of necessity,
and never questioned the number of dollars their
friendly entertainer would have to pay for this
luxury.

II

The Koster establishment looked right into the
Elevated track—trains thundered past the windows
day and night and shook the whole tenement. Yet
no one seemed to notice the noise, and life went on
just as it does in quieter places. Perhaps on any
other night of her life it would have been impossible for the Widow to rest in such an uproar ;
but this evening she was so exhausted that her
one wish was to lie down. She was sent off to bed
immediately, though it was only six o'clock ; for
a harder heart than Mrs. Koster's would have been
touched by the fatigue of body and weariness of
soul which were printed on that old face.

Hector meanwhile was sitting in the parlour
being catechised by Mr. and Miss Koster about
himself and his grandmother—whence they came,
whither they were going.

Miss Cassie Koster was a young girl very much his
own age, but with the complete manner of a woman
of the world, though her long hair was still worn
down her back and tied with one of those huge
hair-ribbons affected by the American schoolgirl.

Hector replied with great dignity to all their

Charlie over the Water

questions : he came from Scotland ; he had never
" crossed " before ; they were going to a place
beyond Memphis called Cypress Creek ; his grandmother was old for such a long journey, and he
knew nothing about railway travel. Miss Cassie
Koster leant back in her rocking-chair, rocking
violently all the time, and listened to every word
that passed between her father and Hector. Then
she said, in her rather sweet nasal voice : -

" Say, father, we'll have to show Mr. MacLean
round a bit."

Mr. Koster nodded.

" We'll show you a thing or two, young man,"
he said. " Like to take a ride on the cars this
evening ?—see the sky-scrapers and Broadway ? "

Hector had not the remotest idea what either a
sky-scraper or Broadway might mean or be, but
he was delighted to see anything that was worthy
to be seen—and said so.

" There, Cassie, you step around lively and get
supper, then we'll go out," the father directed ; and
the elegant Miss Cassie jumped from her rocker
and began the most practical preparations for a
meal.

Hector followed her trim little figure with his
eyes as she flitted about the room, the great ribbon
bow poised like a gigantic butterfly on her head,
and he thought he had never seen anything so
lovely.

Cassie's urban charms were indeed a first revelation of femininity to his country-bred eyes. Her

smartly fitted pink cotton "shirt-waist," high-heeled shoes and lace stockings, made up a whole of loveliness he could scarcely admire enough; and all the time she worked Cassie was talking, asking questions, laughing, smiling, whisking about from one room to another in the most charming manner. Then Mrs. Koster's heavy step came along the passage. She was hot and red in the face from unpacking and then helping the Widow to bed.

"The poor old soul's worn out," she told Hector. "I tell you what it is—she was too old to start on this trip, and that old Uncle Charlie of yours should have known better than to send for her. It was a fool thing to do at her age "—(" seventy-five she is, and never left the Hebrides," she explained in an aside to her husband). Hector sat silent for a moment, feeling very miserable. He felt it would be a relief to confess his guilt to the Kosters, so suddenly he blurted it out.

"It was me that took her," he said. "It was not my uncle that was wanting us—it was me that wearied of the Island altogether."

Mrs. Koster compressed her lips significantly.

"So that was the way of it? Well, I hope you won't ever need to regret it—that's all; remember she's old, though you're young. Not but what I think it was natural of you to do it: I'd sooner die than live on some of your islands—you're just dead there before you're in your coffin. . . . Now then, Cassie, hurry with the waffles; I'm like to die of hunger. . . . Here, Hector, draw in your chair and commence. . . . Koster, you cut the pie and help him." . . . There was an unending stream of such talk all through the meal. Cassie sat next Hector, and plied him with food. She would give his elbow a gentle little nudge, and whisper, " Say, now, have some more pie," or " These waffles are just too perfectly lovely," as she passed him some strange never-before-tasted article of diet. When the meal was over, Cassie whisked away the dishes as if by magic, while Mrs. Koster took her ease in the rocker after all the labours of the day.

" Now then, Poppa," cried Cassie, " we'll take Mr. MacLean out." She came dancing into the parlour, filled with delight at the thought of sight-seeing with their new guest, and Mr. Koster meekly consented to be dragged in the wake of the younger generation.

" Yes, you go right off and enjoy yourselves," said Mrs. Koster from the rocking-chair ; " I'll look after the old lady."

.   .   .   .

That evening was a sort of delirium of bliss to Hector. The rush and turmoil of the streets filled him with sheer delight. To board a car, already hung over with people like a swarm of bees, was to him an exquisite adventure. The Glasgow shops, the Glasgow cars, those whilom favourites, faded into insignificance before the joys of Broadway. He stood entranced under the Flat-Iron Sky-scraper, gazing up at its endless tiers of lights that looked as if they went right up to the gates of Heaven, and

Charlie over the Water

as he stood there he asked himself if this was really the same Hector MacLean who used to herd the cow and work the croft, entirely unaware that all this glittering world existed "ayont the white wave." Ah, youth and age, how tragical is the gulf that separates them! While Hector, drunk with pleasure, was taking his fill of the crowded rushing streets, the Widow lay in the noisy tenement room, her eyes closed, but not asleep. All round her was the thunder and rumbling of the city, and her heart turned back with an inexpressible longing to the little home she had left : no sound there but the waves and the wind or the cry of the gulls—or, och, dear me, the poor cow stirring in the byre! (The cow was a personality to the Widow, almost like another child.). . . .

Sleep was far from her tired eyelids, for this haunting vision of home would pass and re-pass before her brain. She got out of bed at last and fumbled in the pocket of her gown for something—the key of the cottage. Then, clasping it in her hand like a charm, she lay down again, and very shortly fell asleep.

. . . .

"You'll be a day and a night in the cars before you reach Memphis, Tenn.," Koster told his young guest, "and I guess this Cypress Creek you're bound for ain't in Tennessee at all—it's across the Mississippi somewhere, so that'll be a bit more on—you'll need to start that old lady of yours bright and early to-morrow for such a long car-ride."

Charlie over the Water

But when this was told Mrs. Koster she shook her head. " It ain't to be," she said decidedly. " She's not fit ; she's to have the best of the day in her bed to-morrow, whatever you say, and another night's rest before she starts—I know what long car-rides are to one that's not used to them."

Hector hesitated, struck suddenly with the feeling that the Kosters were doing a great deal for him and his grandmother ; but he who hesitates is lost, and Cassie, from the rocker, put in a tempting suggestion :

" You just stay, Mr. MacLean, and I'll take you along to see Cooper's Department Store to-morrow."

This turned the scale.

" Then we will be staying, thank you," Hector replied simply. " I'm thinking mother is very tired."

" She's all that," Mrs. Koster told him. " But lauks ! it's wonderful what a day in bed'll do for an old body. We're real glad to have you—I've a soft side for Scotland yet, laddie."

So another blissful day of sight-seeing in New York was before Hector. He was far too much excited to sleep when at last he went to bed. The thousand sounds from the streets fell harshly on his unaccustomed ear. In imagination he trod again all the wonderful ways he had just traversed ; and always before his eyes there flitted the trim little figure of Cassie, bright and adorable . . . then gradually all the noises seemed to merge into one, and he turned over on his pillow and slept.

Charlie over the Water

Mr. Koster, following a tradition of hospitality which is not uncommon among his countrymen, seemed to have determined to kill his young guest with sight-seeing.

" I've taken a day off from business, young man," he said at breakfast, " so as I might show you around. . . . . There's the Ghetto and the Bowery and China Town all to do ; and Cassie, there, she's anxious you should see Cooper's—I'll leave that to her ; you come along with me."

Domestic duties evidently claimed Cassie during the morning hours, so Hector set off alone with Mr. Koster. What a never-to-be-forgotten day that was ! The wonders of the Ghetto, where hook-nosed men, jabbering a strange language, gesticulated round open-air stalls piled with queer foods. The even greater marvels of China Town, with its mysterious and gruesome resorts, its horrible smells, and the Chinamen with pigtails nearly touching the pavements, who glided past on slippered feet !

From these places Hector could scarcely be dragged away. The morning passed and the afternoon, and still, tireless and enchanted, he wandered through these strange regions. At last even Mr. Koster began to show signs of fatigue.

" That there Cassie of mine'll be waitin' to take you to Cooper's," he suggested. " Supposin' now we were to take a car home ? "

Hector was most unwilling to return, but the thought of Cassie and of food prevailed ; so home they went.

Charlie over the Water

They found the Widow ensconced in the parlour, sipping a cup of strong tea, which Mrs. Koster seemed to think had a peculiar flavour because she had smuggled it.

" Six pounds, more or less, I had on me when I stood jawing with the Customs," she was explaining triumphantly. " Good Scotch tea it is, will last me a while ; Koster and Cassie don't care but for coffee." . . .

The Widow hailed her grandson with delight.

" I'm having a fine cup of tea, and I'm after having a fine sleep all the night," she told him.

Things were manifestly brighter with her. Hector sat down to tell her all his adventures ; but such a multitude of things he had to relate that his scanty English did not suffice for the telling, and he reverted to Gaelic. Cassie clapped her hands in delight. " You listen to that, Poppa ! " she cried. But Hector blushed, suddenly made aware of his own deficiencies, and stopped short in the middle of his recitals.

After an hour's rest, Hector was started off again on his round of sight-seeing—this time under Cassie's guidance.

" It's just perfectly lovely," she told him, as they walked along. " There ain't anything you can name you can't get at the Notion Counter at Cooper's ; and then there's the Fountain—ain't you ever heard of Cooper's Fountain ? Oh, my ! Well, there's a fountain plays right inside the shop, perfectly lovely it is ; and it's a great place for

meeting friends—and girls meet their beaux there :
' Meet me at the Fountain ' is quite an expression
here."

Thus initiated, Hector followed Cassie into the
fairy precincts of Cooper's. They wandered round
and round the huge building (Hector's thoughts
taking in the meantime a rapid journey back to the
store at Balneish), they went three or four times up
in the escalator, Hector becoming each time more
of an adept in stepping off just at the terrifying
last moment when it seemed as though an instant's
delay would have launched him into eternity—
Cassie laughing gaily the while. They then hung
over the Notion Counter for half an hour, and
Hector, in the fulness of his heart, bought a two cent
pincushion in the shape of a red mushroom, which he
presented to Cassie. Finally, they sauntered round
to the fountain and sat down to watch it play.

" It's I that am sorry to be leaving to-morrow ! "
burst from Hector's lips.

" Yes, I'm real sorry," Cassie responded genially ;
then, with a touch of sentiment, she added, " I
guess we shan't ever meet again, Mr. MacLean ? "

The solid earth seemed to reel under Hector for
a moment before he managed to say, " I will be
coming back "; and a moment later, as if the words
had been screwed out of him by torture : " I will
be coming to see you, Cassie."

This boyish confession of admiration was only
what Miss Cassie Koster had expected : she would
have been much mortified if it had not been given.

Charlie over the Water

" Ah, well," she said with a sigh, " that won't
probably be possible, Mr. MacLean ; but you won't
forget me, will you ? "

" I will never be forgetting," Hector blurted out
—terribly in earnest, poor lad. Cassie, on her part,
was gloating over the interesting story she would
make out of this incident to her young friends at
school : " Mr. Hector MacLean, a Highland nobleman of great wealth, who had come to visit them
for two days—two days that had, however, amply
sufficed to light a never-dying passion for her in his
breast : at Cooper's Fountain (romantic spot !) his
passion had been declared. ' I will never forget
you ' had been his words. We parted ; but he
carried my portrait next his heart." To verify the
last clause of this tale Cassie drew from her pocket
a little likeness of herself, about the size of a penny,
made into a locket, and handed it to Hector.

" If you care to have it," she said, " you can wear
it round your neck on a ribbon, or next your heart."

Hector clutched the portrait ; but he felt too
much for speech—it was Cassie who had full command of the situation.

" I guess we must be getting home now," she
said. " Mother said as we mustn't be late. Come
along, Mr. MacLean, and mind you don't let anyone see that—ever—it's an eternal secret between
you and me."

Mr. MacLean, dazed with happiness and completely bewildered by his own novel sensations,
followed Cassie out again into the brilliantly lit

streets, clasping the five cent snapshot tightly in his hand.

. . . .

" I'll see you off myself," Mrs. Koster told the Widow. " I'll speak to the car-conductor and try to get you looked after. It's a longish ride, and I wouldn't wonder but what you'll be real worn out before you get to Cypress Creek."

The Widow was in tolerable spirits—was she not now within two days of meeting Charlie ?

" And is it just sitting in a train we'll be all the time ? " she asked.

" That's it—a long sit, of course, and noisy and shaky, but that's all. I'm fond of a long car ride myself," Mrs. Koster replied.

They had sent off a telegram to Charlie the day before, giving the probable hour of their arrival at Cypress Creek, so they were sure to be met this time. Only one difficulty loomed ahead—a change of trains at Memphis.

" Tuts ! Surely you can manage that now, Hector, since you've been about in cars and trains a bit," Mrs. Koster said.

" I will be managing fine," he replied.

So the moment of their departure came. With many handshakings, admonitions, and good wishes, Mrs. Koster and Cassie said farewell to their guests.

" You'll send us a line when you reach, Hector," Mrs. Koster said. " And tell us how you got on. Get your grannie to eat as much as you can ; there's nothing so good against car sickness as a full

Charlie over the Water

stomach. Ask the conductor if you're in a fix about anything, and keep a civil tongue in your head to the black porter ; then you'll be all right."

Cassie pressed Hector's hand in farewell, and murmured the word " Adieu," which sounded so much more interesting than merely saying good-bye.

She would have liked to think that her heart was broken, but not even her schoolgirl imagination could suppose this, nor could she squeeze out a single tear. It only remained, then, to try to look as tragic as possible ; but in this Cassie succeeded very badly indeed. Hector's feelings were much less superficial, and his heart was in his throat as he stood by the window of the car and waved for the last time to Cassie. He turned to find the Widow looking very disconsolate.

" Och, Hector, we're alone now," she cried, conscious that Mrs. Koster had been left behind, and that they were speeding out into the unknown, carried on by some dread power that was unstoppable. Oh, the terror to her old nerves of those first hours in the railway train ! Yet everyone round about looked happy and composed : how was it that other people were not apprehensive in this dreadful vehicle ? The car was long, and packed with passengers ; it swung from side to side and was suffocatingly hot. Twenty-four hours of this ! The negro porter filled the Widow with unspeakable alarm. " It's the Bad Man himself," she cried at first sight of his black face, and Hector had some ado to quiet her fears. They sat together

Charlie over the Water

by the car window and gazed out at the empty, featureless land studded with advertisement boards and made hideous by unsightly buildings.

The long winter had just ended, and the sudden onrushing American spring had begun. Trees were bursting in leaf; the sere pastures greening over with a film of young grass; everywhere was the urge and promise of coming life. On and on the train went, hour after hour, thundering through unknown towns that seemed to Hector enormous cities. Then out into the country again—always on and on. Late in the afternoon the Widow collapsed entirely.

"I'm ill, Hector; I'm not knowing what will be the matter with me," she said. Her face was very white, and she sat back against the hard seat and closed her eyes. Hector was at his wits' end, and looked round for help. He did not know whom to appeal to. Then with a sudden rally of independence he decided to appeal to no one. Why should he be always helped about everything ?— it was time that he became the helper. Rolling up the Widow's extra shawl into a pillow, he told her that she must lie down along the seat—he would sit on the floor of the car beside her. The other passengers looked on; but no one offered any assistance. It was not a very easy couch, but better for an invalid than having to sit straight upright. Then he remembered a little bottle of brandy, pressed into his pocket at the last moment by Mrs. Koster with admonitions that he had thought nothing of at the moment, so busy was he in looking his last at Cassie.

The brandy was a godsend, and brought back a little colour to the Widow's lips. " She'll be all right now," a man sitting next them said to Hector in an unconcerned tone. " Car-sick the old lady is—you let her lie still."

Hector felt a little reassured. The horrible thought had darted into his mind : what if his grandmother were to die in the car, and never reach Cypress Creek alive ? Now this matter-of-fact assurance from his neighbour was comforting ; but how was the whole livelong night to be got through, he wondered ? At this point of his journey Hector began to learn an excellent bit of knowledge of life —that we often come to places where nothing but sheer endurance is of any use to us. The sooner this lesson of endurance is learned the better for the learner. Here were hours—uncounted hours —still to be got through under these painful circumstances. The car was crowded, and so no one offered Hector a seat in place of the one he had vacated for his grandmother. He crouched beside her on the floor, trying to forget how uncomfortable he was, and from time to time whispering into her ear any word of consolation that he could muster. She would only groan, and make no reply.

The train rushed on and on. Hector nodded with weariness, falling against the corner of the car, helplessly sleepy, yet too cramped to fall really asleep. All round were people in every attitude of fatigue—propped into corners, leaning on bundles, abandonedly tired. Not for them were the sleeping berths and state-rooms that their richer fellow-passengers might enjoy : they must just live through the long hours as best they could. What a strange night it was ! The clanking of the engine seemed to get into Hector's brain ; then he would fall half-asleep for a minute or two and forget it, and waken up again to the tireless clank, clank, clank. . . . Then he would peer out into the darkness they were rushing through and marvel where they were, till sleep like a strong wave would sweep over him once more. . . . A minute later he started broad awake, wondering how his grandmother was. Once or twice the train stopped for a blessed moment or two, and everyone wakened up and wondered what was happening. The next minute they moved on again into the dark.

Thus and thus passed the night, and at last daylight came struggling in through the windows in long white rays. Hector shook himself, rose from his cramped position on the floor, and looked out. They were travelling now through hilly country, with sparse woods just turning green. As Hector gazed out, he gave a sudden exclamation of surprise —he saw for the first time in his life a peach orchard covered with blossom. The starveling Highland spring had afforded no such sight ; the beauty of it took his breath away. With like amazement our earthbound senses may yet behold things undreamed of now. . . .

Charlie over the Water

At last a stirring began among the sleepy passengers. "We'll soon be getting into Memphis," some one told Hector—a bit of news that seemed too good to be true. He leant over the Widow and whispered the glad tidings into her ear.

"The Lord be praised, Hector! Will we be getting out from the train?" she asked feebly.

"Yes, mother, we will be getting out soon, and then maybe you would be having a cup of tea," he suggested. She shook her head; but all the same the thought of leaving this awful vehicle in which her sufferings had been so acute acted favourably on her nerves; she sat up and tried to smooth her few locks of grey hair under her crumpled head gear. Hector made timid inquiry from a man who sat near them, as to how far Cypress Creek was from Memphis? He sucked his teeth reflectively for a moment, and volunteered the information that it must be some six hours or so. The Widow, alas! had caught his words.

"What is he saying, Hector—six hours, is it !— och, och, it's I that will never be reaching Charlie !"

"Maybe he's wrong," Hector said stoutly. The train drew up then, and out the passengers tumbled —a dishevelled, weary looking crew. There was a certain amount of confusion; but Hector was beginning to find himself at last, and did not allow the crowd to bewilder him altogether. He drew his grandmother to a quiet spot on the platform and waited there till the crowd had dispersed. Then he began to ask about the train for Cypress Creek, and was rather dismayed to find that it did not start for fully two hours.

Happily the fresh air had already restored the Widow : she looked much better, and even murmured something about a cup of tea. Hector piloted her along the platform, looking for a bench where she might sit down. Then he was confronted by two signboards : " White waiting-room," " Coloured waiting-room." What could a coloured waiting-room mean ? Well, it sounded more cheerful than a white one, he thought, and boldly opened the door, pushing the Widow before him. She turned back with a scream.

" Och, Hector, the black faces of them ! " she cried ; and Hector, annoyed by his own stupidity, hurried her away to the white waiting-room. He then started in pursuit of a cup of tea for his grandmother. Vain quest ! Such a luxury was not to be had at any price, so he substituted a cup of coffee for it, and returned to the white waiting-room.

The widow had never tasted coffee, and her whole soul longed for a cup of tea ; but so hungry and exhausted was she, that she would have drunk poison, I believe, had it been offered to her. The coffee, however, proved a great success, and under its stimulating influence she consented to take Hector's arm and walk out of the station to look round them a little. Hector was burning with curiosity to see what Memphis was like ; so off they went, as odd a couple as ever trod the streets of that little southern town. Owing to the heat, which

was becoming greater every hour, the Widow had
discarded her large shawl, and now wore only her
little tartan " shawley " over her shoulders.   Hector
was dressed in a complete knickerbocker suit of thick
homespun tweed and a little cap of the same
material—a costume well adapted for the Highland
winter he had left behind him, but strangely ill-
suited for the ardent southern spring he had now to
encounter.   The heat indeed became so great, when
they got out into the sunshine from under the
shade of the station, that Hector took off his coat
and carried it over his arm, walking, as often in
summer-time on the hills at home, " in his shirt-
sleeves."

They walked very slowly, to suit the Widow's
pace ; and as they walked they gazed about them
in surprise.   For they were going through the negro
quarter, and it had that indescribable air of the
population overflowing the houses that negro
dwellings so often wear.   Every cabin seemed to
be fairly bursting with men, women, and children ;
they hung out of the windows, they clustered on
the steps like bees, they squatted on the pavements.
All the cabins seemed to be falling to bits, every
door to lack its hinges, every window to be propped
up with anything that came to hand.   The men
looked far too tall for the low houses, great hulking creatures that they were ; only the children
were supremely attractive as they rolled about in
the dust like happy little animals.

The Widow was at first much alarmed by the

sight of this black population ; but Hector pointed
out a few white people here and there to reassure
her. " If you could be seeing clearer, mother,
you would not be minding," he told her. He longed
to go on farther, but the Widow's steps began to
flag, so they turned back to the station. It was
at this point that a dreadful discovery was made—
one which Hector had been anxious to keep from
his grandmother.

" What day will it be, Hector ? " she asked him.
" I'm after losing count of the days."

He would have liked to tell a fib, but could not.

" It's the Sabbath, mother," he said. She gave
a cry of dismay.

" And we on the road, Hector ! Ochone, that I
should ever be doing such wickedness ! "

" It couldn't be helped—with the train taking
so long," he explained ; but the old woman would
not be comforted.

" To think upon it ! " she wailed. " And they
will be in the church at Balneish now. What time
is it, laddie ? Will they be at the singing or at
the prayer at Balneish ? "

Hector was unable to grapple with differences of
time between the countries, so took it for granted
that twelve noon at Memphis must be twelve noon
at Balneish.

" They'll be at the singing, I'm thinking," he
said. The words seemed to transport him back to
the little church at home, where, rain or shine, he
had sat every Sunday since he could remember

Charlie over the Water

anything—every Sunday till this one and the one
before it ! He seemed to hear the old " precentor "
" reading out the line," as it is called in Gaelic
singing. Then the company of worshippers, after
learning the words, join in with the tune. At that
moment Hector could have sworn that he heard
again the long-drawn quavering notes of the old
psalm tunes—and here were he and his grandmother, thousands of miles away, walking among
the black people in Memphis ! . . .

" I will be going back into the station and saying
a Psalm to myself," the Widow said ; it was the
only tribute she could pay to the day.

So Hector led her back to the waiting-room, and
set her down in a corner to rest. There with closed
eyes she sat, and tried to shut out all the noisy
secular world ; her lips moved, though no words
came from them. Hector wondered, rather with
awe, what she was saying. These, if he had only
known, were the words :

> " By Babel's streams we sat and wept
>   When Sion we thought on."

She muttered the lines over and over, forgetting
some of them, and then suddenly came upon words
that seemed to voice her own need :

> " O how the Lord's song shall we sing
>   Within a foreign land ? "

It comforted her to know that another had felt
like her.

Charlie over the Water

The train for Cypress Creek came up at last.

" We will soon be reaching now, mother," Hector said, feeling that their troubles were nearly over, as he helped her once more into the car. It was filled with a motley company, and our travellers retreated to their seats and watched their fellow-passengers in surprise. A lot of foreign emigrants filled some of the seats, and another group were playing cards.

" What will they be doing with the bits of pictures ? " the Widow whispered to her grandson.

" These'll be playing-cards, mother," he said, having learned as much as that (and a little more) on board ship. He would have liked, indeed, to join the game ; but his grandmother's horrified exclamation put an end to that. She had never seen a card in her life, and knew of them only as some mysterious evil.

" Eh, Hector, and on the Lord's Day ! " she sighed. Her Sabbatarian views were getting many a shock just now. Hector then began to look out at the window. They were crossing the Mississippi, and the rushing, tawny flood of the great river filled him with delight. They came after that into a strange region, where the train seemed to run through shallow lakes ; water was round and round them, with great cypress trees rising out of the swamps. Then the swamps seemed to dry up again, and they went through forests. There were clearings here, and white men's houses, easily distinguishable from the deplorable negro cabins.

Charlie over the Water

It was about two o'clock now, and the fervid heat of the afternoon sun struck in through the windows of the car. Would the journey never end? Even Hector's interest began to flag; and as for the Widow, she felt as if she were in a bad dream—a dream of endless clanking noise and dust and heat, and wild strange faces all round her.

She leant back and closed her eyes, and her mind travelled across the weary leagues that lay now between her and home. As clear as day she saw the cottage, its brown thatched roof dripping in the rain, the blue peat smoke curling up from the chimney. . . . With a quick movement she felt in her pocket for the key—the blessed key—and clutched it fast : it seemed to her a charm, a pledge, something to hold on to when everything round her was unreal. Then in her utter weariness she dozed again, and another hour was got through. Three o'clock—they had lost all sense of time, and had no watch to set them right. The train stopped once or twice, and people got out and came in. Each time Hector started up, asking if this was Cypress Creek, and always was told " Not yet." They might have been travelling on into Eternity—far, far beyond the limits of Time. . . . Hector, too, fell asleep, and was wakened by a tap on his shoulder and the voice of the negro porter speaking thrilling words :

" Now then, sah ! Cypress Creek—step lively."

Hector dragged himself up out of the abyss of sleep, and essayed to waken his grandmother, who had again been wrapped in slumber. She woke with a start.

" Och, Hector, I was after dreaming of a cruel long journey I was taking ! " she cried. She sat up, blinking her tired eyes. Could it be she found herself in her own chair at home ? Alas ! there were only the horrible strange faces round her, some of them laughing at what she had said, and Hector calling to her to be quick and get out of the train, for they had reached Cypress Creek at last !

They seemed to have arrived at the very world's end—just a cluster of wooden houses set down on the edge of the forest ; the railway track running through this pretence at a village, and two or three negroes and whites loitering about to look at the train.

With some difficulty the Widow was hoisted out of the car. She found herself standing on the solid ground once more, but dazed with fatigue and blinded by the blaze of the afternoon sun as it struck across her dim old eyes. Groping, with her hands held out before her as she went, she stumbled forward. A tall man was coming towards her.

" Eh, mother, it's yourself ! " he cried, with that quite indescribable note of the exile's voice in his cry. She ran forward—yes, ran, as if those old limbs had suddenly become young again—and fell into his outstretched arms.

" Och, och, it's Charlie—it's Charlie ! "

In a moment she had forgotten everything—the unutterable strangeness of her surroundings, the

weary sea and land that she had crossed : she had
got to Charlie at last, her dim eyes had seen him
again, her dull ears heard his voice.

People at the window of the car looked out and
smiled at the meeting—at the funny-looking old
woman in her tartan shawl holding on to the big
man ; but some of them had tears in their eyes, too
—for with most of them partings had been commoner
than such meetings.

.   .   .   .

During the first few days of their stay at Cypress
Creek Hector lived in hourly expectation that his
fraud about the letter would be discovered. But
whether it was that his grandmother had got so
confused by all she had gone through that she
forgot about the letter, or whatever it was, nothing
happened, and very soon Hector began to forget
the matter himself. The new life that opened
round him now appeared wonderfully vivid and
interesting. For here at " MacKay's Place," as
the neighbours called Charlie's clearing, there was
work enough and to spare, and Hector rejoiced in
this. Work—the men of the Old World didn't
know the meaning of the word ! In comparison
with what the settlers here got through in a day,
the labours of men at home seemed like the scratch-
ings of mice.

Nature was being conquered and held by the
throat, as it were, all the time ; the land had been
slowly and painfully reclaimed from the forest inch
by inch ; the great trees fired, with reckless waste

of timber, and then their roots dug and torn out of the soil to make room for crops. All round about the clearing Hector watched the same sort of thing going on. Men toiled like cattle to win this rich land for themselves and their children. An incessant war it was, splendid and triumphant, where man was always the victor in the end, and Nature, at last subdued, obediently yielded up her fruits into the hands of her conqueror.

To join in the battle—what more would any man ask ? Hector wondered. His spirit kindled to the work. It was new and exciting, often dangerous, always difficult ; but work for men. He looked back with a blessed sense of escape at the little stony croft on the island where he had worked so long. What child's play it had been ! No adventures, no risks—above all, no prizes to win : just picking away at the barren soil, reaping the thin little crops, and scraping the ground once more, over and over again. And now he had escaped from it all. He thought contemptuously of the long idleness of the crofter's winter, and laughed with glee to have said good-bye to it for ever. You may be sure that a lad with Hector's views was fully appreciated by his uncle. It was not easy to get "help" enough for all the work ; the negroes were lazy and difficult to manage, and white labour was scarce. No wonder, then, that Hector found himself in great request. He toiled late and early, getting burnt almost black with the sun, growing taller and stronger, and enjoying himself mightily.

Charlie over the Water

There was a curious, not altogether desirable, population round Cypress Creek. All nations and peoples and tongues were there, and among these, too, a large sprinkling of the descendants of the convicts who had been sent out to the plantations in old days. These you could distinguish from the other settlers by their very air; there seemed to be a streak of untameable wildness somewhere in them—it sparkled in their hard defiant eyes, and lurked at the corners of their thin lips. A strange composite society it was altogether; in truth a change of mental atmosphere from the few decent crofter families of Balneish!

Hector's relative had lived long enough in America to have thoroughly absorbed one of its cardinal doctrines—that everyone must look for himself. So beyond a word or two of warning now and again, Hector was left to take his own way.

The Widow in the meantime was having some new experiences too, as you may imagine. The first weeks of her stay had been a sort of confused yet happy dream. She had reached her son; she had finished her terrible journey. But then things began to wear another complexion. The heat became overpowering—there was no escape from it day or night; and sometimes in her simple way the old woman would " put up a prayer " that coolness might come. The thunderstorms terrified her when they burst above the little house with a strange crackling sound, and the very earth shook. Then, when evening came, there was sometimes a breath

of fresher air, and Charlie would take her to sit
out by the door. Away in the distance they could
still see the lightning playing, like great swords
thrust down out of heaven into the forest, and the
Widow was scared by it. In the swamps the frogs
kept up a constant chanting that she could not get
accustomed to, and, worst of all, an occasional
rattlesnake would appear.

" Och, it's the Evil One himself—I will have read
it in the Good Book ! " she cried, almost beside
herself with terror. Mosquitoes, too—who could
be doing with the like of them ? And nothing
would ever reconcile her to the negroes. So what
with one thing and another life did not appear in
its liveliest colours.

But these outside disagreeables would have
mattered not at all if everything had gone smoothly
indoors.

Alas ! before many weeks had passed, difficulties
began to crop up between the Widow and her
daughter-in-law. Mrs. Charlie MacKay proved to
have " a temper," and along with it a fiercely
jealous nature. She could not see her husband's
devotion to his mother without resenting it ; and
when the Widow also won the affections of little
Donald it was more than she could bear. Like
all jealous people, she tried to conceal her jealousy,
and showed it in undeserved outbursts of anger
about nothing. But she took good care never to
lose her temper in this way before Charlie ; it was
always when he was out that these horrible scenes

Charlie over the Water

occurred. Then the old woman would cower before her, and take refuge in silence, always hoping that things would mend with time. Of course, instead of mending, they got worse and worse. The Widow began to wear a bullied, almost frightened, expression, and Charlie asked her often if she felt quite well. " It will be the heat," she always told him, anxious that he should suspect nothing. Then they would return to that unending converse they held together about the Island—that converse which so provoked and angered Charlie's wife. Why, she asked, why in all the world should her husband be wanting to know all the foolish things he was forever asking his mother about ? He seemed to wish to know about every stone on the road, every bush on the hillside ; and as for the questions he asked they were purely childish : ' Had the big boulder on the roadside still got the blasting-hole in it ?—he remembered how he (and poor Andrew that's dead and gone) used to play at filling up the hole with mud on wet days ; and was there a gate now where the path from the shieling joined the road to Balneish ? What sort of gate was it ? And was it true the byre needed new thatch ? Did old John Matheson do the thatching yet ?—he must be getting up in years.' . . .

So their talk ran ; and Charlie's wife listened with very ill-concealed irritation. He could apparently never hear enough of the Island, and every evening when he came in from work would sit down beside his mother to hear more. It was just extraordinary the silly questions he found to ask. These hours of talk became the only happiness of the Widow's life —for them she lived through the long, hot, weary days, bearing with her daughter's ill temper. One night (but the wife was out then) she drew from her pocket the clumsy old key of the cottage door, and showed it to Charlie.

He held it reverently in his big work-marred hands for a long time, turning it round and round ; then he gave it back to his mother without a word, but he drew his hand across his eyes as he did so, and the Widow gave a great sob. How well that no one was there to behold their folly !

It was getting on to the month of August, when one day Hector came in very full of excitement, for something had happened. He had been at Cypress Creek, and there at the saloon had met some horse traders from Mexico. These gentlemen, with their fringed leather gloves, slouched hats and sashes, had completely captivated Hector's imagination—how could it possibly have been otherwise ? They had allowed him to mount into their high Mexican saddles, and had even complimented him on his lately acquired accomplishment of sticking on to a horse. Finally, they had proposed that he should return with them to Mexico for a couple of months to try how he liked their style of life. Hector was wildly anxious to go ; his answer was to be given next day. But here Charlie was as adamant. Nothing would make him approve of this scheme. The horse traders from Mexico were, as he expressed it, "too tough altogether" for a lad like Hector to go with—he must stay where he was.

This verdict put Hector into something perilously like a bad temper. He would scarcely speak all the evening, and finally marched off to bed in silence.

"The lad's disappointed," Charlie said, with a smile.

"Och, Charlie, he's but young, for all he's so tall and strong," said the Widow indulgently; "I'm thinking you were liking your own way yourself once."

"To be sure I was, mother, and Hector's a fine lad; I'd have given him his way if I could," said Charlie. Then he forgot all about the boy, and returned to his eternal talk of home.

The next morning, however, Hector did not appear at breakfast.

"He will be sleeping, I'm thinking," said the Widow, always anxious to defend her grandson.

Charlie's wife rose impatiently, and went to rouse the boy, grumbling as she went. But in a minute she returned, holding a bit of paper in her hand.

"Here's for you, grannie," she said, thrusting the paper at the Widow.

"I cannot be seeing it, Charlie," she said; and Charlie took it from her and read out:

"I have gone off to Mexico, because I wish to see more of the world. I will be coming back in two months' time. Do not be anxious for me, mother; I will be getting on all right.

"Your dutiful grandson,
"HECTOR."

Charlie over the Water

" Dutiful grandson, indeed ! " Mrs. Charlie cried, and even Charlie was roused to indignation by this defiance of his authority. Only the Widow tried to soften down Hector's transgression, and pled with her son to remember the boy's youth and spirit.

But Charlie in stern haste set off there and then in the mule cart in pursuit of Hector ; only to find on inquiry at Cypress Creek that the horse traders had made a mysterious departure in the small hours of the morning.

It was impossible to catch them up. Hector must be left to look after himself.

.   .   .   .   .   .

August and September went slowly past, October began, and still Hector did not return. He sent a letter once to the Widow, telling that he was well and happy ; that was all. Many an anxious thought she had for him during these weary months, you may be sure.

But at last one morning Hector walked into the house, without a word of warning, as coolly as possible, and quite as if he expected to be made welcome there.

His aunt, however, greeted him but coldly.

" It's you, is it, Hector ? You might have sent word that you were coming ; but you weren't over-civil when you left, so perhaps we couldn't look for it now," she said.

" Where's mother ? " Hector asked, ignoring her words.

Mrs. Charlie put down the dish she was drying on

to the table before she replied : " She's in bed : I don't know what's the matter with her, I'm sure."

Hector strode across the kitchen and ran up the little wooden stair that led to his grandmother's room. Opening the door, he stood for a moment on the threshold and looked in.

The Widow was propped up in bed and lay with her eyes shut. There was an expression of humble weariness on her old face that was infinitely touching. " I am so tired," it seemed to say ; " but I must just wait ; there is nothing I can do."

Everything round her was clean and comfortable —far more comfortable than the old box-bed at home—but still . . .

Hector stepped across the floor softly, thinking she was asleep. In a moment her eyes opened at the sound of his footstep.

" It'll be yourself, Charlie ? " she asked, for her eyes were getting dimmer than ever.

" No, mother, it's Hector," he answered.

She gave her old cry of delight : " Och, Hector, and you're back safe and sound ! Wherever have you been all this long time, my laddie ? "

" Just seeing the world," said Hector. " And what's the matter with you, mother ? Is it sick you are ? "

" I'm not knowing ; I'm thinking it's the end coming," she said.

Hector had a sudden flash of intuition at that moment and a stab of conscience. He sat down on the edge of the bed and took her wrinkled hand in his, that was so young and strong.

" Tell me, mother, are you not liking to be here ? " he asked in a whisper. She held on hard to his hand, and the long pent-up misery of all these months found speech at last.

" I'm wanting home, Hector ; I'm wanting home to die—I couldn't be resting in the strange earth here. . . . Och, och, that I ever left Balneish ! " she moaned.

" But then you'd not have been seeing Uncle Charlie again," Hector said, with another stab at the heart. " And would you like to be leaving him now—him that's so good to you, mother ? "

The Widow pulled Hector's face down towards her that she might speak low into his ear.

" It's Charlie's wife that's wanting to be rid of me, Hector ; she'll be saying things to me every day. She will have said it was a mistake that ever we came—*they were never wanting us ;* but, och, dear me ! she'll not be troubled long with me now." The old woman sobbed aloud as she gave this melancholy testimony to the hardness of human nature. Hector sat still, holding the old hand firmly in his. A terrible moment it was to him—the harvesting of the only lie he had ever told.

" I'm to tell you something, mother," he said at last. " It was me made up the message from Uncle Charlie in the letter—he never sent it ; I was wearying of the Island, and couldn't get away."

Then, in a perfect agony of self reproach, poor

Charlie over the Water

Hector knelt down by the side of the bed and prayed the Widow's forgiveness for what he had done. He had never thought it would make her unhappy; he had only thought she would like to see Charlie—and now she was miserable, and it was all his fault ! In a moment a thousand fond excuses had leapt to her tongue. Forgive him ? She would never be thinking about it again ! But Hector would listen to none of all this. One road lay before him, and only one ; it would be a bitter road, but he determined there and then to tread it.

"I'm to take you home, mother," he said.

She caught at his hand and peered into his face, trying to read there whether this blessed suggestion could be true.

"You'll be joking, Hector," she said sadly. But Hector shook his head.

"I'm to take you home whenever you rise from the bed," he said doggedly.

"Eh ! and what will Charlie be saying ? she asked. "I'll never be telling him about the wife."

They were indeed on the horns of a dilemma— how to make Charlie, the best of sons, understand why his mother wished to leave him in her age and frailty.

"I'm thinking you should tell him this, mother," Hector said at last, "that you're wanting to die at home." A moment later he added reflectively, "It's him that'll understand that."

.   .   .   .

You would have thought that nothing could have

Charlie over the Water

put strength enough into the Widow's poor old
limbs to rise from her sick-bed and to start off once
again on the "terrible long road" for home. Yet
with the hope of home came the strength to try to
reach it.

In vain Charlie protested against the proposed
journey, using every argument he knew to make his
mother stay with him. She would only make one
reply : " I'm wanting home, Charlie ; I cannot be
staying, I wouldn't be resting in the strange earth."
It seemed natural enough to Charlie, after all—too
well he understood her feeling, though he tried to
argue it down. A little desolate graveyard stood
on a bit of rising ground half way to Cypress Creek.
Wooden crosses marked the graves in this stoneless
land for a few years ; then they fell to pieces and
were never replaced. Many a time had Charlie
shuddered as he passed the place, fearing some day
to be laid in that alien earth, under the blinding
sun, in a forgotten grave. The Celtic strain of
ineradicable superstition was strong within him ;
like his mother, he feared he could not rest there—
that his uneasy ghost would somehow have to re-
cross the ocean to " walk " for ever round the dear
home of his childhood. " I won't be hindering you,
mother," he said at last. " Maybe you're right."

Charlie's wife was palpably delighted to be getting
rid of her mother-in-law, though in her husband's
presence she begged her to make a longer stay.
But the Widow was all impatience to be off. She
seemed filled with a feverish strength, and declared

Charlie over the Water

herself quite ready to start whenever Hector was willing to do so.

It was with a heavy heart that the poor lad saw that there was no escape from the path of renunciation, and realised what it meant for him.

In a fortnight's time, or thereabouts, he would be back again on the Island, with only the croft to work, the cow to herd, and with the long idle winter opening out before him with its dismaying vista of emptiness. All one night Hector lay awake in an agony of despair. At one moment he thought of begging Charlie to take his mother home, and let him stay to work the place in his absence. But he quickly realised that a travelling companion was not all that the Widow needed; she could never be left alone in her old age with no one to work the croft or look after her, and Charlie could not stay with her always. Then another possible loophole of escape suggested itself: would there be enough of money to take them home again? The fifty pounds had dwindled down amazingly. But this hope was quickly extinguished.

"I'll be paying for anything extra, Hector," Charlie said. "And, mind, you must take her home comfortably—she's not fit for much now."

Hector was ashamed to feel his own disappointment at these words. Every day that their departure was put off the Widow became more impatient; she was like a child clamouring for something.

"When will you be for starting, Hector?" she

would say each morning ; and always there would
be some unthought-of preparation to be made. . . .

Charlie, of course, proposed to write to the mythical Mrs. MacDonald who had so unaccountably
failed to meet them on their arrival in New York ;
but Hector, with a bright blush that was inexplic-
able to his relation, said they would prefer to be
met there this time by Mrs. Koster : he would write
himself about it, he added.

This caused a week's delay ; then a note, written
on pink paper, arrived to Hector one morning. It
seemed to please him mightily, though he only said
in an off-hand manner that Mrs. Koster would be
kind enough to put them up for a few nights before
they sailed.

This matter being arranged, there remained no
other pretext for delay, so the 17th October was
settled for the homeward start. On the last evening Hector left the Widow sitting with Charlie, and
went out alone into the warm autumn night. He
sauntered along the fields to the edge of the clearing
and sat on the fence to rest. The frogs were chanting in the swamps with their curious solemn note,
and away across the clearing in one of the negro
cabins someone thrummed on a little stringed in-
strument. Then the soft negro voices began to
sing in chorus. Hector knew by this time the
pensive old words that they were singing ; but to-
night they seemed to bear another meaning to him :

> " Swing low, swing low, sweet char-i-ot,
> Comin' for to carry me home."

Charlie over the Water

He rose impatiently and walked away; but the plaintive chorus of the hymn carried far in the quiet night—he could not escape from it. The negroes were singing it over and over again:

"Comin' for to carry me home."

.   .   .   .   .   .

Charlie came as far as Memphis with them, and there bade them good-bye. He tried hard not to let it be a sad farewell, because, said he, perhaps he might be coming across the water himself next year. What would his mother say to that?

They kept holding on to this hope all the way to Memphis, speaking of it as almost a settled thing, even planning how the Widow was to drive down to Balneish in the Matheson's cart to meet him on that blessed day when he should return to the Island. But when the moment for parting came, Hope dwindled down into a mere phantom; and Separation and Distance, Age and Death, took on shapes of horrible actuality. Would he and his mother ever really meet again face to face? It seemed unlikely; she so old, he so bound to his new home by a hundred ties.

When the bitter moment had come and gone—when she had looked her last at Charlie and given him her blessing—the Widow, to Hector's surprise, seemed wonderfully sustained by something. He discovered a few minutes later what it was. "Charlie will never have heard from me, Hector, that the

Charlie over the Water

wife did not make me welcome," she said proudly, as she wiped her eyes.

. . . .

As you may have seen, a tired horse suddenly mends its pace when turned in the direction of home, so the Widow scarcely noted now the leagues of land and sea that had still to be gone over; she knew that every hour was bringing her nearer home ?

She fared better on this journey than on her first, for had not Charlie insisted that she should travel in a sleeping-car like any lady ? So the long night was passed in slumber, and the next day, though wearisome, was comfortable; and then, lo, they were in New York again, being greeted by Mrs. Koster and Cassie ! It was Hector, however, who managed everything this time ; or rather, an altogether different Hector from the one who had arrived in New York six months before. The change did not escape Mrs. Koster's eye.

"My ! ain't he smartened up ? " she said admiringly. "Well, I'll say this for the States, if there's one thing they *can* do it's to make men look alive."

Cassie, too, was watching her Highland Nobleman with admiration ; she noted his added inches, as well as his added alertness of speech and manner, and his look of being able to take care of himself. But, with all this, Hector could not be said to be looking happy ; he was very silent, and scarcely brightened up even under the sunshine of Cassie's smiles.

Charlie over the Water

" I know what it is," Mrs. Koster told her husband, when their guests were disposed of for the night ; " I know what it is—he don't want to go home, poor lad, that's what it is ; and no wonder either—just stepping into his grave before the time, I call it."

Koster agreed with her most heartily : " A real smart man we'd make of him here ; pity he can't stay this side."

But Hector, with the dignity and reserve which characterises the Highland nature, asked no pity from anyone. Whenever the Kosters tried to find out what he felt about going home he shut up like a trap.

" I'm hoping to come back some day," was all they got him to admit. Neither would he delay their sailing any longer than could possibly be helped.

" Mother's wishing to get home," he said. " It's not for me to put it off."

In vain Cassie tried her most seductive wiles ; Hector would not be beguiled. Only on the night before they were to sail for Scotland he found an opportunity to beg Cassie to write to him.

" The winter's terrible long on the Island," burst from his reluctant lips, " terrible long and dull."

" Oh, I'll send you a picture post-card now and again," Cassie said gaily ; " and if you could just kindly send me the same, it would be nice—I'd add them to my collection."

" I'll remember," Hector assured her.

.   .   .   .

Charlie over the Water

The sea was like a mill-pond all the way across. Even the Widow could not feel uncomfortable, and used to walk daily up and down the decks on her grandson's arm, while every day her face looked happier and her step grew stronger. Her talk was all of home.

" Och, Hector! how will we be finding the cow? I'm thinking she'll be glad to be back to the old byre! And will the hens be knowing me again? I wonder is Chuckie, that had the broken leg, still going? She was a fine bird "—and so on and so on. Hector then told her that by Mrs. Koster's suggestion he meant to take her to see an eye-doctor in Glasgow. " It's not blind she is, it's only spectacles she's needing," Mrs. Koster had said. The Widow would not believe this; she had tried on John Matheson's spectacles two years past, and didn't they just make the sight worse? Oh no! it was the old eyes were gone these ten years and more. However, it made an excellent subject of conversation, and Hector was glad to have it. He had some difficulty in persuading his grandmother to consent to the extra day's delay it would entail; she was counting the hours now till they could reach the Island—if she could have entered on such a calculation she would have counted the minutes also.

So the ocean was crossed again; the low green shores of Ireland came in sight, and home was nearly reached at last. The Widow wept with joy as the ship came into the dock.

Charlie over the Water

" Is it true, Hector, or is it dreaming I am ? " she cried.

But Uncle Neil's hearty greeting had nothing dream-like about it certainly.

" So y're back already to auld Scotland ! Ye've no made a long stay. Welcome hame to ye baith —there's nae place like hame, the song says ! "

Alas ! Hector could have cursed the song for its falsity to his own case ; but he tried to affect good-humour and to join in the jocularities of his relative —he was not going to be a kill-joy, and above every-thing he refused to be pitied.

All the next day he went about cheerfully, and no one guessed at the fox that was gnawing his vitals.

The Widow, with many protestations, was taken to the eye-doctor in the afternoon. Hector stood beside her as the spectacles were one by one placed upon her nose. Each time she would shake her head and groan, and exclaim that it was blind she was, what was the gentleman troubling with her for ? But all at once she gave a cry of joy and held out her hands to her grandson.

" Och, Hector, I'm seeing you as clear as the day ! " she cried. " And you're grown to be a man altogether ! " It was a wonderful moment indeed, and Hector laughed with pleasure to see her gazing round and round the room in the sudden possession of her sight again. This miracle of healing came as a boon to Hector, for the Widow was so full of her recovered vision all the evening that she could think and talk of nothing else, and her garrulity made his silence less noticed. Next morning they were to start again for the Island, and Hector was as impatient now as his grandmother—on the sound principle that if one has a disagreeable thing to do, the sooner it is done the better.

" Y're a wee thing glum, Hector," Uncle Neil said jocosely. " Ye've maybe left yer hairt in Ameriky."

"Maybe," Hector retorted laconically, with no answering smile.

. . . .

A day and a night—and the next day as evening fell the steamer came in to the quay at Balneish.

They were almost the only passengers, for the tourist season was over. The little quay was empty, except for a cart and a man with it. In the dusk a light or two twinkled in the windows at Balneish. Everything was very still.

" There's John Matheson, mother, with the cart ! " Hector cried ; " he will have come for you and the box."

The Widow gazed through the grand new spectacles at the well-known outlines of the Island, pointing out each house and naming its owner— if the light had not failed she could have named each horse and cow, I believe. Hector sprang down the gangway and held out his hand to help her across it ; a moment more and she stood again on the dear shores of home—shaken with excite-

Charlie over the Water

ment, and worn with the fatigues of her long journeying, but oh, at home once more !

The kindly dusk hid her tears—her foolish tears of joy—as the cart rumbled along the stony road to the croft . . . and John Matheson in the meantime was pouring out microscopic bits of so-called news to Hector—all that had happened at Balneish in the six months since they had left the Island : Rob MacLeod's cow had choked on a turnip in the summer ; and Hamish MacLeod, he was bad with the asthma, but his daughter Jessie, she that's in Glasgow, was after sending him a bottle to take— oh, it was grand stuff, and helped him at times. There had been good crops ; yes, just fairish good of the hay ; there was a boat got washed away from the pier in September, and John Farquharson's horse had gone lame in the right knee. . . . Hector listened and responded to it all, feeling exactly as if he had wakened from a dream of extraordinary vividness. Was it true that they had ever crossed the sea and seen Charlie ? . . . All manner of funny scenes crowded into his memory, and here was Matheson droning away about a horse with a lame leg, and a cow that had choked on a turnip !

The cart stopped : they had reached the path up to the cottage. It was dark now, and Hector had to help the Widow up the rough bit of ground—she stumbled and would have fallen if his arm had not held her up.

" Och, Hector ! it's old and useless I am," she said.

In spite of the fact that the door-key had been all

Charlie over the Water

this time in the Widow's pocket, the Mathesons had effected an entrance to the cottage somehow, and sorted it up for the return of its owners. A big peat fire burned on the hearth, and a table stood spread by the fire. All this they saw through the window, and then, producing the key, they solemnly turned it in the rusty lock and stepped across the threshold. ("God forgive me," Hector thought; "I was never meaning her to come back!")

Surely that moment of home coming compensated the Widow for many a weary hour. She sank down on the old, hard, uncomfortable wooden chair in the chimney corner, and gazed hungrily round and round the little room as if she could never have enough of it.

Hector, with one tremendous effort, pushed away his thoughts of the past and turned his energies to the present.

"I'll not be taking you across the water again, mother, I'm thinking," he said with a laugh, as he lifted the big black kettle on to the fire to boil. He drew the table up beside his grandmother's chair and laid away her shawl for her as gently as a daughter might have done it.

No voice was there to whisper comfort to Hector at that moment : he had never heard of Carlyle or his gospel ; but none the less he arrived in some obscure way at the same conclusion as that stern old philosopher, " *Here or nowhere was his America* " for the present.

Charlie over the Water

Charlie came across the water next year and saw his mother again as he had promised to do, and some two years later the Widow went on another journey, from which she never came back—crossed an uncharted sea and landed on the shores of a New World. Then Hector, wiser grown, sighed as he said farewell to the shieling for ever and turned his face towards the future.

MYSIE HAD A LITTLE LAMB

MYSIE HAD A LITTLE LAMB

MYSIE'S had been a dull day : storm outside, and Mother, with a big baking on hand, a little cross when the child wanted to " turn the scones " on the girdle by way of amusing herself.

Mysie was only six years old and could not reach high enough to see whether the scones were burning or not, so perhaps it was just that she should be refused the job ; but she felt aggrieved none the less. She wandered across to the window, and gazed out through the small panes at the hillside and the brooding grey-white sky above it. A vast frown seemed to have gathered over the face of the world —the grimness of it made her afraid. Snow had fallen early, and then, because it was late in the season, had thawed quickly and now only lay in the hollows to any depth, though a thin coating still spread over the hillside. Every boulder stood out black as ink against the whiteness, and crows were wheeling about in the dark sky—not an enlivening prospect at all. The draughts that blew from the keen outer air into the warm kitchen were as sharp as knives ; but Mysie did not heed them. She pressed her nose against the little window and gazed out—something was moving on the hillside.

Mysie had a Little Lamb

" What's that y're seein', Mysie ? " Mother asked from the fire, turning a scone as she spoke, " Is't yer faither ? "

" Aye, it's Faither an' Jock."

" He'll have had an' awfae coorse day on the hill," said Mother, dusting the flour from the last scone with a bunch of feathers. A delicious smell of burning flour spread through the kitchen and Mysie sniffed with pleasure—tea was not very far off now. Mother swung the girdle off the chain, and put the kettle on so as to be ready when Father arrived, and Mysie jumped down from the chair by the window.

" I'll gang oot," she cried, her little hand stretching up to the snib of the door in vain ; she never could reach it unaided, though she was always making the attempt.

" Bide where ye are, Mysie—you've got the fidgets the day," said Mother quite crossly. " What for would ye gang oot intil the snow, and you wi' sic a dose o' the cold last week ? "

Poor Mysie ! Evidently she must cultivate patience. She settled down at the window again and watched the black specks on the hillside as they came slowly nearer and nearer. Jock, the great black collie who lorded it over hundreds of trembling sheep, came bounding down ahead of his master. The shepherd himself seemed to be walking very carefully.

" Faither's walkin' gey slow," Mysie sighed ; her mother came across to the window and looked up the glen too.

Mysie had a Little Lamb

"Aye, he's no hurryin' himsel'" she admitted after a minute's survey.

At last the latch was lifted, a blast of wind rushed into the kitchen, and the shepherd and Jock made their entrance.

"Eh, man, shut tae the door!" cried Mother. Mysie slipped down from her perch and stood beside her father, plucking at his coat—she just reached up to his knee.

"What's yon?" she piped out. It seemed her predestined trial never to be able to get high enough to see what was going on in the world. Just now she could make out that up there in her father's arms something lay—but what that something was she could not possibly see from where she stood.

"See here, Mysie," her father said, stooping down to her level at last; "here's for ye." The something in his arms looked like a hank of wet wool.

"What is't?" Mysie asked, putting up her hand to touch it.

"Come awa an' see, then," said Father.

He knelt down by the fire and laid the bundle ever so carefully on the warm hearth-stone.

Mysie drew near, her eyes large with interest:

"It's a wee lambie!" she cried at last, as the shepherd spread out its four tiny black legs towards the blaze. The hank of wool began to take on form; she could distinguish a little black face now among the drenched fleece.

Mother drew near too: "Is't no' deid, Tam?" she asked.

Mysie had a Little Lamb

" She's gey far through onyway : get a drop warm milk, Maggie," he directed.

Mother bustled about to get the milk, and Father strode out of the kitchen, crossed to the barn, and returned carrying a bunch of wheat-straws.

Mysie crouched down on the floor to watch what was going to happen. Her father had lifted the lamb again and was feeling round its tiny black muzzle—so tightly shut . . . how big his hands looked, thought Mysie ; how wee and dead the lambie ! Its little mouth was shut, as if with an iron clamp, and Father didn't seem able to get it open. . . .

" Hoots, Tam, gie her tae me," Mother said at last. She sat down on the old chair beside the fire and directed him to lay the lamb on her knees. To all appearance life was gone ; the pitiful little black head fell down on one side helplessly.

But Mother, whose hands were not so big and clumsy, began to force the lamb's mouth open, till Mysie cried out in delight :

" It's got a wee bittie o' a tongue, Mither ! "

Mother was far too absorbed in her task to answer. She took a mouthful of the warm milk, and holding the lamb's mouth open, put one of the wheat straws in at the side of it. Then very slowly she directed a trickle of milk down through the straw. Drop by drop the milk went down, but still there was no sign of life. " I maun jist sit here a wee," said Mother, " an' see if she'll come roond." After twenty minutes or so, another spoonful of milk was conveyed into the lamb's mouth. Father had

Mysie had a Little Lamb

lighted his pipe and sat down on the other side of the hearth; Mysie on her three-legged stool kept close to Mother and the lambie, and Jock had squatted on the other side, his bright eyes fixed unwaveringly on the thing he had helped to rescue.

It was a half-hour of breathless interest.

"Mysie," Mother whispered, as if a sleeping child was on her knee, "gang you tae the drawer and find a bit rag for me, like a good lassie."

Mysie could reach up to the drawer, so she proudly did her mother's bidding; but she wondered what the rag was wanted for.

"Pit it in the milk," Mother directed, "an' syne gie it tae me."

Mysie handed her the rag dripping with milk, and saw the end of it laid upon the lamb's tongue. Father took his pipe out of his mouth and leant forward to watch, Jock jumped to his feet and wagged his tail—what was happening, Mysie wondered?

"She's sookin' noo!" Mother exclaimed in a voice of triumph, and Jock gave a yelp of excitement, understanding perfectly all about it. Languidly, as if reluctant to take up this painful business of living, the lamb sucked at her rag. Slowly, drop by drop, the milk went down, and a tremor of vitality began to pulse in the hank of wool.

"She'll dae fine," said the shepherd. "Gie's oor tea, Maggie—I'd clean forgot a' aboot it."

Mother gave a laugh of relief and deposited the lamb on the hearth again, while Jock waved his plume-like tail joyously as if to say "How clever we are!" Mysie gave a croodle of satisfaction.

Mysie had a Little Lamb

" I want the lambie for mysel'," she demanded, plucking at her father's coat.

" Weel, maybe—see here then, Mysie, tak' the stool an' sit near hand an' watch her : see the sticks dinna drop oot on her—tak' the wee tongs in yer hand an' sit quiet like a fine lassie."

What a delightful task that was ! Perched on her three-legged stool, armed with the old twisted iron tongs, Mysie sat there as immovable as a little Buddha, watching her lamb. When a stick fell out upon the hearth, she made a grab at it and replaced it on the fire, her eyes fixed jealously on the lamb, lest any spark should fall upon its fleece.

" Come awa' til yer tea," Mother cried at last, but Mysie protested :

" I dinna want my tea : I'm mindin' my lambie."

" Hoots, Jock'll mind the lambie ; come awa'," said Father, who had much more confidence in Jock's guardianship than in Mysie's.

At the sound of his name, Jock, now asleep after his labours, raised his head and looked at the shepherd, waiting for orders.

" Watch her," said Father, and Jock walked across to the hearth with the grave, responsible air of a human being, to see that all went well with the lamb.

Thus released from her charge, Mysie came gladly enough to the tea-table. She was a great pet of her father's, and would often sit on his knee at meals, to be stuffed with scones and jam, or porridge

Mysie had a Little Lamb

and treacle (when the cream was scarce), to an alarming extent.

This evening she heard all about where her lamb had been found. How Jock had discovered a dead sheep in a snowdrift, and how they had thought that the lamb was dead also.

" I didna think there was ony life in her," Father said, laughing ; " but Jock there, he wadna leave her ; he aye yappit at me an' gave a bit pat tae the lambie, an' syne he'd look up an' yap again.—Dod ! he's an' awfae wise beast is Jock ! "

" He's that," Mother agreed.

Then just as Mysie was fishing up the last delicious sticky mouthful of sugar from the bottom of her teacup, a faint, thrilling cry went up from the hearth.

" *Ma-a-ah*," and again, " *Ma-a-aha*."—It was a bleat of desolation that no pen can describe : all the helpless, orphaned woe of the universe seemed to be in the sound.

Jock gave a yelp of excitement. Mysie slipped off her father's knee and flew to the fireside, and the lamb lifted its feeble little black face and gazed up at the child and the dog.

" She's greetin' ! " Mysie cried—" Mither, she's greetin' ! " She thought something was wrong with her lamb that it could utter such a plaint.

" Hoots, Mysie, she's no greetin' ava, she's fine noo ; wait a wee, an' she'll be on her legs."

This prophecy was very quickly fulfilled, for in about half an hour the little creature struggled up on to its shaking legs, gave a ridiculous wriggle to

Mysie had a Little Lamb

its tail, and then took a tipsy gambol across the floor.

" See yon," said the shepherd. " Ye'll hae yer wurk wi' her, Maggie, noo she's come-to sae weel ; ye maun get a bottle for her."

" I've Mysie's bottle ben the hoose," said Mother —it was not so very long ago that Mysie had been quite as helpless as the lamb.

" I'm thinkin' she'll be waur tae manage than ever Mysie was," said Father, with a grin.

Now that the lamb had come alive and found a voice, it was difficult to keep Mysie away from this new toy. Her solitary childhood had known no such pleasure. She would have liked to be allowed to administer the first " bottle," but Mother insisted on doing this herself ; so Mysie had to be content with keeping close to her new-found delight, stroking its tightly curled fleece and small black face, and gazing into its glassy eyes.

But after a few days Mother would fill the bottle and allow Mysie to feed the lamb. This was an exquisite delight to the child, and an ever-recurring employment : to see the lamb suck up a bottle of milk made Mysie scream with pleasure, and the little creature became so attached to the hand that fed it that Mysie and her lamb were seldom apart.

In a fortnight's time " Buckie," as Mysie chose to call her pet, was as strong as possible, and began to gambol about the kitchen to such an extent that Mother opened the door and drove the child and the lamb out on to the hillside to play.

Mysie had a Little Lamb

The late snow had disappeared; there was a sense of approaching spring everywhere. Under the dry grey stalks of the heather that had been fired the year before, delicate blades of brilliant green grass sprang up, and the bare twigs of the birch trees in the glen were purple. Moreover, something wonderful had happened—an event that is welcomed by many a country child : the frogs had come. The old peat cutting at the back of the cottage was suddenly all a-hum with them ; they seemed to have arrived in one night, out of nowhere, Mysie thought. It was quite a puzzle to her.

" Whaur dae the puddocks come frae ? " she asked. " Dae they come loupin' ower the hill when I'm in my bed ? "

" Aye, Mysie, they maun loup frae somewhere," Father said, laughing.

Mysie had funny dreams of the frog army arriving across the hill that night, and in the morning she resolved that she and Buckie would go down to the peat cutting and visit them. She said nothing about this to Mother, though, for she had often been told not to go near the bog. Of course, it was for that very reason the most coveted spot in the glen. The peat was rich and black, and beautiful patches of bright red moss grew upon it, while, looking down into the pools between the moss-islands, one saw all manner of funny live things. Mysie had no name for them, but they interested her intensely, and often when Mother's back was turned she would run down to the bog

Mysie had a Little Lamb

and lie on her face to peer down into the mysterious pools where so much was going on . . . it was a joy, too, to poke in the peat with a stick. This morning Mysie watched a favourable moment when Mother was busy making broth, and called Buckie to follow her. The little couple ran out at the door together, and Mother, peeling turnips, called after Mysie : " Dinna gang far frae the door, bairn."

" Na," Mysie called back, aware that she was strictly within the truth in saying so, for the peat bog was delightfully near. She frolicked about before the door with Buckie for a few minutes— just to make Mother think that all was right—and then set off as fast as she could run towards the bog, Buckie gambolling after her. As they came near it, a fascinating sound like very distant singing de- lighted Mysie's ears ; on the edge of the cutting she stood still to view the life of the frogs. Hundreds and hundreds of them were there, with their sprawl- ing legs, wide mouths, and goggle eyes. Looking very closely, she could see their throats pulse as the humming noise came from them. The bog pools were covered with great masses of frog's eggs floating there like lumps of jelly. Was there ever a more interesting sight ?

Mysie squatted down on the edge of the cutting with her arm flung round Buckie's neck, and gazed at the frogs. Buckie, who naturally did not find any interest in the sight, became restive and wanted to run about ; but Mysie would not give in to the

Mysie had a Little Lamb

lamb's wishes on this point—frogs were not to be seen every day !

One big, wide-mouthed croaker had landed on an old tree-stump in the middle of the bog, and sat there like a king. Mysie thought how delightful it would be to get a long stick and poke him till he jumped off his little island with a splash. This was not very difficult to manage. She ran off to the thin birch wood that grew near the house, and tugged at a stick twice as long as herself which lay among a pile of brushwood. It seemed as if it would never come out, but when it did it proved wonderfully long, and Mysie trailed it behind her, back to the peat cutting, Buckie of course gambolling at her heels.

The frog still sat on his island, goggling and croaking. Mysie sat down again to observe him, and then cautiously, with immense difficulty, stretched out her long stick towards the frog king. " Alas, alas ! the stick was too heavy and she had stretched too far ! Mysie gave an ear-splitting scream, clutched at Buckie, and down they both went together into the black abyss of the peat bog. There were not more than six inches of water in it, but to the child it seemed as deep as the sea. Oh how she screamed in her agony of terror, down there in these slimy depths among the frogs !

Buckie was floundering beside her, and gave forth a melancholy bleat. Was there ever such a helpless little pair ?

The next moment help came. For at the sound

Mysie had a Little Lamb

of Mysie's scream, Jock came across the hillside like an arrow from the bow. He had been at the sheep fank with his master, and recognised the note of terror in Mysie's cry. With a bound he came into the mud beside her, took a large mouthful of her frock, and dragged the child up on to the dry ground. Then down again he went once more, and this time rescued Buckie. Spattered with mud, panting, he stood beside these two ridiculous mites so unable to take care of themselves. Only speech was wanting to express his contempt for their folly. . . . . Once safely on the dry ground again, Mysie set off as fast as her short legs would carry her towards the cottage, howling as she went. She arrived there a tear-stained little image, woeful to behold. Jock in the meantime was driving Buckie home by means of soft barks and an occasional gentle nip ; he had compassion upon the silly thing, not yet come even to the idiotic maturity of a sheep.

"Gosh me !" Mother cried, and again, "Gosh me ! sic a pair o' ye ! "

Mysie would have come in for chastisement in all probability, if Father had not appeared very opportunely for his dinner. His roars of laughter at sight of Mysie and Buckie at first made Mother cross, but finally made her laugh too.

"You sort Mysie," said Father, "an' I'll try ma' hand wi' Buckie."

That indeed was a cleaning up. Mother got a tub into the kitchen, and Mysie, divested of her peaty garments, was scrubbed in the hot, soapy

Mysie had a Little Lamb

water. Her very hair was filled with " glaur," as
Mother expressed it, and her little feet were as
brown as if they had been dipped in walnut juice.

" There, noo, ye'll gang til yer bed a' the day ;
that'll maybe teach ye tae keep awa' frae the bog,"
Mother said, polishing up Mysie's face till it shone.
Signs of renewed weeping appeared at this sentence,
so it was commuted by Father's pleading :

" The bairn's been feared, Maggie—pit her intil
the box-bed there ; she's better by you." So into
the box-bed Mysie went, instead of being consigned
to the little room off the kitchen where she generally
slept, and in its fusty depths she cuddled down
gladly enough after her cold adventure.

The washing of Buckie was then begun, and that
was a terrible business. Pail after pail of water
was soused over the lamb before her curly wool
became even tolerably clean. Then she was tied
to a big chair near the fire to dry, the kitchen floor
was wiped up, and the unfortunate incident (in
newspaper language) was closed.

. . . .

This unpleasant adventure seemed only to
strengthen the bonds of love between Mysie and
her lamb. They were never apart now—" wherever
Mysie went the lamb was sure to go " in fact. When
some three months had passed, Buckie's fleece had
grown long and white, and budding horns appeared
on her head. Then alas ! it is sad to relate, greed
became the master passion of the lamb. She was
so impatient to get at her bottles of rich new milk,

that she would knock Mysie over in her haste, so Mother had to administer them.

There was not much gentleness noticeable in the creature then : she sucked at the bottle with such eagerness that her eyes stuck out with the effort, and the milk frothed round her greedy black mouth. By-and-by the number of bottles was diminished, and Buckie found that she must look elsewhere for some of her nourishment. She began to crop delicately at the greenest grass that was to be found, rejecting all but the most tender blades and munching these with the air of an epicure. Mysie took pleasure in discovering exquisite green patches among the heather, and would lead Buckie to them that she might enjoy the tender fare. Then Mysie would make wreaths of heather and ferns and hang them round Buckie's neck, and twine them round the budding horns, and lead her home crowned like some sacrificial animal decked for the altar. At first Buckie did not resent these adornments, but as time went on they began to tease her, and she gave an impatient toss of her little horned head, as much as to say, " Leave me alone : I want to eat." Mysie did not mind the playful toss in the least ; it was all part of the endless game that she and Buckie had played the whole summer through.

The autumn was coming on again, however, and it was too cold for Mysie to sit out on the hillside any longer, so there was nothing for it but that Buckie should be admitted as an inmate of the kitchen again. The creature was certainly a good

Mysie had a Little Lamb

deal in the way, for she had grown enormously, and had not the best manners imaginable. But, as Mother well knew, it would be a distinct gain to keep Buckie and feed her for another winter, for the shepherd's wife who rears a lamb by hand always gets the fleece as a perquisite. So Buckie was going to be well looked after; it would not do to let her merge into the herd upon the hill.

At first Mysie was delighted with this arrangement; but ever so slowly a disillusionment set in. Buckie might almost have known the value that was put upon her, for she began to presume upon it, to assert herself, and to establish rights. On cold autumn days she now took up a position right in front of the fire, where Mysie used to sit; and the child had to content herself with the chimney corner instead. After this Buckie discovered that Mysie always got a " piece " in the morning; and it became her object to filch the bit of bread and butter from the child and eat it up. Nor was this all: the creature developed an extraordinary slyness and knew perfectly well that it would not do to steal Mysie's " piece " when anyone was there to see.

One day there was, in consequence, a sad scene. Mother had spread a great big delicious scone with treacle, and given it to Mysie to eat while she went down to the burn for water.

Mysie was sitting on her three-legged stool in the chimney corner; Buckie, to all appearances unheeding of anything that was going on, lay as

Mysie had a Little Lamb

usual before the fire. But no sooner had the door closed behind Mother, than Mysie heard the tap, tap of Buckie's hoofs on the floor, and the next minute the scone was twitched out of her hand. Mysie decided to fight for her treasure and gave Buckie a vigorous shove; but a savage thrust from the now quite formidable horns made her retreat discomfited to the door. There she watched the disappearance of the scone.

"Buckie grabbit my scone and treacle!" the child cried, as her mother came in, "an' she butted at me!"

"Haud yer tongue, Mysie, and dinna tell lees," said Mother. "Y're ower fond o' scones and treacle; y're wantin' anither, but ye'll no get it."

Certainly appearances were against the child and for the lamb: Mysie's mouth was well smeared with treacle, whereas Buckie lay on the same spot of floor she had occupied when Mother left the house; she wore an air of lamb-like innocence, and there were no smears of treacle round her mouth. Of course no refuge but tears was possible for Mysie; she was all beslobbered with them when the shepherd came in half an hour later.

"What ails the bairn?" he asked his wife.

"She tell't me a lee, Tam; dinna speak tae her," Mother answered. Buckie by the fire paid no heed to what was going on, and the shepherd (a great disciplinarian in his way) gave Mysie a grave look.

"Ye ken whaur bairns that tell lees gang, Mysie," he said darkly.

Mysie had a Little Lamb

" Can lambies gang til the bad place ? " sobbed the child, stung by the injustice that was being done her. But Father did not understand this remark in the least ; he only thought it profane.

" Haud yer tongue, Mysie : dinna be sayin' sic things," he said.

After this incident a distinct coldness grew up between the former playmates. Taught by sad experience, Mysie always ran out and drew the door shut after her when she got her " piece." The shepherd told his little daughter that she was not as fond of Buckie as she used to be.

" Na ; she's ower big," was the cautious reply, " an' she's no' the same."

Mother would sometimes pass her fingers through Buckie's splendid fleece in admiration, calling her husband's attention to it. " She's an awfae fine fleece on her," she would say ; " I'll get a frock for Mysie yet off her."

During the winter months Buckie learnt a new accomplishment. She chose now to join the family at tea and get a drink out of a cup like any Christian. The shepherd one day in joke substituted tea for the usual milk ; but after a preliminary sputter and sneeze, Buckie quaffed off the tea with infinite relish. After this her craving for tea became inordinate, and every day she ran to the table, bleating, and would give them no peace till she had had her longed-for stimulant. It was the funniest sight to see her stand on her hind legs, placing her two front ones on the table, and utter " *Bah-Bah-*

Mysie had a Little Lamb

Bah" as she gazed at the teacups. The shepherd roared with laughter and encouraged the new game. One evening, to tease her, he hid an oatcake in his pocket, and Buckie began searching for the food as a dog might have done. At last she managed to poke her nose into the shepherd's pocket, but instead of the oatcake she drew out a long bit of twist tobacco. There was a yell of derision, as Buckie turned away with the bit of tobacco hanging from her mouth.

" Whisht ; wait or we see what she'll dae wi' it," said the shepherd.

Buckie stood irresolute for a moment, not sure how to attack this new foodstuff, then gave it a vigorous chew, finally swallowed down the whole twist.

" Dod ! was there ever sic' a sheep ! " they all cried.

Very quickly this new passion for tobacco grew as marked in Buckie as the passion for tea. Men that came to the house would tease the creature, holding out bits of twist to her, and then hiding them in their pockets till she searched them out. Mysie would join in the laughter that followed when Buckie successfully found and ate the tobacco ; but though she laughed at Buckie she never caressed her now.

" It's near aboot Buckie's birthday," the shepherd told the child as spring came round again. " D'ye mind the wee bit bundle she was yon day, Mysie ? "

It was certainly difficult to believe that Buckie

Mysie had a Little Lamb

was really the same creature as the pitiful bundle of wool that had lain on the hearth one short year before. What with all the rich milk she drank and the quantity of mixed feeding of one sort or another that she had assimilated, Buckie had grown to a portentous size in her one year of life. Her wool was thick and white, untorn by bramble or heather —the hardy outdoor sheep on the hill, with their ragged grey fleeces, scarcely seemed to be of the same breed as the fatted house-sheltered creature. But by the inexorable justness of things, gentle timid hearts beat under their tattered fleeces, while Buckie's easy life seemed to be developing almost human vices in her nature. Mysie, who would have walked alone and unafraid among hundreds of the hill sheep, did not now like to be alone with Buckie in the kitchen for five minutes !

It fell on a day when the spring was well advanced, and all the world green again, that an urgent message came for Mother to go down the glen to a cottage where some one lay ill. Mother was sewing by the window ; she glanced at the clock : " It's near four," she said ; " Tam'll be in the noo—I'll can leave Mysie a wee."

" I'll come wi' ye," Mysie whimpered, plucking at Mother's apron.

" Ye canna, Mysie ; ye'd be in the road. Ye'll bide oot by an' play at a shoppie till Faither comes in—will ye no', dearie ? "

This was such a tempting proposal, that Mysie fell in with it at once. A small burn ran beside

Mysie had a Little Lamb

the door, where any child might play in safety ; and here Mysie had an old box set up to act as a shop, and white and grey pebbles from the brook did duty for various articles of commerce. She would often spend hours there, perfectly content, without anyone near her—why not now, then, when it was so necessary? It seemed an obvious arrangement.

" Ye'll hae yer tea when Faither comes doon off the hill," Mother said, " an' ye'll bide here like a good lassie for half an 'oor."

All was well with Mysie for quite an hour after Mother left her. The play was delightfully realistic, for she had been provided with " a puckle tea," a handful of sugar, and half a dozen currants. The child never even looked up to see the last of Mother, so happily contented she was with her mimic stage. Why can we not carry with us into later life the glowing imagination that inspired our childish games ? How poor we are now, when our gold must really be gold, in comparison with that exhaustless wealth of childhood which turned every withered leaf into a nugget !

A whole procession of interesting characters visited the shop asking for all manner of things. The King and Queen came first, in a coach and four, wearing of course crowns of solid gold, and trailing robes of velvet : curiously enough (though it did not strike Mysie as being at all out of the picture) they came to buy tea and sugar, and there had to be a great fussing and doing up of bits of paper into bags, before their Majesties drove away with their homely purchase.

" It'll be the best y're wantin', yer Majesty, the kind Mother tak's at 1s. 2d. ? " Mysie asked innocently, and the Queen replied with the same artlessness. " Aye ; yon'll be the kind."

There was, of course, a slight difficulty in making both questions and answers oneself, because one knew what the answer was going to be ; but what is imagination good for if it cannot surmount such a tiny obstacle as this ?—" barriers are for those that cannot fly."

After the King and Queen came the Minister and his wife, then the farmer's wife down the glen, finally some tinkers begging, who were relentlessly shown the door.

Then Mysie looked up suddenly ; the sun was no longer high ; a chill breeze was blowing ; the game had come to an end ; the shop wasn't a shop any longer, only an old box covered with stones, and worst of all the King and Queen, the Minister and his wife, the farmer's wife and the tinkers had all disappeared, and Mysie was horribly alone !

" I want m' tea," she cried, and ran up to the house to find Father—but when she got there, there was no sign of him. All round about the child the stillness seemed to become of a sudden terrible, oppressive—a thing to be escaped from at any cost. She rushed into the kitchen. The clock was ticking with its usual tranquil sound, the fire had burned low, and before it stood Buckie. She pattered across the floor to Mysie at once, and the child, though shrinking a little from the creature, would have welcomed almost any companion in that hour of loneliness.

" I'm awfae hungert, Buckie," she said, glad to hear her own voice.

" *Bah-Bah*," Buckie answered, quite intelligently —they were evidently of one mind.

Mysie went across to the dresser and opened the door, to see if any scones were to be found. She knelt down on the floor, and reached into the darkness of the cupboard. But just as she was feeling about there for the scones, Buckie shouldered up against the child and began to investigate matters for herself. In a minute she had her big, horned head right inside the press. Crash went a pile of plates, one on the top of the other : Buckie did not mind in the least, but went on rummaging to right and left in search of food. Down came an open jar of treacle and fell out upon the floor, spreading in a lazy black stream across the well-scrubbed boards. Crash went another heap of plates, over went the sugar basin, and the sugar mixed with the treacle. This stayed Buckie's career of destruction for a time ; she was very fond of sweet things, and fed greedily on the sticky mass till it had all disappeared.

Mysie in the meantime, filled with dismay, made an effort to get the cupboard door fastened, but Buckie would not be interfered with—she lowered her horns threateningly at the child and returned to search into the cupboard again. A pile of oat-

Mysie had a Little Lamb

cakes was the next find. Buckie, bewildered by this profusion of good things, tried to eat half a dozen of the cakes at once : nibbling the corner off one, she would toss it aside in favour of another which looked nicer, then it would be discarded and a third one chosen—so it went on till all the cakes lay broken and trampled on the floor.

Mysie began to cry bitterly now, powerless to stop this destruction. She was very hungry, poor child, to add to her troubles, and in her humility she took up one of the cakes that Buckie had rejected and began to eat it.

In a moment Buckie had twitched it away : Mysie was not even to be allowed to eat the refuse.

" I'm hungry, Buckie," the child sobbed, appealing as if to a human tyrant ; Buckie only stamped and butted in reply.

Mysie had now reached an extremity of hunger and fear. She looked round for help. If only she could get up on the top of the dresser, then Buckie couldn't reach her !

Waiting till she saw Buckie, head down, gorging on a pat of butter, Mysie seized a scone from the floor, drew a chair to the side of the dresser, and climbed up in triumph to a blessed haven of safety.

Buckie looked up, but could not reach her— Mysie drew a breath of relief and munched her scone. It was not very pleasant to stand there perched on the narrow dresser top ; yet our poor little St. Simon Stylites could do nothing else. She sustained a prolonged siege, for Buckie, very

Mysie had a Little Lamb

vindictive, came and stood below her and gave a savage butt at the dresser. It shook under the blow and a couple of plates crashed down from the rack above Mysie's head and fell to the floor. But the dresser was old and firm, so this was all that Buckie's evil temper could accomplish. Secure that she was out of reach of her enemy, Mysie stood there and contemplated the wreck of worlds below her.

Scones and cakes that were to have fed the household for a week now lay scattered over the floor, stamped on and wasted. Buckie had walked backwards and forwards through the pool of treacle, and sticky black imprints of her hoofs were everywhere to be seen. She had begun to eat a pound of butter where it fell, but at each lick it had been pushed farther along the floor, and by evil chance had landed in front of the fire, there to melt away into a large pool of grease. The broken dishes had been tossed hither and thither by Buckie's impatient horns . . . a woeful scene indeed! Mysie in her loneliness and dismay had begun to cry again, when she heard the sound of Jock's well-known bark. The next moment he bounded into the kitchen. Just for a second he paused and looked about him, then made straight for Buckie, who had taken up a defiant attitude before the fire, beside the melted butter.

Now Buckie had hitherto, for obvious reasons, been very respectful to Jock; but this fateful afternoon seemed to have wakened in the creature a realisation of her own powers. Jock had teeth,

Mysie had a Little Lamb

it was true ; but had she not horns ? Some such train of reasoning must have passed through her brain, for she lowered her head menacingly at the dog. In a moment the kitchen was turned into pandemonium. Over went the chairs and Buckie with them—Jock bounded across the furniture biting, barking and snarling at the sheep in wild indignation.

Mysie, from the dresser, screamed aloud, and in her terror brought down more dishes from the rack above to add to the confusion. Then Buckie got on her feet again, and began to drive Jock into a corner : once there, pinned against the wall, horns would be better weapons than teeth. But just as things had come to this pass, in walked Father. Like heavenly music to poor little Mysie's ears, were those awful curses which were hurled broadcast at Jock and at Buckie, as the shepherd strode across the room and seized Buckie by the fleece !

" Sae ye'd kill Jock, wad ye, ye deevil ? " he cried, apprehending Jock's predicament in a moment, pinned there into the corner under Buckie's wicked horns. For one terrifying moment Mysie wondered if Buckie was going to get the better of Father too ? —then she saw the sheep a mere struggling defiant bundle of wool being hurtled out at the door, with Jock barking gaily behind her.

Ah, the comfort of that moment, when Father came back into the kitchen, reached up his arms to Mysie, and lifted her down from the dresser with words of endearment !

Mysie had a Little Lamb

" Were ye feared, my wee dearie ? Whaur's Mither—did Buckie fear ye ? Hoo long hae ye been on the dresser ? "

The Shepherd sat down by the fire, took the child on his knee, and kissed her little tear-wet face, while she began the tale of her sorrows :

" Mither gaed oot, an' I was wantin' my tea, an' I went til the press for a scone, and Buckie pushed me awa', and pit her heid intil the press, an' the plates fell oot, an' she grabbit at the scones, an' they fell oot, an' the treacle fell oot, an' the sugar, an' I wantit a bit oat-cake an' Buckie grabbit it frae me, an' I took a chair an' got ontil the dresser, an' Buckie butted on the dresser, an' the plates cam' doon an' Jock cam in an' they commenced tae fight. . . ."

It all came out in one long woeful sentence, punctuated by sobs and tremors, as Mysie nestled down into her father's arms with a blissful sense of security.

" Weel, weel," said the shepherd ruefully, looking about him at the awful disorder of the kitchen, " I maun sort up a wee afore Maggie comes hame—sit you there, Mysie, on the creepie; there's a fine lassie."

Though a little afraid to get down from her father's knee, Mysie had to obey. She perched herself on the stool by the fire and watched the tidying up. It was no easy job. Before the problem of how to remove a sea of black treacle and a pound of melted butter mixed up with pashed oat-cakes off a wooden floor, the manly spirit of the shepherd speedily

Mysie had a Little Lamb

quailed. He gathered up the broken dishes, set the upturned chairs on their legs again, took a shovel and scraped up a certain amount of the débris—but at the sight of the treacle and butter he stood aghast and grinned.

"I maun jist leave it tae Maggie," he said. "There's things a man canna' attemp'—we'll tak' oor tea, Mysie."

Somehow or other they gathered together the materials for a meal, and were eating it with the greatest contentment in the dirty kitchen when Mother made her appearance.

Mysie crowed with delight, pointing to the treacle-covered floor as the greatest joke ; while Father, roaring with laughter, described the scene he had come in upon. As was natural, perhaps, Mother was not inclined to take such a humorous view of the matter

"Gin ye had the scrubbin' o' yon floor, Tam," she said, "ye'd no' be lauchin' that wye," and she added bitterly, "Buckie 'd need a fine fleece tae pay for this day's work."

·   ·   ·   ·   ·   ·   ·

There was now a sort of armed neutrality between Jock and Buckie. Whenever the dog came into the kitchen he lifted his lip and snarled, and the sheep lowered her horns in response. But they were both sharply looked after, so no open battle was possible.

"Buckie's getting tae be an awfae fash," Mother said often, then she would look at the creature's

Mysie had a Little Lamb

splendid thick fleece and thriftily decide to endure all things for it.

Mysie now openly hated her former playmate. She would never stay alone with Buckie, though her parents laughed and told her "no' tae be a wee silly, feared o' a sheep." Even they, however, could not deny that Buckie's character was not improving: every week her temper became more imperious, her attitude more aggressive—one might have thought that the cottage belonged to the creature.

About this time a family of "lodgers," as they were termed, came to a farm farther down the glen. They may have been excellent young people; but they became the instruments of the decline and fall of poor Buckie. One afternoon two of these lodgers came up to the cottage to buy some milk. They were idle young men, and seeing the pet sheep, thought they would play with it. Mysie, emboldened by their presence, stood by to watch, and gave a shrill utterance to her hatred of Buckie :—

"She was my wee lambie, but I canna' bide her noo." Questioned more closely, Mysie explained the reason of her dislike, and gave a description of Buckie's appetite that astonished the young men.

"Try her wi' a bit baccy," Mysie urged. She had perched herself on the top of the dyke, out of reach of her enemy, and could enjoy the scene.

One of the lads took out a tobacco-pouch, and proffered some of the mixture to the animal. She nibbled it up as if it had been corn. Then with a shriek of laughter one of them placed a bowler hat

Mysie had a Little Lamb

on Buckie's horns, and got her to prance for a minute on her hind legs by means of dangling the tobacco-pouch out of reach above her. Mysie too screamed with laughter. There was no eye to notice the complete degradation that had been worked on the poor beast that stood there like Samson of old, making sport for the Philistines! After this the lads came often to the cottage to tease Buckie and play with her. They fed her on tobacco and sweets and encouraged her to butt savagely on the smallest provocation. "It's a good thing shearin's no' far off," Mother said.

Just before the shearing, "Uncle Geordie," as Mysie called him (though he was really her mother's uncle, not her own), arrived from Glasgow to pay his annual visit to his relations. Uncle Geordie was a retired tradesman, reputed to be "gae weel aff"; but his affluence had not kept the poor man from acquiring chronic rheumatism in his knees, which made it necessary for him to walk leaning on two sticks. In spite of this infirmity, however, he had unfailing good spirits. His little, deep-set eyes were creased all round with innumerable wrinkles caused by laughter, and he seemed able to find a joke everywhere.

"When I've naething else tae lauch at, I jist set the ae thoomb to lauch at the tither," he used to tell Mysie, holding up his thumbs like two little mannikins bowing to each other, till the child screamed with amusement. Seated on the bench by the cottage door with Mysie beside him, Uncle

Mysie had a Little Lamb

Geordie was a great deal happier than the proverbial king. Buckie was encouraged to be one of the party, for Mysie was not afraid of her when Uncle Geordie was there—a vigorous thrust with one of the sticks would generally keep the sheep at a safe distance.

Uncle Geordie kept a large supply of "conversation lozenges" in one pocket for Mysie, and quids of twist tobacco in the other for Buckie. It became a favourite game with him to try to cheat both the child and the animal. Diving his hands into his pockets, he would then hide them inside his coat and deftly change the sweets into the tobacco hand and *vice versa*. Finally he held out both hands, repeating the old rhyme of

"Knick-knack, which hand will ye tak'?"

Buckie invariably scented out the tobacco long before Mysie had made up her mind where the sweets were to be found. Never was sheep so depraved: she would have chewed tobacco all day long if she had got it to chew. One day she even stole into the kitchen and ate up a whole dish of sliced ham prepared for Uncle Geordie's dinner. No one would have believed that Buckie was the thief if she had not been seen coming out of the door with a long slice of ham hanging from her mouth, munching it in guilty haste as she went. . . .

"Maircy! the beast's awfae," Mother cried, but she added darkly, "A good thing the shearin's no' far off."

Mysie had a Little Lamb

The shearing was a great day in the glen. Mysie loved it, and was allowed to run about at will among the crowd of shepherds and collies. Hundreds of sheep had been brought down from the hill, and were now penned into the stone folds, waiting to be clipped. The whole air smelt of wool and tar, and echoed with the bleating of sheep and yelping of dogs. There was a sense of excitement and bustle everywhere.

Mysie, who was a great favourite with the shepherds, was lifted on to the broad turf top of the sheepfold wall so that she might look down into the crowded pens. The sheep were huddled together so closely that you could not have put your hand down between them. Now and then, to Mysie's huge delight, Jock, or one of the other dogs, would bound into the fold and walk across on the backs of the sheep as if on solid ground.

Then the gate of the fank would open, and two of the shepherds would clutch at a sheep and bear it out struggling to the shearers, who sat on funny long wooden stools just outside the gate.

Oh, how the sheep struggled, and how helpless they were in the hands of the shearers! Thrown on their backs, with their stiff black legs beating the air, they had to lie and be snipped and clipped at by the awful shears. White as snow, shorn and naked looking they lay there, and another heavy grey fleece was thrown on the ground. Then Mysie always held her breath and leant forward to watch that thrilling moment when Father dipped a long iron rod, with a circular thing on the end of it, into a huge bubbling pot of tar, and approached with the dripping rod to where the beautiful snow-white sheep lay. Down went the round end of the rod on to the white wool, and a great black letter was stamped on the sheep.

Mysie could never get over the impression that it hurt them somehow, tho' Father had told her a dozen times that it didn't. To-day there was special interest about the shearing, for was not Buckie to be shorn ? The whole morning Buckie marched about all unconscious of the fate in store for her. On every side she was greeted with jeers and laughter :

" Hoo are ye the day, Buckie ? "

" Are ye for a pipe ? "

" Ye'll be braw the nicht wantin' yon fleece ! "

And Buckie shouldered her way through them all, a privileged character, butting fiercely at her enemies the dogs—a sight to be seen for size and rude behaviour. She came impudently up to the gate of the fank and stared in at the trembling sheep huddled behind it—poor things that they were, to be held there in durance by a few men and dogs !

As she stood thus by the gate staring contemptuously at her fellow-sheep, two shepherds came up behind her and caught her by the fleece—that wonderful fleece that had not its equal for thickness in the whole flock. There was a stiff encounter between Buckie and the men ; they were tall and strong, but it took all their strength to cope with

Mysie had a Little Lamb

Buckie. She reared on her hind legs, beating the air with her hoofs like a savage horse, then suddenly lowered her big horned head and tried to butt, then stood stock still, her forefeet driven into the ground. What insult was this that was going to be offered her? She refused to be hustled along. But hustled she was, relentlessly, and flung like any poor, common, timid sheep on to the clipping stool, there to lie helpless under the awful, glittering shears. It was vain to struggle now; in that ignoble position strength availed not at all; but if a sheep can think, certainly dark thoughts of vengeance passed through Buckie's brain at that moment. . . . Slash went the shears through the thick wool, slash, slash, again and again, and once the shearer cut too deep and blood gushed out scarlet over the snow-white wool . . . they took a dab of tar and clapped it over the cut . . . another offence this cut and this tar, added to the long account that Buckie was adding up against mankind her enemies.

Mysie, on the top of the wall, had watched up to this time in silence ; now so great was her interest that she burst into speech.

"Eh, Faither, is Buckie tae be markit ? " she cried.

"Aye, Mysie," Father called up to her. He was approaching, as he spoke, with the tar-dipped brand ready for use.

"But, Faither, Buckie's got a name, what for will ye gie her anither ? "

Mysie had a Little Lamb

" I've nae time for yer clavers," said the shepherd, who was indeed busy enough in all conscience. And with that he planted the brand deep into Buckie's lovely white wool, leaving a big, black letter M upon it.

" There she is—ye'll no ken her noo," he said. Thrown upon her feet again, Buckie stood perfectly still for a moment, dazed and trembling, then went off with the grotesque lamb-like gambol that sheep give when they feel themselves rid of their heavy fleeces.

" Ye canna' get at me noo, Buckie ! " Mysie jeered, from her stronghold on the wall. Buckie however was never thinking of her old playmate. In the distance, far up the road beyond the fank, Uncle Geordie was hirpling along on his two sticks : tobacco might be obtainable—she set off in that direction, and was merged among the other newly clipped and branded sheep that were feeding about everywhere. Mysie returned to her absorbed contemplation of the shearing, and Buckie was forgotten for the time being.

Buckie shorn was so unrecognisable that Uncle Geordie paid no attention to the sheep that came bounding across the hillside towards him. But an imperative tweak at his pocket made the old man stand still in amazement.

" Gosh me ! it's Buckie ! " he exclaimed. " It'll be baccy y're wantin', ye limmer, is't no' ? "

He halted on his sticks and felt in his pocket, holding both sticks in one hand as he did so—a distinctly perilous thing to do, for his balance was not secure.

" Na—I've left my pooch in bye," he said aloud ; he shifted his sticks into the other hand as he spoke, to feel if by any chance the missing pouch might be in the left-hand pocket. Buckie dashed round to wait for the coveted mouthful.

" Ye'll hae tae want it," the old man said, shaking his head ; " it's no' here." But Buckie would not accept this explanation. She was cross exceedingly, and wanted something to make up for the indignity of losing her fleece and being snipped and plastered with tar and branded. The time had come to assert herself. She therefore stepped back a yard and then ran full tilt against Uncle Geordie. The old man went down on the ground like an overturned nine-pin, his sticks knocked out of his rather feeble grasp, and there he lay helplessly at the mercy of Buckie. She began a deliberate rummage through his pockets for the tobacco she felt must be there. " Revenge," said Bacon, " is a sort of wild justice," and in the obscure recesses of the sheepy mind some such feeling may have been at work. A few minutes ago Buckie had been helpless under the hands of the shearers ; it was just that Buckie, who had been shorn and hurt, should now pillage and hurt in her turn. With her greedy black nose she tugged at the old man's pockets till she tore the lining inside out and extracted some grains of tobacco dust that lingered in the corners of the lining.

Uncle Geordie in the meantime could do nothing

to help himself, for whenever he moved Buckie gave a threatening toss of her head, as much as to say, " You lie still or I'll make you."

True to his nature, the old man laughed aloud at his own ridiculous predicament, then shouted at the top of his voice, thinking that some of the shepherds might hear and come to his rescue.

It was not the shepherds, however, but Jock who heard these distressful cries. Idle for a moment at the gate of the fank, he pricked his ears, and then dashed suddenly across the hillside in the direction of the shout.

Buckie had just decided that no more tobacco was to be found in Uncle Geordie's pockets : she stood and looked contemptuously at her victim : these men that had shorn her and cut her flesh and branded her with hot tar, were poor things after all, easily knocked over, easily kept flat on the ground once they were down—why had she not mastered the others as she had mastered this one ? —Then lo, across the heather came Jock with fearful, snapping jaws, and lolling red tongue . . . primeval terrors stirred in the heart of Buckie—the heart that had seemed of late almost human in its degradation. Blind ignominious fear took hold upon her; she was a sheep once more, and nothing but a sheep. Panic-stricken, trembling, panting, fleeing before the hereditary foe of her race, you would scarcely have recognised the doughty Buckie of half an hour before.

And alas, Jock too seemed to have changed back

278

Mysie had a Little Lamb

to the primitive beast of prey, to have come near
forgetting all his man-taught restraint and gentleness. His old grudge at Buckie rose up hot within
him; he wanted to bury his teeth in her throat and
revenge himself for that bitter moment when he
had been driven into the corner and humiliated.
And this was the dog who had found on the hillside
that pitiful bundle of wool and known it to be a
lamb ! Well, well, such is life !

It is not difficult to say what the issue of the
chase would have been, had the road not led
past the sheep fold. Mysie, from her watch-
tower, was the first to give warning ; her shrill
cry of :

"See Jock after Buckie !" drew the attention of
the shepherds to what was going on. A volley of
curses, frightful to hear, stopped Jock as suddenly
as if a bullet had gone through his heart. He came
towards his master trembling and contrite, and
Buckie fled on down the stoney road at a tremendous
pace. Mysie called out again another and more
startling bit of news :

" They've knockit doon Uncle Geordie—he's lyin'
east the road ! "

There was general consternation at this, and
Father set off running to see what was wrong with
the old man. Mysie, too, slipped down from her
perch and followed Father, while Jock, humble
and anxious, came also, as one of the family. With
some difficulty Uncle Geordie was raised on to his
stiff old legs, and supported on his sticks ; but

instead of complaining about his accident he would do nothing but laugh as he related how it had happened.

"Eh, yon sheep! Yon Buckie! She's an' awfae beast yon!" he cried, wiping his eyes with his red pocket-handkerchief; "she knockit me doon, and syne she ate a' the linings o' my pockets—see til them!" He turned out all that remained of the linings as he spoke. "I'd be there yet if it hadna been for Jock," he added; "she got a fine fleg when she see'd him comin'!"

Jock wagged his tail humbly, not quite sure yet of his master's forgiveness, and the old man went on :

"Gosh me! tae think a sheep could master a man—I'm a puir bit mannie, I'm thinkin'!" And off he went into another chuckle of laughter.

But it was recognised at last that Buckie's time had come.

"We'll no' can keep her anither year," the shepherd said grimly, and Mysie plucked at his sleeve.

"Dinna keep Buckie—I'm feared o' her," she whispered.

"Hoots, Mysie," said he, not wishing to encourage her fears ; but his determination was made none the less.

Buckie's splendid fleece was brought into the kitchen at evening to be admired.

"There's for ye, Maggie—the finest fleece I've seen this long while," said the shepherd. "But

Mysie had a Little Lamb

ye'll no' hae anither—I'm sendin' Buckie awa' the morn."

"Tae the—?" Mother began; but a glance at Mysie silenced her. She need not, however, have thought her daughter so sensitive—as after events proved. It was two days later that the lodgers from down the glen came up as usual to buy butter and have a game with Buckie: they could not find her, to their great disappointment, and asked Mysie what had become of her pet.

Alas, there was unmistakable glee in the child's voice as she made shrill reply:

"The butcher's got her."

.   .   .   .

Late that night, as Father, Mother, and Uncle Geordie sat round the fire in the kitchen, a scream came from Mysie's sleeping place.

Mother jumped up from her chair to see what was wrong, but before she could cross the kitchen Mysie herself had appeared. Her curls were all tousled over her face, her eyes wide with fright; she ran blindly to the shepherd, scrambled on to his knee and buried her head against his shoulder.

"What is't, dearie? Were ye dreamin'?" Mother asked.

"I saw the butcher, and he'd a muckle knife an' he kilt—he kilt—he kilt . . ." Mysie's voice died away in an agony of sobs; she could not voice the awfulness of her dream.

The elders exchanged meaning glances across the hearth.

Mysie had a Little Lamb

" Was't Buckie he kilt ? " Father inquired, and with a fresh burst of weeping Mysie got out the words at last.

" Na—it wasna Buckie—Buckie's a bad beast—it was my wee white lambie."

Impossible at that moment it seemed, to disentangle the confusion in the child's mind ; but Uncle Geordie had a sudden inspiration, of the sort that only comes to the real child-lover.

" Hoots, Mysie," he said, reaching across and lifting her on to his knee, " d'ye no ken what came of yer wee white lambie ? "

Mysie lifted her tear-stained face incredulously—only too well, she thought that she knew.

" I'll tell ye then—it was this wye," Uncle Geordie went on. " It was late in the gloamin' an' you were in yer bed, when the wee fairy folk came doon the glen—there must hae been near about a hunder o' them, a' in green ye ken, an' awfae wee, wi' gold croons on them. Weel, they saw Lambie oot bye feedin', an' ane o' them jumpit on til her back, an' they a' clappit their hands an' made sic a noise that Lambie ran off up the road, awa' up the glen miles an' miles. Syne they were that pleased wi' Lambie they thocht tae keep her, sae they jist caught an awfae beast they caed Buckie an' drove her down the glen tae the door, an' there she was in the mornin' when ye wakened up."

" An' Lambie's wi' the fairies then ? " Mysie asked, her sobs already a thing of the past.

Mysie had a Little Lamb

" Aye is she : eatin' fine bits o' green grass an' wee flowers, an' made a deal o' by them a'."

'' An' the butcher didna " — Mysie's voice shook.

" No' he : the fairies dinna hae butchers. See, Mysie, here's a gran' conversation lozenge for ye, an' Mither's tae pit ye til yer bed again."

Mysie slipped down off his knee, grasped the conversation lozenge, and pattered off contentedly to bed : in her young mind Buckie the tyrant was dead and gone, and her wee white lamb was alive and happy forever among the fairies.

THE DEIL'S MONEY

THE DEIL'S MONEY

DAFT JIMMY came down the High Street of East Lenzie jingling his money in the old stocking that served him as a purse. He was a tall, red-haired man, with mild, vacant blue eyes, and a gaping mouth. The light within his brain had been blown out from his birth, and Jimmy had stumbled on through a long mental twilight ever since. Vagueness was all around him; dim shapes of men and women moved before his unseeing eyes; faint sounds reached his dull ears; only hunger and thirst were realities to him—terrible, ever-recurring things that found their way somehow through his befogged senses with startling clearness.

Jimmy really understood what hunger meant. More than once he had experienced it in his wretched adolescence; now a grown man, his great fear in life was that he should ever be hungry again without the means of satisfying himself. By tiny accumulations of experience he had at last grasped the idea that money was his safeguard against this hideous enemy hunger. He had never heard of that hypothetical island political economists are so fond of, where a man might have all the wealth of the world, yet starve to death. In Jimmy's simple creed a

The Deil's Money

" bawbee " would always buy food, and this was the beginning and the end of his political economy.

With this end in view, then, Jimmy went from door to door through the whole county of Eastshire —a privileged beggar, whose pitiful infirmity seldom failed to gain him the money he sought. His form of appeal was invariable :—

" Gie's a bawbee, mistress, to buy a bit bread ! " And when he had got it :—

" Thank ye, m'hen," he would say, using that quaint form of endearment so often heard in Eastshire.

Jimmy had learned, with great difficulty, that when he had collected twelve pence they should be changed into another and smaller coin. At first he had been very unwilling to change his twelve precious heavy pennies into anything so insignificant and light as a shilling. Then a friendly baker, by the exercise of infinite patience, at last managed to teach him that he could buy whole two dozen cookies for one of these despised little shillings, instead of buying only two for one big, heavy penny.

After this Jimmy's passion for " siller " became more and more marked, and shillings accumulated in his old stocking at a wonderful rate, till, weighed down by his burden of wealth, poor Jimmy had to come again to his friend the baker and explain to him how difficult it was to carry about all his siller. The baker had another plan to suggest then ; it was possible to change shillings into gold. But

The Deil's Money

here a grave difficulty arose, for Jimmy wanted to
get a sovereign for twelve shillings, and could not
understand why twenty were needed. It was a
terrible business ; but at last he was convinced.
The little gold coins—there were three of them—were
wrapped up in a bit of newspaper and thrust deep
down into the toe of the stocking for greater safety,
then a stitch was given across the stocking to
keep them secure. This had been the beginning of
Jimmy's hoard. For years he went on adding every
few months another pound to his store, till he carried
a considerable sum of money about with him.

To-day as Jimmy came down the street of East
Lenzie he paused at an open door, attracted by the
sound of voices inside the house.

" Haud yer tongue, Agnes. I'm fair seek tellin'
ye it canna' be," said a woman's voice.

" I'll no' haud my tongue, mither ! " yelled another
voice, younger in its tone, but shrill and defiant.
" It's a sin an' a disgrace if I'm put to the dress-
makin', and me sae cliver at the school ! "

" If ye dinna haud yer tongue, Agnes, I'll leather
ye ! "

" Ye will not ! "

" Get awa' wi' ye, ye besom, whaur'll I get money
to make a teacher o' ye ? " . . . Then the sound of
an overturned chair, and out through the door flew
a lanky, fair-haired girl, with sharp features and
thin lips. She almost ran into Daft Jimmy, standing there on the threshold. His unvarying petition
was on his lips :—

The Deil's Money

" Gie's a bawbee, mistress, to buy a bit bread ! "

" I've nae bawbees—ye've mair yersel'," said
Agnes roughly, as she pushed past him and ran off
down the street. Her narrow grey eyes were red-
dened with tears, and she sobbed as she ran.

Jimmy knocked again, and this time the girl's
mother came to the door. Mrs. Cockburn had just
the same sharp, unpleasant expression as her
daughter—no man in possession of his senses would
have asked an alms from her ; but Jimmy had no
sense at all, so he mumbled out his usual appeal :—

" A bawbee, mistress, to buy bread ! "

" I've mair tae dae wi' my bawbees," said Mrs.
Cockburn, and with that she slammed the door in
poor Jimmy's face. He slouched away down the
street, giving a little chink to his stockingful of
coin, as if to reassure himself.

.   .   .   .   .   .

That was a cheerless autumn afternoon. Grey
skies, a grey, tossing sea, the very thorn bushes on
the wind-swept Links bending themselves lower
before the rush of the squalls that blew in from the
sea. But Jimmy had set his face to reach Eastlaw
that night, and so he plodded along the Links, not
giving much heed to the weather. It was heavy
walking across the uneven sandy ground. Sometimes he would sit down under the shelter of a
thorn bush and gaze vacantly out to sea ; sometimes he took a crust of bread from his pocket and
chewed it, but always his poor mind, or what
served him for a mind, kept worrying round one

The Deil's Money

perplexing point : his stockingful of coin was getting too heavy to carry about with him.

It is probable that clouded minds such as his are much prompted by bodily sensations. Because Jimmy was annoyed by the weight of his stocking he tried to think what to do with it. The money was dear to him : it represented food. Yet he wanted to get rid of the burden of carrying it. What, then, was to be done ?

He must have gone through some sort of process of reasoning, for at last he took out from his various pockets all the pence he had collected during the week, and spread them out upon the ground. Jimmy could not count one, two, three in words—he had just somehow learned to know by the look of the pennies when he had got a dozen of them. Sometimes the row was a little too short, and, after considering it, with his foolish head hung to one side in an attitude of speculation, Jimmy would slowly add another penny to make the row up to the right length. Sometimes his eye told him that the row was too long, and then a penny had to be taken away. This afternoon he made three rows of twelve, very deliberately, then swept the coppers together and put them back into his pockets. After this he produced a great brass pin from the collar of his coat, and pinned together the mouth of his precious stocking. All the time he muttered to himself, looking round every minute or two to make sure that no one witnessed his preparations. Suddenly Jimmy noticed a rabbit sitting by its

The Deil's Money

burrow, and at sight of the creature his face lit up. Why not leave the money in the burrow? The rabbits were a friendly people. Jimmy liked to sit in the dusk and watch them whisking in and out of their holes, little dumpy shadows with white tails. He had often laughed aloud, his awful mirthless laugh, as he watched their gambols.

Jimmy approached the burrow, and knelt down. The rabbit had disappeared down its hole; but unaffected by this sign of distrust, Jimmy pushed his stocking in after the creature.

" Hi ! my mannie ! " he said, " ye'll keep my siller in yer wee hoosie for me ? "

The rabbit kept a prudent silence, but Jimmy was quite satisfied that he had done something very clever. " For they dinna want siller," he said, and plodded off along the Links, relieved of his burden, and chinking his remaining pennies cheerfully in his pockets as he went.

.   .   .   .

Mushrooms grew on the East Lenzie Links, and the children used to go out in little bands to search for them. Agnes Cockburn was a specially good mushroom-finder. She somehow always managed to secure a large basketful.

Agnes had no intention of eating the mushrooms, however; she was far too practical for that. Already, at thirteen years of age, she had a passion for making money, and that curious instinct of how to make it which belongs to certain natures as a talent for music or painting belongs to others.

The Deil's Money

Her fertile brain had quickly conceived the idea of hawking the mushrooms round to the larger houses in the neighbourhood. With this end in view, she rose early one morning and sped along the Links while they were still hoary with dew to get the first harvest that had sprung up through the night.

Agnes knew that her school friends, Jeanie Peden and Bella Ross, were going on the same quest whenever school was over. Thought Agnes—"I'll be afore them." It is true she intended to join the afternoon expedition also, but her reasons for doing so were sinister to a degree. She explained these to her mother with great plainness.

"I'll ken where the best anes is, an' I'll tak' Jeanie and Bella the other way!" Agnes was displaying a great basket of exquisite pinky brown mushrooms as she spoke, the fruit of her early search. She stood there, like the mad maid of Herrick's verse, 'all dabbled with the dew,' breathless from her long run home across the Links, her grey eyes glinting with excitement.

"I'll sell them afore Jeanie and Bella's oot o' their beds!" she cried triumphantly.

"You're the one!" Mrs. Cockburn exclaimed in admiration. They often fell out, this mother and daughter, but on one point they were in the completest harmony—the mother even aided and abetted her child in all her schemes for making money. So Agnes went off to sell her mushrooms, and in an about an hour's time returned with two

The Deil's Money

shillings held tightly in her thin, red hand. She spread out her palm to display the coins, and laughed aloud with pride of her bargaining.

" My certy, Agnes, but y're cliver ! " said the admiring mother. " What are ye to buy wi' them ? "

" Buy ? " said the girl contemptuously. " They'll be in the Savings Bank the nicht."

Not a word of her exploit passed Agnes' lips at school that morning. She joined in the most whole-hearted manner in the proposal to hunt mushrooms in the afternoon. So whenever school came out at four o'clock the three little girls set off on their search. Jeanie and Bella were two years younger than Agnes, but she liked this, because her word carried authority with it in consequence.

At first the children ran along the sands for a mile, then, when they reached what might be called the mushroom zone, they climbed up on to the Links and began the hunt. Agnes was far too acute to mislead her companions at once. In fact she gave them two or three rich finds by way of encouragement, and to inspire them with confidence in her leadership. Then she deliberately began to lure them away from their quarry.

" There was awfae good yins last year east a bit —behind thae thorn bushes," she directed, halting where she stood, and pointing forward with a gesture of command. They dived through the low thickets of hawthorn and briar, tearing many a rent in their frocks, and came out upon a likely enough spot, green and bare, with short, rabbit-cropped

The Deil's Money

sward. But no mushrooms were to be seen, and Agnes, with well assumed disappointment, shook her head dolefully.

" They've no' come up the year," she said. " Maybe it was a wee thing further on they were."

" See here, Agnes, what'll this be ? " cried Jeanie Peden. She held up something in her hand.

" Hoots, it's a stocking, Jeanie," said Agnes, not much interested in the discovery.

" Aye, but it's full o' money ! " Jeanie exclaimed. She took the pin out of it, and fumbled at some stitches that held the coins in to the toe of the stocking. The next moment a shower of gold and silver poured out upon the sandy ground. There was a babble of voices from all three children at once—

" Whaur did ye find it, Jeanie ? "

" It was pokin' oot frae the rabbit hole."

" Wha's 'll it be ? "

" There's an awfae heap o' siller there ! " Then, in a flash of inspiration, Jeanie cried out—" Eh, I ken wha's it is ! It's Daft Jimmy's. I se'ed him wi' it when he gaed doon the street a week syne."

During this short discussion Agnes had been apparently thinking hard. Now she gave an unexpected turn to the situation by uttering an awful scream. It seemed to go right to the hearts of the other children like a knife. At the same moment she dashed off through the bushes, calling to her companions—

" It's no Jimmy's, it's no Jimmy's ! It's the Deil's money ; and He'll get ye if ye touch a penny

The Deil's Money

o' it—He'll get ye!" Her cries terrified Jeanie and Bella, for panic spreads among children like fire among dry wood. They scarcely waited to catch up their baskets; but charged off through the bushes after Agnes, tearing many a screed in their poor little frocks as they ran past the thorn bushes that seemed to catch at their raiment like detaining hands. With sobbing breath and eyes wild with terror, they tore along, trying to make up to Agnes, who was very fleet of foot.

"Wait, Agnes! Dinna leave us! Wait!" they cried, their panic growing as they saw how Agnes fled from the accursed spot. But Agnes would not wait; on she ran, threading her way in and out among the bushes, and always from time to time casting a fearful glance behind her as she ran. At last down she sank, breathless, and caught her foot in her hand. She was nursing it, and rocking herself to and fro, when Jeanie and Bella came up.

"Eh, Agnes! Agnes!" they cried, flinging themselves down beside her, and huddling together in their terror.

"Rin on—rin you on, Jeanie; rin, Bella!" Agnes admonished them. "Dinna bide wi' me. I've got a stob intil my tae. I canna' rin ony mair."

But staunch little Jeanie would not run.

"I'll no' leave ye yer lane, Agnes," she sobbed. "I wouldna like it mysel'. I'll bide wi' ye."

Bella, more selfish by nature, urged her to come on, and Agnes clinched the matter by an unanswerable argument—

The Deil's Money

" It was you found His siller," she said, giving an awful backward look over her shoulder that conveyed unspoken terrors. " Sae it's you must rin. He'll no meddle wi' me. I niver pit a finger on it—rin, Jeanie ! " she commanded. " Dinna ye hear what I'm tellin' ye. He'll no' want me ! "

The suggestion that she might, Persephone-like, be drawn down into Hades, was too much for poor little Jeanie. She fled on without another word, followed by Bella, and Agnes was left alone, nursing her injured toe.

.   .   .   .

For about ten minutes Agnes sat still. Then she rose, stood upright, and gazed round her. Far off she could just see two tiny figures disappearing round the corner of the bay at a great pace. That was all right. Agnes smiled, and began to retrace her steps as quickly as she could through the bushes. Her heart beat fast ; this was a real adventure. Oh, how long the way seemed, and how rough ! Each clump of thorn bushes looked so exactly like every other that she was several times deceived, and thought she had reached her destination when still far away from it. But at last out she came upon that smooth green sward, and there, before her greedy eyes, lay the Deil's money.

Two or three rabbits had come out, and were frisking beside the little heap of coin. It did not, as Jimmy with the wisdom of the simple had divined, possess any value for them. Everything was very quiet. There was no wind, and the only sound

The Deil's Money

was the swish of the long waves curling in on the sands below.

Agnes stood still and gazed at the money. She looked round ; there was no one anywhere in sight. Even the rabbits had disappeared into their holes. She bent down then, and lifted the stocking, then looked up again with a guilty fear that some one might be there after all. But no—she was quite, quite alone. Down she went upon her knees and scraped together the whole heap of money, cramming it into the stocking without making any attempt to count how much there was. All Agnes wanted was to make sure that not a single coin was left behind. When at last this was quite certain, Agnes took off her garter and tied up the mouth of the stocking with it. Then she pinned her skirt up round her waist, and dropped the stocking into the bag thus formed. So she began her homeward way. Agnes was very tired, but she walked quickly at first, then more slowly, till, as she entered the village, she limped painfully. It would never do to meet Jeanie or Bella with her toe miraculously healed.

" I'll bide frae the school the morn," she thought, determined that her part was to be well acted when she was at it.

.   .   .   .

" Mither," Agnes cried, as she came limping into the cottage, " lock the door, an' light the lamp, an' shut up the hoose. I've something here for ye."

The Deil's Money

"What is't, Agnes—what for would I lock the door and it not six o'clock?" Mrs. Cockburn demanded.

"I'm no wantin' onybody in," Agnes said darkly.

"Weel, then, turn the key yersel', and I'll pit on the shutter," said Mrs. Cockburn. But even these precautions did not satisfy Agnes. She insisted that one of her mother's shawls was to be pinned across the chink of the shutter. "I've whiles seen the bairns lookin' through the crack," she explained.

Mrs. Cockburn's curiosity was fully roused at last. She waited impatiently for Agnes to reveal her secret. But when the stockingful of money was laid upon the table a dead silence fell between the mother and daughter. Both of them knew to whom the money belonged. Too often they had seen Daft Jimmy pass down the street, stocking in hand, to have any doubt at all upon the subject. They looked at each other across the little table. At last the mother spoke—

"Hoo muckle's o' it?" she asked, her voice hoarse and unsteady, her eyes fixed on her child's face.

"I dinna ken—I didna take time to count."

"Whaur did ye find it?"

"East the Links, in a hole."

"Was ye wi' Jeanie an' Bella?"

"Aye."

"An' they se'ed ye take it?"

"No' them! I tell't them it was the Deil's

The Deil's Money

money, an' we maun rin or He'd hae us ; syne I
gaed back an' took it mysel'."

" Gosh, Agnes, but y're cliver ! "

Mrs. Cockburn opened the stocking then, and
poured out the money on to the table. She began
to count it out, but Agnes longed to feel the gold
between her own fingers.

" I'm to coont it, mither ! " she cried. Her
quick, clever fingers separated the gold from the
silver with almost the dexterity of a bank clerk.
You would have thought she had been handling
money all her days.

" It's close on five-and-twenty pound ! " she cried,
her voice shrill with excitement. " We'll can start
a shoppie ! "

" Aye, Agnes, fine, an' a licence tae sell baccy."

" Sweeties—sweetie shops aye prosper," said
Agnes.

" Aye, sweeties an' tobaccy. But we maun bide
a wee, or folks would talk—they wouldna ken whaur
the siller came frae."

Agnes was quite sharp enough to see the wisdom
of this remark. "Aye, we maun bide," she
assented.

It never seemed to occur either to the mother
or daughter that the money should be returned to
its owner ; they purposely did not mention his
name to each other, and the agreement between
them on this point, if tacit, was profound.

" Hoo long maun we bide, mither ? " Agnes
asked wistfully.

The Deil's Money

"Twa years an' mair, lassie ; then maybe we might commence talkin' aboot a bit shoppie."

"Can we pit it intil the bank ? " Agnes pursued, her sharp little features puckered with care.

"No' here, onyway—maybe in Edinbury."

"Eh, yon would be fine. We'd hae interest ontil't for twa years an' mair ! "

"You're the lassie ! " Mrs. Cockburn cried again, struck afresh with admiration for the financial capacity her daughter displayed.

.   .   .   .

School did not see Agnes next day ; she sat at the cottage door, her foot tied up in rags, and supported ostentatiously on a wooden stool. Visits of sympathy were duly paid her by Jeanie and Bella, and together they went over in detail the horrors of their flight across the Links.

"I was that feared," said the graphic Agnes, "I didna look the way I was goin', till I cam' doon wi' the awfaest dunt on my tae, and when I got hame there was a stob near as big's a peen intil't."

"My ! " echoed her companions. "It maun hae hurt ye awfu', Agnes ? "

"Aye—mither took it oot wi' a needle, but my tae's a' swelled up."

"I thought shame to leave ye there," said Jeanie, her tender conscience pricking still.

"Dinna mention it," said Agnes grandly, feeling herself very magnanimous.

Jeanie, who was a sensible child, now put forward another idea.

The Deil's Money

"D'ye ken, Agnes," she said, "father said we was jist sillies to think yon was the Deil's money. He said it maun hae been Daft Jimmy left it ; and he gaed a' the road across the Links seekin' it last night, but he couldna' find it."

"Dinna you believe him!" Agnes cried, with the air of a young prophetess. "The Deil pit it there, an' the Deil liftit it again. If it was Daft Jimmy's, d'ye no' think it would hae been there yet ?"

Jeanie did not know whether Agnes should be believed or her father ; but as they sat discussing the mystery, Daft Jimmy himself came down the village street. And as he slouched along he cried aloud, so that all might hear, a most melancholy chant—

"I want my siller! I want my siller! I want my siller!"

Now the children were a little afraid of poor Jimmy, and used to shrink inside the doors as he passed by. But to-day, urged by a strong impulse of pity, Jeanie Peden ran into the street and plucked at his sleeve.

"Hi! Jimmy!" she cried, terrified to find herself so close to those vacant, staring eyes, yet determined to give him such help as she could. "Jimmy, hae ye lost yer siller, man ?"

"I want my siller! I've lost my siller!" he chanted.

"I se'ed it away east the Links," Jeanie panted ; "near hand the Eastlaw burn, stickin' oot o' a rabbit

The Deil's Money

hole, an' I pu'ed it oot, and then I was feared, an' ran awa' an' left it, an' maybe it's there yet."

Quite a little crowd soon gathered round Jimmy and the children, for Agnes and Bella had come to add their testimony to Jeanie's. It never occurred to anyone to doubt their story, and when one or two lads offered to go off in search of the lost treasure, Jeanie at once volunteered to guide them to the place.

Only Agnes Cockburn tried to discourage the search-party. " Ye'll no' find it ; it wasna Jimmy's money. I'm tellin' ye gospel truth—it was the Deil's money ! "

" Hoots, lassie, haud yer tongue ; ye're speakin' nonsense," some of the older people told her.

Then Mrs. Cockburn joined the throng, shrill in support of her daughter's theory. " Agnes was cleverer than any one of them. . . . Agnes knew what she was talking about. . . . Agnes had come home in a pretty like fright. . . . She would tell the minister all about it any day. . . . It was gospel truth she had spoken, &c."

In fact, the part was ever so little over-played by both Agnes and Mrs. Cockburn, till the neighbours retired into their houses, shaking their heads.

" I misdoot me if Agnes Cockburn doesna ken a' aboot it," said Jeanie Peden's mother darkly.

She had heard a great deal from her daughter.

Somehow this got whispered through the village, and for a short time the Cockburns were not very popular in the community. But months slipped on into years, and no signs of prosperity appeared in

303

The Deil's Money

the Cockburn household. The sinister rumour died down, and no one except Daft Jimmy remembered anything about the Deil's money.

His melancholy cry became well known in the countryside, as he went along lamenting his lost treasure—

" I want my siller ! I want my siller ! I want my siller ! "

 . . . .

It must have been quite two and a half years later that Mrs. Cockburn and Agnes appeared in church one Sunday in handsome mournings. The neighbours knew of no bereavement in the Cockburn family, and eyed the new blacks with great curiosity. Then Agnes told Jeanie Peden a wonderful bit of news. It appeared that a distant cousin in Australia had died and left them a legacy. " An' mither an' me was that taen aback gettin' the money when we never looked for't, we didna ken what to think ; but mither, she's an awfae yin for blacks, an' says she, ' Agnes, when he's left us siller we maun wear murrnins oot o' respec' to his mem'ry.' "

" My, Agnes, ye'll can be a teacher noo ! " cried Jeanie, delighted by her friend's good luck.

" Na : we've talked it ower, an' we're to start a sweetie shop—it's mair profitable," was the quick reply. Agnes was ʏa big, well-developed girl, getting on to sixteen years of age now, so the neighbours often wondered why she had not yet settled down to any calling. But this sweetie shop scheme appeared to decide her future in a very easy way.

The Deil's Money

Agnes seemed predestined by Heaven, or perhaps by Hell, to be a shopkeeper. All that there was to know about sweetie shops Agnes had at her finger ends. How she had acquired the knowledge suddenly no one could imagine. Some mysterious instinct taught her which " gundy " would be most irresistible to children, which peppermint most popular with old women. Her astute fancy pointed out to Mrs. Cockburn how many decent bodies among the neighbours " tasted a wee " at times, and were unwilling· that their weakness should be known. Were there not special preparations of clove made for such purposes of concealment ? These had a grand sale. Then Agnes speculated in a bankrupt chemist's stock of cough lozenges, and sold them for twice what she had paid for them. Finally she adopted an ingenious, though simple, method by which she took exactly one sweetmeat out of every pound, half-pound, or quarter-pound that she made up. It was surprising how many additional pounds she got for nothing in this way, and sold at the usual price. No one ever detected Agnes in this trick : she was much too clever for that, and would even contrive to make her customers believe that she flung one or two " extras " into their poke.

Agnes began to put up her hair about this time, and to wear a becoming white apron. She was improving in appearance with prosperity, and knew that prosperity would also improve with appearance, for nothing succeeds like success. For two or three

The Deil's Money

years Agnes was content with the sweetie shop, then she mooted another plan to her mother—

" Mither," she said ," what d'ye think o' starting a public ? It's gey slow work makin' money oot o' sweeties."

" Eh, Agnes, what are ye sayin' ? There's fower publics in East Lenzie a'ready ! "

" Aye," said Agnes deliberately, " but d'ye no' ken that if there was six publics they'd a' pay ? Did ever ye hear o' a bankrupt public, mither ? "

" No' that I mind on, Agnes," Mrs. Cockburn admitted.

" It'll pay fine, mither. Ye'd wunder whaur they find the money whiles—but they hae it."

" Weel, we may jist as weel get it as ony ither body," said Mrs. Cockburn, perhaps visited by a momentary pang of conscience, which she tried to stifle with this very old argument.

They were standing in the shop as they spoke. It was getting late, and business was slack, but a step sounded on the threshold, the door creaked open, and some one looked in.

" I want my siller ! I want my siller ! " chanted poor Jimmy at the door, and then, changing his refrain, he took up his old plea—

" A bawbee, mistress, to buy a bit bread ! "

Agnes dashed to the till, and, without counting what she took out of it, literally flung some half-dozen or so of coins across the floor to Jimmy. He looked at her in amazement, then stooped down

306

The Deil's Money

humbly to pick up this reckless gift from the hand
that had robbed him.

" Thank ye, m'hen," he said, as he slouched away
down the twilight street.

. . . .

It was amazing how the public-house flourished.
As they sat and counted out their gains Agnes and
her mother would say to each other that they didn't
know where the siller came from. " Ye'd hae
thocht the ' Eastshire Arms ' got a' the custom was
goin' this end o' the toon ? " Mrs. Cockburn would
ruminate ; but Agnes, with her crafty smile, made
answer—

" We've got them that thought shame to gang
til the ' Eastshire Arms.' Ye see, they jist slip in
like, here, an' a'body doesna ken ; syne they canna
do wantin' it, an' it's a glass here an' a glass there
a' through the day—they get the habit easy."

" Eh, it's an awfae habit ! " sighed Mrs. Cockburn,
who had no sense of humour at all, and so could
moralise over the evil ways that she was doing her
best to encourage.

" Weel, folks maun look oot for theirsel's," said
Agnes tartly. " It's a fine habit for them that
keeps publics."

She was so clever, and kept her eyes so wide open
that there was no fear of Agnes herself falling into
this fine habit, as you might have expected she
would : not a bit of it. Agnes could stand all day
in the smell of whisky, and serving it out, without
wishing to taste a drop of it.

The Deil's Money

"I'm no' sic a gowk," she would say, as she watched some poor be-fooled neighbour go stumbling away down the street from her door.

.　　.　　.　　.　　.　　.　　.

Agnes married " well," and gained in worldly prosperity year by year. She had children, of whom she was inordinately proud ; in fact, she flourished like the proverbial green bay tree. Yet a more miserable woman than she was in her later life you could scarcely imagine. For all the faults of her own character began to be pitilessly reproduced in her children. She who had never regarded the things of others was now in her turn disregarded. Her sons did not care in the least if they broke their mother's heart ; they had just the same indifference to her feelings that Agnes had always had for the feelings of her neighbours. Two of the lads ruined themselves with drink, and the third stole £25, and was sent off to jail.

"Eh ! to think he'd bring disgrace on us for five-and-twenty pound ! " cried poor Agnes ; but even as she spoke a thought drove through her heart like a sword—"It's the Deil's money again— the Deil's money ! " she screamed.

"Wheesht, woman ; what's that y're sayin' ? Are ye daft ? " said her husband anxiously, afraid that the neighbours would hear her terrible cry.

But Agnes never explained what she meant by these strange words.

THE LOVE BAIRN

THE LOVE BAIRN

" MADE in the image of God " : the words seemed blasphemous when applied to James Gilchrist—he had travelled so far away from all God-like attributes, become hardened into such insensate clay. Modern teachers tell us that no man is altogether vile ; perhaps they are right, but if they had known James well such teachers might have reconsidered their doctrines. A bad Scotchman can indeed be more odious than a sinner of any other nationality, because he adds to his transgressions the crowning offence of affected respectability. Now it is difficult to believe in a creature hideous enough to take upon his lips the language of the Saints while he is living the life of a sinner ; yet if you are to understand the character of James Gilchrist and, alas, that of many of his fellow-countrymen, you must acknowledge this national tendency.

Night after night all week through James was drunk ; then on Sunday he had a good shave, put on a black suit and went to church, looking an image of respectability. He cannot have thought it possible to deceive his neighbours ; they knew him too well for that, so it must have been an obscure

The Love Bairn

idea that his God was more easily taken in which prompted the action : " He seeth not as man seeth " might read two ways.

If drink had been Gilchrist's only fault it would have been well. Far graver sins were laid at his door. " Eh, the dirty man ! " the neighbours would say expressively, for he had such a vocabulary that women turned away and shut their doors as he reeled through the village. Worst of all, there was a dark story about a weak-minded woman, Lizzie McTavish by name, who had two children belonging to James. She was the daughter of a widow on one of the loneliest crofts ; the widow was old and helpless, and there had been no one to make James marry the girl, so he had never dreamed of doing it : " An' 'deed the poor crater's better wantin' him," was the perfectly wise opinion of Lizzie's neighbours.

The children, however, were not better wantin' food—that was quite another matter. It seemed always perfectly easy for James to find money for drink (he would say with a gleeful twinkle of the eye, " *The dru'ken man has aye his dru'ken penny* "), yet only the terrors of the law could wring anything from him for the support of these wretched children. At last poor Lizzie was fortunate enough to die. James rejoiced openly : " They'll maybe no' want sae muckle for the bairns noo," he said, basing his hopes on the fact that the widow was too old and frail to extort the money from him herself—she would probably rather allow the children to starve.

The Love Bairn

He might wait and see how long it would be before she claimed anything.

.   .   .   .

It is said that every man alive can find some woman ready to marry him. But James Gilchrist's neighbours could scarcely " believe their ears," as they expressed it, when some two years after poor Lizzie's death James told them he was going to be married. He had been in Glasgow, and there had found a wife—this was all he said when sober ; in his cups he boasted of the fine lass he had chosen, " wi' a bit tocher o' her ain," he added, with horrid glee. At first the announcement was treated as a joke, then James went off again to Glasgow, this time to be married, and the neighbours had to believe in his story at last. Finally, the new Mrs. Gilchrist appeared in church one Sunday in a grand bonnet that smacked both of Glasgow and of money. She was not a " lass " at all ; rather, as they said, " A weel-come-through woman." So much the better : no young creature could have been expected to cope with James Gilchrist.

" My certy ! she'll no' look sae braw for long ! " was the general verdict. " There's no enough o' the daur aboot her." (In other words, she could not frighten her husband into good behaviour.)

.   .   .   .

With Heaven knows what illusions Kirsty had arrrived at her new home. A quick process of disillusionment began there and then. James had represented himself as a small farmer, and she

The Love Bairn

found that he was a crofter, and a poor one at that.

"The hoose is awfae bare-like," the bride said timidly, glancing round her in dismay. A few cracked dishes stood on the dresser; two broken chairs, a table, and a box-bed completed the furnishing of the kitchen. It is true there was another room "ben the hoose," but it had evidently been unused for years and smelt like a tomb. The paper was hanging off the damp walls in strips; an old horse-hair sofa stood crazily on three legs; mice had nibbled at the stuffing till half of it had fallen out. There was a round table in a corner, and a dilapidated wicker chair was the only seat.

Walking between these two poverty-stricken rooms Kirsty had, as I say, exclaimed at their bare appearance : her remark did not meet with approval.

"Gin it's no' braw enough, ye can buy mair for 't," Gilchrist had said, adding : " I'm awa' tae the village "—a phrase of which Kirsty had still to learn the full significance. She said nothing in reply ; but after he was gone she went to the door and stood looking round her new home. All about the cottage there was nothing but dirt and disorder. A heap of manure from the byre lay at one side of the door, a rubbish heap of tin cans, broken bottles, and scraps of old iron at the other. Some ill fed moulting hens scratched about in an unending search for a livelihood, and in the weedy field behind the cottage a miserable dirty cow was feeding.

Town bred as Kirsty was, she could scarcely

The Love Bairn

imagine this to be a farm. Why, the Gallowgate of Glasgow was scarcely dirtier or more forlorn! She drew in her breath expressively, and tried to make excuses to herself for everything. But an awful little voice whispered at her heart that this was only the beginning of sorrows. James had deceived her in this, what would she find out next? She turned back into that miserable house and looked round it again. Evidently the first thing to be done was to clean up the kitchen. Soap, however, was nowhere to be found . . . a little tea in a tin box, half a loaf on the shelf, this was all she could see in the way of food. But inside the dresser a surprising accumulation of black bottles attracted her attention: the corks had all the same smell.

"My certy! there's been a deal o' whisky here," she thought The phrase "inhibition" would have conveyed nothing to Kirsty, yet it is possible to act without giving a name to our actions: Kirsty "inhibited" the rising terror in her heart, the sudden conviction that the whisky bottles explained everything—she would not admit the thought for a moment.

"I'll gang ower tae the village mysel'," she said, "An' buy a' the things that's wantit—it's easy seen there's no' been a woman here."

The village yielded a supply of comforts that quite surprised Kirsty. She paid for everything out of her own purse, not having yet broached the delicate subject of finances with her husband, and came home laden with soap and soda, black lead and whitening, as well as all the materials for a substantial meal. If it was possible to make the house look comfortable and home-like, Kirsty was determined to do it. First of all the floor had to be scrubbed clean from the accumulated dirt of years. Then the chairs and table had to be scrubbed; then the grate, red with rust, must be "black-leaded," and the dark, greasy hearthstone whitened into startling and cheerful contrast. The window panes, too, were rubbed clear of dust, and a splendid fire was lit in the clean grate. It shone into every corner of the little room, and was reflected in the dark panels of the old box-bed. Then Kirsty drew the table near the fire and laid out upon it all the provisions she had bought at the village shop. She smiled to think how pleased James would be when he came in—he wouldn't know the room, and how he would enjoy this fine tea, the buttered toast, the eggs, and the big slice of deep-coloured, strong-smelling cheese !

Even as the thought passed through her mind, the door opened and Gilchrist appeared.

" Eh, James, there ye are ! I'll mak' the tea in a minit. Ye'll no ken the kitchen, I'm thinkin' ? " she cried out in the pride of her heart.

James had paused on the threshold, and Kirsty interpreted his attitude as a tribute to the changed aspect of the room. He did not reply to her question, however, and Kirsty looked up quickly from the teapot to see what was wrong. James was holding on to the latch of the door, and now he

The Love Bairn

lurched forward and caught hold of the back of a chair to steady himself. The chair was not very firm on its legs, and did not supply the necessary support ; James fell forward against the table, and only avoided the fire by a drunken man's luck.

Kirsty, on the other side of the table, said never a word ; she just sat there and realised in one terrifying moment the misery that she had entered upon.

.   .   .   .

What she could not realise all at once was the light in which she would gradually come to regard her husband. At first she went on for a little hoping against hope that things would mend, trying to make excuses for the man, telling herself it was a madness that would pass. But before very long Kirsty had to confess that " the drink was the least of it " ; for every day she lived with James stripped off from him another rag of the character she had thought he possessed. There are men who can be drunken and lovable in spite of their fault ; but with fuller knowledge of the man she had married, Kirsty came to see there was nothing anywhere in his nature that it was possible to love. He took no pains now to conceal from Kirsty that her money had been her attraction in his eyes. A pitiful enough little fortune it was of twenty a year ; but to working people, who live always from hand to mouth, " invested money " has a sound of almost fabulous wealth. Gilchrist stopped all pretence of work until he had drunk up every penny that Kirsty had brought with her to Inverawe, then he refused to believe that no more could be had before spring, when the dividends were due.

"There's a pound owin' at the shop, James," Kirsty told him one day.

"What for d'ye no' pay it then?" he asked insolently.

"I havena the money," she answered.

"Haud yer tongue, ye lying ——," said James, striking her full across the mouth as he spoke.

It was the first time in her life that Kirsty had heard such language, the first time she had felt a blow. She scarcely knew which hurt her most. She wiped the blood off her bruised lips, but the words could not be effaced from her memory.

In vino veritas, and Kirsty was to get awful insight now into the mind of her husband. Sometimes she would run out of the kitchen, her fingers in her ears, to shut out the sound of his words. There she would sit, in the damp, icy back room, rocking herself to and fro in fear and disgust unspeakable. Worst of all, Gilchrist had a blood-curdling habit when only half drunk of having long family prayers. He would come to the door of the room and summon his wife :—

"Come awa', Kirsty, I'm tae pit up a prayer (hic). Are ye there, lassie? Come ben an' kneel doon afore the Lord (hic). . . . 'O Lord God, Thou knowest how vile we are, what filthy rags our righteousness is, but Thy salvation is full and free' (hic)."

Poor Kirsty, compelled to join in these horrible

The Love Bairn

devotions, knelt there and trembled—trembled because she thought that surely fire from above must come down and slay the man whose impious breath thus took the name of God in vain. James would sometimes keep her on her knees for hours : at other times, as the fancy took him, he would spend the night in nothing but cursing—not varied cursing, only the one word, " Damn," repeated over and over and over just like the ticking of a clock— " damn, damn, damn "—on and on he went with it, hour after hour, and each time the word was repeated, he seemed to find a fresh depth of intonation put into it. Kirsty used to wonder what he had found in life to curse so deeply—perhaps just the lost soul of himself ?

There was quite a long account standing at the village shop before Gilchrist began to work again. Kirsty was miserable about the debt, so when her husband announced that he had got a job of thatching to do " east the road," the news was a comfort to her. Something had evidently put James into strangely good humour too ; he was like another man. Kirsty felt a flicker of hope ; perhaps work was what he wanted.

" I'm glad ye've got a job," she said, " there's no' muckle in the hoose, an' there's a good few things standin' at the shop."

James grunted contemptuously, and set off to his work.

The farmhouse that was to be rethatched stood on the hillside ; at the back of it there was a little,

The Love Bairn

old, seldom-used graveyard, the dreariest place
surely that the eye could light upon. The en-
closure was utterly uncared for : nettles and dockens
grew high above the grass, and the headstones were
all fallen away. So few burials now took place
there that the iron gateway was all grown across
with weeds and grass, and the gates would scarcely
turn on their rusty hinges. This morning, however,
they stood open, and in the farthest corner a pile
of freshly turned earth showed that a grave had
just been dug.

James went round to the barn and collected all
the materials for his thatching. He looked like
anyone else, quiet and workman like, as he walked
about there ; but the heart of him was a little
hell that morning—a hideous, unnatural delight
filled it ; one of Lizzie's boys had died two days
before, and he had only heard of it yesterday. The
news had but one signification for him—more
drink for himself.

As he worked there among the golden straw,
his mouth creased and watered with anticipation.
Only one child to provide for now ! There was a
burden off his shoulders. He threw down the
straw he was sorting into bunches, and walked into
the graveyard to have a look at the newly made
grave. So small it was—so damp and deep a bed
for a little sleeper to be laid in, you would have
thought that no man born of woman could have
endured to look down into it. But James was
entirely untouched by the sight ; he kicked a stone

The Love Bairn

into the grave, as if to measure its depth, then turned away and spat upon the ground expressively.

Getting out a ladder, he climbed on to the roof and began his work. All round him was the golden October world. Far below the farm, the loch lay like a mirror that has been breathed upon, motionless but dim—it gave a blurred reflection of the brown and golden woods. Wisps of thistledown flittered across the roadway on some almost unfelt breath of air. The bracken on the hillside was coloured like a lion's hide ; the smoke from the cottage chimneys, undeflected by any wind, rose like some serene intention, and in the rich, still atmosphere the faintest sound was magnified. Now as Gilchrist sat there on the roof at his work, he heard the creak and rumble of a cart coming up the stony road to the graveyard. He looked down and saw that a cart, drawn by an old white horse, was approaching. Two men walked beside the horse ; there was some straw in the bottom of the cart, and a little black box lay upon the straw.

An evil spirit impelled Gilchrist to begin to whistle. In spite of the loud rustling he made with the straw, each one of the approaching footsteps seemed to strike upon his ear . . . he whistled " Duncan Gray " and roped down another handful of straw.

The cart stopped at the graveyard gate, and James broke off his whistling, to crouch behind the chimney and watch and listen.

A few words passed between the two men below,

then one of them lifted the little coffin in his arms, and they both went through the gates into the graveyard.

Very cautiously James raised himself till he could look across the ridge of the roof, straight down to where the two men stood beside the new-made grave. He seemed to gloat, to feast upon the sight ; as each spadeful of earth was flung in on the coffin, he smacked his lips and nodded his approval: " Aye, pit the beggar weel doon—*pit the beggar deep doon !* " he muttered, with an indescribable gusto of intonation . . . behold and see if there is anything in Nature so cruel as the heart of a man ?

When he had seen the last sod flattened down over the humpy little mound, James Gilchrist swung himself on to the ridge of the roof again, and recommenced his thatching. One of the men below looked up at him.

" Y're surely verra busy the day, James ? " he called up to him sarcastically. " Ye micht hae gi'en us a hand wi' the bairn."

Gilchrist made no response to the taunt. He appeared to be occupied with his work to the exclusion of any other matter.

.   .   .   .

Kirsty had some conversation with her husband that evening as they sat at their tea. He seemed to be in such good temper that there was plenty to talk about.

" There's some poor body lost a bairn, James," she said, " I se'd the funeral gae past—jist a cairt

The Love Bairn

wi' a coffin intil't, and twa men walkin' alongside
—d'ye ken whose bairn it would be ? "

" Ou—jist a wee by-blow o' a crater," said James,
cutting himself another bit of bread.

" Was it the faither was walkin' behind ? "
Kirsty persisted.

" No fears o' him ! he'd mair tae dae," said
James ; " it was just Mackenzie the wright, him that
made the coffin, an' Fraser that drove the cairt."

" Eh ! it's an awfae-like thing tae pit awa' a
bairn like yon ! " Kirsty cried.

But James checked her sentimentality.

" Wha's wantin' a bairn like yon ? " he demanded,
" it's better deid."

" Eh, James ! " Kirsty said, and sighed—partly
at his hard-heartedness, partly at the thought of
the little grave that no one had wept over—for her
heart was as soft as his was hard.

.   .   .   .

Torrents of rain fell that night and all the next
day. The golden world had disappeared, the hills
were wrapped round and round in mist, and every
burn by the roadside was swollen into a rushing
stream.

Then the mists cleared away and the first sharp
autumn frost nipped the country.

That sudden frosty night, Kirsty sat up late
waiting for James to come in. At midnight she
went to the door to watch for him. Overhead in
the frosty sky myriads of stars were sparkling ;
not a sound could she hear anywhere ; there were

The Love Bairn

no footsteps coming along the road ; in the cottages on the hillside all the lights had been put out long ago. " Whatever's come over him ? " Kirsty wondered. She came back into the kitchen with a patient sigh, and made up the fire again. It was tolerably certain that when James did come in he would be drunk. She did not try to disguise the fact from herself, and only made a distinction in her mind between talking drunk, mad drunk, or dead drunk—all three phases she knew only too well now. Kirsty leant back in her chair waiting for the sound of the uncertain footsteps, and as she sat there the poor soul looked ahead into life with a fainting heart.

Not yet forty years of age, strong and " like life " for many a day to come . . . without calculating on any great longevity for either herself or James, she might have to endure thirty years of this misery still. Thirty years of disgust, thirty years of terror —how were they to be lived through ?

Long ago any liking Kirsty had ever felt for James Gilchrist had entirely disappeared, and now her hopefulness and her faith in life were also dying rapidly.

She had made no friends among the neighbours, because pride would not let her confess her misery— she was as lonely as if she had been stranded on a desert island. Occasionally Kirsty had wild thoughts of leaving James, and indeed she had every right to do so ; but again pride had stepped in : what would her people in Glasgow say ? She would be

The Love Bairn

a laughing-stock to them all, if she left her husband. There was nothing for it then, she thought, as she sat gazing into the fire that autumn night—nothing for it but just to shut her mouth and bear her misery as other women had done before and would, alas, do again ! Every year she would come to hate James Gilchrist more ; there was no possibility of reformation in the man—and probably he would treat her worse and worse as time went on. How she hated him already : his foul speech, his fouler mind, his long, drunken prayers that were worse than the oaths he swore !

Kirsty thought over all these things, and then her thoughts passing from particularity into confusion, she nodded, overcome with weariness, and at last slept soundly. The fire died down to ashes in the grate, and she woke to see the white daylight peering in through the little window—and James never in yet ! She flung a shawl round her head and went out into the still, icy morning air. Could anything have happened to James, she wondered ? He had come home so often drunk, that she had ceased to think he might be in danger. She ran down to the gate and looked along the road ; no one in sight there ; then turning to look the other way she saw that in the ditch, not a hundred yards from his own door, James must have been lying all the night. He was still asleep, but his face was ghastly and blue with cold. The ditch had water in it, so he was soaked through and through. Kirsty shook him, called out to him

The Love Bairn

before she could get any answer. At last, stiff and stupefied, James dragged himself up to a sitting posture and looked round about him.

"Gosh me! but it's cauld, lassie—gie's a hand oot o' here!" he exclaimed.

Kirsty leant down and caught hold of his arm. He stumbled up on to the bank, but could scarcely stand when he got there.

"Hae ye been there a' the nicht, James?" Kirsty asked.

"I had a fa' . . ." he said, looking round him stupidly, as if he did not understand her question. His teeth were chattering with cold, he was almost too numb to move. She gave him her arm and helped him along the bit of path to the cottage.

"Ye maun gang till yer bed, James," she told him, "ye've got an awfae chill."

.   .   .   .

Poor people do not send off for doctors on the slightest provocation as their richer neighbours are apt to do, so Kirsty "wrought away" as she would have expressed it, alone with James for the next twenty-four hours. By that time it was evident that further skill was needed, all her simple nostrums having failed.

"It's the infulmation, I'm thinkin'," she said to herself, "I maun get the doctor."

James was tossing from side to side of the old box-bed, muttering ceaselessly to himself. His face was flushed, his eyes staring. Sometimes Kirsty thought that he seemed to see things unseen

The Love Bairn

by her, for he would sit up and point into the corner of the room, crying out, " What's yon, Kirsty ? "

" What's that ye're seein', James ? " she said kindly, but he never answered. Then there would be silence for ten minutes or so till he cried out again. . . . This went on for hours, but as the dusk began to fall his fears took a concrete shape.

" Tak' it awa', Kirsty—tak' it awa'," he called angrily; " what's the bairn wantin' here ? . . . it was a gey sma' grave, but bonnie an' deep . . . I dinna ken hoo he's come oot—Gosh ! but they pit the beggar in deep—an' what's he doin' here ? "

" There's no' a bairn, James," Kirsty said, trying to soothe him.

" Aye is there—it's Lizzie's bairn—him that died a week syne."

Kirsty drew near to the bed : " I dinna ken aboot Lizzie," she said curiously.

" Hae ye no' heard tell o' Lizzie, her that had twa bairns tae me ? "

Kirsty shook her head : she was not quite sure whether James was to be believed or not, yet she wished to hear more.

" It's no' jist verra good for ye to be speakin' the now," she told him. But James would not be silenced :

" I'm tae tell ye a' thing, Kirsty," he cried, " an' there's a deal tae tell. . . . Ye see, I didna break the commandments, I pit them under my feet and trampit them . . ."

327

The Love Bairn

He sat up in bed and clutched hold of her hand as if she could protect him :

" There's awfae wurds I mind on noo," he went on wildly. " D'ye mind them? ' *For all these things will God call you into judgment* '—that's ane o' them; an' there's anither, ' *to every man according to his works;* yon's an awfae wurd, Kirsty . . . ! "

" Whisht, whisht, James ! "

" I aye grudged the siller for the bairns, ye ken. . . . I let them want whiles ; an' whiles she'd be needin' claes for them, but I let them want the claes. . . . Yon bairn sittin' by the fire's gey cauld like, I'm thinkin' . . . he's jist the wee bit shift he was chestit (buried) in . . . that's the way he's sittin' by the fire . . ."

Kirsty turned round, half expecting to see the naked child there. She lit a candle, to see if the light would calm James, and told him that he must not speak more. But he would not be silenced. On and on he went, pouring out the tale of his transgressions into her unwilling ears.

" Will I get the minister for ye, James ? " she asked him in despair.

" Na, na, I ken a' the minister has tae tell me—an' mair," he said.

" Maybe the doctor'll help ye," Kirsty suggested.

But the doctor, when at last he came, had not much comfort to give—he had no medicine to offer the sick soul : " Keep him warm and quiet—if you can—he seems to have something on his mind," he said impotently, as he went away.

The Love Bairn

An appalling night followed for poor Kirsty. A thousand terrors seemed to have taken hold upon James Gilchrist: he would babble on and on with an endless stream of texts, till one more poignant than the rest occurred to his memory, when he would scream aloud in indescribable anguish of mind.

Kirsty stood beside him the long night through, doing all that woman could do to ease his pain, yet powerless to help him in his extremity. She had forgotten all his faults, and the many injuries he had done her—they were swallowed up in an overwhelming pity for the man.

"Eh, James, dinna you be thinkin' on thae awfae words," she said, trying to soothe him. "There's others in the Bible forbye these."

"No' for me, Kirsty!" he cried. "An' it's death that's on me!" He rose up again in the bed, crying out with that terrible coward's voice of his: "*Death! and after death the judgment!* Eh, Kirsty, can ye no' help me, woman?"

So abject was his fear, it would have made any heart quail to watch him. He tossed from side to side of the bed, desperate, agonised with remorse. The cold morning light was beginning to come in now, and Kirsty could see that the fever was going down, leaving his face deadly white.

Very gradually the feverish strength began to desert him and he became as weak as a child. In a few hours' time he could scarcely move his hand, and his voice had a curious far-away sound. It was a mercy to see him quiet though, Kirsty thought,

The Love Bairn

after these terrible hours of agony. She sat down and took his hand in hers—that unloved hand which had struck her many a blow : it was all she could do for him now, all the help she could offer him as he went down uncomforted into the darkness. Thus hour after hour went past. From time to time Kirsty would give James some brandy, but it scarcely raised his pulse a beat now. Once his lips moved, and she bent down to catch the words he spoke. He said quite distinctly :

"*Behold the Judge standeth before the door,*" and Kirsty understood that ; but the last words he uttered were unintelligible to her : "*Pit the beggar deep doon,*" he said, and never spoke more.

.   .   .   .

James Gilchrist was dead and buried : the poor house " redd up " after the " buryin'," and Kirsty sat alone in it, all her terrors past for ever. She was considering what she was going to do now.

The neighbours had been very kind to her. Of course James would have had the funeral of a lord, and gone down into his grave with honour if drunkenness had been his only sin ; for in Scotland a man who has never exceeded can scarcely be said to be universally respected ! But the man's other offences, his meanness, his want of heart, weighed heavily against the popular failing, and sympathy had gone with Kirsty. She had not been left alone till this evening, one or other of the neighbours having come to stay the night with her that she might not be alone in the house with the dead man. Now that

The Love Bairn

all was over, however, Kirsty told them she " wasna feared," and would "manage fine" by herself. She had a great deal to think about, and one important decision to come to—a decision which might alter her whole future. This is what had happened. During the two days and two nights which passed between the time of her husband's death and that of his burial, Kirsty had held much whispered conversation with one old woman, Mrs. Fraser by name. She was so old, so wise, so grimly cheerful that her presence had been very welcome in the house of death. Sitting together in the firelight, Kirsty ventured to ask Mrs. Fraser a question that she burned to know.

"Can ye tell me, had James twa bairns ? The last night he was aye speakin' o' them. I thocht maybe he was wanderin'. . ."

The old woman shook her head.

"Aye had he—twa bairns, and ane's in the kirkyaird."

"Did they ca' their mither Lizzie ?—he aye spoke o' Lizzie," Kirsty said, hesitating yet intensely curious.

"Aye, Lizzie they ca'ed her, a puir half-witted crater—she died three years syne."

"An' what's come o' the ither bairn ? " Kirsty asked.

"He's wi' his grannie in the Glen—I'm thinkin' he'll no' be coaxed tae live : wee Wullie that's gone was awfu' sma'—they werna' gettin' their meat, the bairns."

The Love Bairn

There was a short silence between the two women
—both knew what the other was thinking, yet
neither would utter a word against the man who
lay dead " ben the hoose."

" Weel, weel ! " was all Kirsty had said ; but as
she uttered the ejaculation, a thought fixed itself
in her mind like a barbed arrow. All the next
day she went about conscious of the thought sticking there obstinately—only now she had time to
examine into it. Her processes of reasoning were
quite obscure : indeed she did not rightly reason out
the subject at all ; but gradually two pictures
formed themselves distinctly before her mind's
eye. The first she had seen with the bodily sight—
a cart, with a tiny coffin lying in it, and two men
walking alongside. The second she had to imagine ;
but it became as real to her as the first—a child,
small, ill-fed, ill-clothed, and, above all, not wanted
by anyone : it was very like James Gilchrist to
look at. Well, Kirsty mused, James had been a
bad husband to her ; he had ill-treated her, used
her money, done everything a man could to make
her life miserable. But was that any reason why
his child should be starved and neglected ? To
some natures it would have been a quite sufficient
reason—Kirsty was built on larger lines : " *A bairn's
a bairn*," she said to herself darkly.

.   .   .   .

The next day was wet and windy ; but early in
the morning Kirsty began to make various preparations. She tidied up the house, spread a com-

The Love Bairn

fortable meal on the table, as if to await the coming of two persons, made up the fire so that it might keep in for many hours, and finally pinned her skirt up round her waist, put on a heavy cloak, and issued out into the rain. She had made many and precise inquiries from old Mrs. Fraser, and was now setting out to verify them, undismayed by wind or weather.

Following the high road for quite three miles, Kirsty passed through a gate, and began to walk up a stony track which led through the Glen. It was very lonely—a little brawling burn flowed beside the path, and secretive looking thickets of alder grew close down by the edges of the stream. At the sound of Kirsty's footsteps the sheep lifted their heads from the heathery grass and bounded off, afraid of the intruder.

Thick mists covered the hills on either side of the Glen, as if great curtains had been let down from heaven to hide something. It was eerie enough, Kirsty thought, as she plodded steadily on up the rough road. At last she came to a little bridge thrown across the burn, and right before her was the cottage of her quest.

A low roofed, tumble down place, scarcely fit for the housing of human beings, it might have sheltered cattle and not done very well even for that. Smoke was rising from the chimney, and the door stood open.

Kirsty knocked : there was a stir inside the cottage, and a half dressed young woman with bare feet came to the door.

The Love Bairn

"Does Mistress MacTavish bide here?" Kirsty asked.

"Aye, she's in bye."

Kirsty stepped into the house and looked round; the fire had been smoking so badly that she could scarcely make out who was in the room. At last she saw that an old woman sat beside the fire, very bent and shrivelled. Kirsty stood before her.

"I'm James Gilchrist's wife," she said, "an' I've come for Geordie, the bairn your Lizzie had tae James."

The announcement, so bald, so unexpected, did not seem to annoy the old woman. She peered up at Kirsty curiously through the smoke, and then pointed across the hearth.

"There's Geordie," she said. "He's no' weel; I dinna ken what ails the bairn, he'll no' take his meat since Wullie dee'd."

"He'll gang the same way Wullie did," the young woman interpolated, with no sign of feeling whatever. She held a hairpin in her mouth, and was trying to twist up her hair into some sort of tidiness for the visitor.

Kirsty crossed to where the child sat, that she might get a nearer view of his face. Oh, such a small, pinched creature, sitting limply on a three-legged stool, one thin bare foot resting on the other, his little hands folded in a singularly unchildish fashion, almost with the attitude of resigned old age!

"He's wearyin' on Wullie," the young woman

334

The Love Bairn

explained. " He'll greet till he's done, an' syne he'll sit yon way."

Kirsty drew a chair up beside the child ; she threw off her wet cloak, and lifted the little creature on to her comfortable knee. " Sit you there, my wee man, till ye see what I've got for ye," she said. It was bribery and corruption of the basest sort, but Kirsty had not known what other weapons to use. Out of her pocket she drew a bag of those gundy balls beloved of youth, brown and glossy, with a white streak running round them.

" Here's for ye," she said invitingly. The small hand closed over the sticky ball ; something like the ghost of a smile passed across the pinched, bluish lips. He gave a furtive glance at the old woman in her chair, then licked the gundy with intense, sudden relish.

" It's fine," he whispered. Kirsty passed her arm round the thin little body in a quick impulse of tenderness, but the child was so unaccustomed to caresses that he was almost frightened, and gave a wriggle like a caught rabbit that tries to escape from its snare. Kirsty set him down from her knee at once, too wise to try to hold him against his will. He sidled away from her, and seated himself on his little stool to enjoy the gundy ball in safety. There he sat, lick, lick, licking at it in an ecstasy of enjoyment it is impossible to describe, and all the time he never took his eyes off Kirsty, who had given him this wonderful thing to eat.

The old woman now began to ask Kirsty for some

The Love Bairn

details of James Gilchrist's end. But her curiosity got little satisfaction.

" It was that sudden, there's no muckle tae tell," Kirsty affirmed, quite decided that her lips would utter nothing against the dead. Then she added, " He said a deal aboot the bairns tae me—that's the way I've come for Geordie there—I'm tae tak' him wi' me."

" They say ye've siller o' yer ain ? " the old woman asked, with a nasty smile. " Puir Lizzie had nane, ye see."

There was a disagreeable silence for a minute after this passage of arms. Then Kirsty drew a purse from her pocket, opened it, and took out four half-crowns. She laid the little heap of silver on her hand and held it out across the hearth to the old woman.

" I'll gie that for Geordie," she said laconically.

.   .   .   .

The bargain had not taken very long to strike, because there was no false delicacy to be overcome on either side. Kirsty was frankly anxious to get possession of the child, the old woman as frankly anxious to get rid of him.

" I'll tak' his claes wi' me," Kirsty said, " it's a long road tae come for them again."

The young woman went into a back room and began to rake in a kist that stood there ; presently she returned, tying up a small bundle in a ragged bit of cotton stuff.

" He hasna' muckle," she said curtly, " James Gilchrist was gey near." Kirsty received the bundle

The Love Bairn

in silence, then turned to Geordie and held out her hand.

"Come awa', dearie, we'll gang doon the Glen thegither," she said, in a reassuring voice.

She half expected the child to refuse to go with her, but he did not hesitate.

"Wullie gaed doon the Glen in the cairt—I'll maybe get tae Wullie," he said, a sudden light in his woebegone eyes. Kirsty turned away without answering. She would not tell the child a lie, yet she must get him to come with her. He put his skinny little hand in hers with no shadow of fear now. Kirsty felt it necessary to assure the grandmother that she would see Geordie again:

"I'll bring him up whiles," she said, as she took her departure.

"It's a gey long road; ye needna fash bringin' him," said the old woman.

So Kirsty and Geordie stepped out together into the rain, and there was no pretence of regret over the child's going.

"I'll show ye whaur Wullie an' me makes hooses doon by the burn!" Geordie cried, running ahead a step or two. Then he turned back, all the joy gone out of his little face: "But I'm no' carin' for them till Wullie comes back," he said. "Maybe ye ken whaur Wullie is?"

"Aye, Geordie, I ken fine, but I canna' tell ye the now," Kirsty answered. Instinct told her that this cheerless hour, while he was being led by a stranger he knew not whither in rain and wind, was not the time to tell Geordie the truth. She changed the subject briskly :

" Y're tae have a grand tea when we get hame," she told the child. " It's waitin' on us, a' ready by the fireside—wi' scones an' butter an' a wee thing jam, an' maybe an egg if y're a good laddie."

Geordie's eyes gleamed. " I like an egg fine," he said, " I've no had one this long time."

Kirsty found it easy to believe this as she looked at his thin little legs, scantily covered by a tattered apology for a kilt. He had no strength to come and go upon, she noticed, and before they had reached the gate at the mouth of the Glen, Geordie's steps were lagging.

" Ye'll be tired, dearie ? " she asked anxiously, thinking of the three long miles still ahead of them.

" Na," said Geordie stoutly, and plodded along for another half-mile. Kirsty seemed to recognise some indomitable stuff in the puny creature ; he would not give in to be being beaten. She must try a more subtle method of address, one that did not hurt his pride.

" Are ye tired, my wee man ? " she queried this time, and his manhood once acknowledged, Geordie collapsed in a burst of weeping.

" Aye, *awfae tired !* " he cried.

Well, there was nothing for it but to try to carry him, Kirsty thought. He was not much too heavy for her, only the miles still to be got over were formidable with any burden to carry. She lifted him up and made her way slowly along the road.

The Love Bairn

The child was so tired that he lay like a dead thing in her arms. The rain beat against her face, but Kirsty was quite undismayed; she would not have laid down this self-inflicted burden for anything you could have offered her. On she went, " Wat, wat, and wearie," as the old song says, yet strangely happy. She pressed the child close to her warm heart, sheltering him from the wind with a mother's tenderness.

They were passing just then close under the old graveyard on the hillside where Willie lay, fast in the cold arms of his Mother Earth. Geordie did not know how near he was to his lost companion, but Kirsty quickened her steps and cast a look behind her as she went by—the jealous look of one who fears to be deprived of a great possession.

" He'll no' get tae Wullie if I can help it," she said to herself.